Baby, You're The Best

Baby, You're The Best

MARY B. MORRISON

Kensington Publishing Corp.
http://www.kensingtonbooks.com

DAFINA BOOKS are published by

Kensington Publishing Corp.
119 West 40th Street
New York, NY 10018

All Kensington titles, imprints, and distributed lines are available at special quantity discounts for bulk purchases for sales promotion, premiums, fundraising, educational, or institutional use. Special book excerpts or customized printings can also be created to fit specific needs. For details, write or phone the office of the Kensington Special Sales Manager: Attn. Special Sales Department. Kensington Publishing Corp., 119 West 40th Street, New York, NY 10018. Phone: 1-800-221-2647.

Library of Congress Card Catalogue Number: 2015937821

Dafina and the Dafina logo Reg. U.S. Pat. & TM Off.

ISBN-13: 978-1-61773-068-9
ISBN-10: 1-61773-068-8
First Kensington Hardcover Edition: August 2015

eISBN-13: 978-1-61773-069-6
eISBN-10: 1-61773-069-6
Kensington Electronic Edition: August 2015

10 9 8 7 6 5 4 3 2 1

Printed in the United States of America

Heavenly "Forever34" Hillton, I will always love you.

Acknowledgments

Life, like love, should be a continuance of experiences, not a series of encounters. Encounters are easily forgotten. Experiences are long remembered.

Thankfully, I can testify that I've utilized some of the gifts God has bestowed upon me for a greater humanitarian purpose. There are a few more talents I'm preparing to unleash to entertain my audience before this book is in print. God willing, we shall see!

Individually and collectively each of you, my readers, are blessings. I appreciate your continued support. Where would I be without you? I never want to know.

Since my previous publication of *If You Don't Know Me,* major things have happened. I've relocated from Oakland, California, to Atlanta, Georgia. I was peachy already. Now I'm truly ripe, y'all. I'm in a new and exciting space. I've penned two nonfiction books, produced my stage play, *Single Husbands,* and starred in a reality show. Okay, I'm speaking all of this into existence.

Believing no man is an island, I have several people who have stood by me throughout my life. I'll mention them as I continue, but right now I'd like to say, "I'm proud of my son, Jesse Byrd, Jr." He's completed his first novel, *Oiseau: The King Catcher.* He's closer to standing at the altar to exchange wedding vows with his beautiful fiancée, Emaan Abbass. I pray all great things for them and other couples—irrespective of gender—uniting in matrimony. Everybody deserves love and happiness.

Family, friends, fans, and faith are the unbreakable bond that sustains my literary career, which is stronger than ever. You guys make me feel amazing!

ATL welcomed me into the open arms of concert promoter Jeremy Hill, radio personality Missy E. the Partydoll, Realtor Dianna Crawford, journalist Michelle Gipson (and her mother Mary), my sisters Regina Morrison and Margie Rickerson, author friends Marissa Monteilh, Stephanie Perry Moore, and Tamika Newhouse, my friends Vanessa Ibanitoru, Shannette Slaughter, Marlon Hamilton, June Grant, and Marcus Darlin. Each of you helped me settle into my new environment. Your loyalty is priceless and appreciated.

My unmarried husband, Richard C. Montgomery, tricked out my new loft crib. He was my co-executive producer extraordinaire for my stage play, *Single Husbands*. I couldn't have done it without you! Divorce is not an option for us. I love you, man!

A special shout-out goes to Roland Morrison, my nephew who is also my personal assistant and trainer. You are amazing! To my cuz, Edward Allen. You are the smoothest dude I know. To Ed's wife, Tasha Allen, you're the greatest. Through your marriage, I've witnessed the unconditional love you have for one another and your son, EJ. That's my boy. Carroll Hawkins, thanks cuz for always keeping in touch with the fam. You're solid C, and for real, you deserve the Father of the Year award, every year.

Daniel Markell, VP of Development at Sirens Media, you're the classiest act ever, man! Thanks for the opportunities! You have to star me in *Literary Divas* reality show.

Kendall Minter, no entertainment lawyer reps like you and I'm blessed to be your client and friend. You support me on levels that I can never repay you for.

Everything must change but the constants in my life are my siblings. Wayne, Andrea, Derrick, and Regina Morrison, Margie Rickerson, and Debra Noel, I love you guys.

This chick here is incredibly supportive. Author Lisa Renee Johnson, I love you and I'm going to miss your husband's gumbo. I might have to make it back to Cali for y'all'z Christmas party.

I have a friend who has the gift to read. One day we were sitting in my room at the Twelve Hotel in Atlanta and she asked me to place my hands in hers. When she connected with my parents and told me things I'd never revealed to her, she closed a void in my life. It was burden-lifting to understand how my mother, Elester Noel, loved not only me but all my siblings equally. My father, Joseph Henry Morrison . . . was far more abusive than I'd imagined. My friend helped me to comprehend why my mother committed suicide. I'll leave it at that. Thanks, Shannette!

To Natalie Nervis, I appreciate your gift, insight, and countless prayers.

Boss bitch, Christal Jordan, owner of Enchanted PR, put me on the map in the ATL. From promoting *Single Husbands* to launching my Google Hangouts to getting me on Foxie 105 FM as the relationship sexpert, you're top notch. A shout out goes to Cathy Hughes and Radio One for embracing me early in my literary career and now. My fam at Foxie 105 FM are truly number one. BabyJ and Georgia drive-time on-air with you guys is a rush.

What's life without social media, baby (pumping both palms toward the sky)! I can never have enough Facebook fans, Twitter, Tumblr, and Instagram followers, and McDonogh 35 Senior High alumni supporters, but I can say, "I love you for checking me out!"

Much heartfelt appreciation to my editor and friend, Selena James at Kensington Publishing Corporation. At Kensington, I'm family. Undying praises to Steven Zacharius, Adam Zacharius, Karen Auerbach, Adeola Saul, and everyone else at Kensington for growing my literary career since 1999.

Laurie Parkin, I hope you're enjoying your retirement. Lesleigh Irish-Underwood, I pray for continued success in your new career. Carol Hill Mackey and Karen R. Thomas, your efforts in elevating my literary works will never be forgotten.

Latoya Smith, muah! You're an incredibly talented editor. *Single Husbands* stage play was a huge hit in part to Grand Central Publishing's support.

Behind the scenes, I have scintillating agents and attorneys. Andrew Stuart and Claudia Menza, Kenneth P. Norwick, Esq., and Kendall Minter, Esq., I appreciate each of you.

My thirtysomethings are a blessing beyond measure. Heavenly Hill-ton, Dominique McClellan, Marlon Hamilton, and Bryan "BWats" Watson, you are truly unique.

Wishing each of my readers peace and prosperity in abundance. Visit me online at www.MaryMorrison.com. Sign up and invite your peeps to do the same for my HoneyBuzz newsletter. Join my fan page on Facebook at TheRealMaryB, follow me on Twitter at marybmorrison, Instagram at maryhoneybmorrison, and Tumblr at HoneyBMorrison.

This is novel #1 in The Crystal series

PROLOGUE

Alexis

"Thanks for everything. I enjoyed serving you."

You? You? Not this shit again! That bitch waited on us for two hours. I'd kept my mouth shut when the "What would *you* like to drink" was directed toward my man only. I had to interrupt with my request for a mai tai.

We'd adhered to their protocol by writing our orders on the restaurant's request forms meaning there was no need to ask what we wanted to eat. The repeat for confirmation, "So you're having the fried wings, rice and gravy, and steamed cabbage and the vegetable plate with double collard greens, and fried okra?" was asked of my man as though he was going to eat it all by himself.

Now that the check was here I was still invisible? *Aw, hell no!* I pushed back my chair, stood tall on the red-bottom stilettoes my man had bought. The hem of my purple halter mini dress was wedged between the crack of my sweet chocolate ass but I didn't give a damn. That working-for-tips trick was about to come up short.

I leaned over the table, pointed at the waiter, then said loud enough for all the people on our side of the restaurant to hear, "My man is not interested in you!"

James held my hips, pulled me toward my seat. Refusing to sit, I sprang to my feet, then told him, "No, babe."

Nothing was holding me back from the inconsiderate asshole that obviously needed customer service training. I stepped into the aisle. The only thing separating us was air.

"Not today, Alexis. Please stop," James pleaded.

I extended my middle finger alongside my pointing finger, and my nails stopped inches from the waiter's face when my man reached over the table and grabbed my wrist. I was about to put both of that dude's eyes out.

He posed, one foot slightly in front the other, tilted his head sideways, put his hand on his hip with a bitch-I-dare-you attitude.

The room was cold. I was heated. The guests became quiet. A woman scrambled for her purse, picked up her toddler, then rushed toward the exit. I didn't give a damn if everybody got the hell out!

"One of these days, sweetheart, I'm not going to be around to intervene," James said. He handed the waiter a hundred dollar bill.

I snatched it. "Give his ass whatever is on the bill and not a penny more."

James handed that jerk another hundred. This time the waiter got to the money before I did. He stuffed the cash in his black apron pocket, rolled his eyes at me, scanned my guy head to toe, then said, "Thanks. You can come anytime you'd like. Let me get your change."

He stepped back. I moved forward. I didn't have a problem slapping a bitch that deserved it. I swung to lay a palm to the left side of his face. His ass leaned back like he was auditioning for a role in the next *Matrix* movie.

"Don't duck, bitch, you bold. If you feeling some type of way express yourself." I shoved my hand into my purse.

He screamed, "Manager! Manager!"

I didn't care if he called Jesus. "Say something else to my man. I dare you." If I lifted my gun and put my finger on the trigger, I swear he wouldn't live to disrespect another woman.

James swiftly pulled my arm and purse to his side, then told the waiter, "Sorry, man. Keep the change."

The waiter stared at the guests. "Y'all excuse my sister, she forgot to take her meds." A few people laughed.

"Take your lame-ass jokes to Improv Comedy Club for open mic, bitch. You weren't trying to be center stage before my man tipped you."

"I got you, boo." He pulled out his cell, started pressing on the pad.

"You so bad. Stay turnt up until the po-po comes." He turned then switched his ass away.

James begged, "Sweetheart, let's go."

Some round short guy with a sagging gut dressed in a white button-down shirt and cheap black pants hurried in our direction. "Ma'am. Sir. You need to leave now."

The old lady seated next to our table said, "Honey, you're outnumbered in this town. You gon' wear yourself out."

I told my guy, "Walk in front of me."

Shaking his head, James said, "You a trip," then laughed. "You go first. I have to keep an eye on you."

That was the other way around. Atlanta was a tough place to meet a straight man who cared about being faithful. The ugly guys had a solid five-to-fifteen females willing to do damn near anything to and for them. The attractive ones had triple those options. The successful good-looking men with big egos and small dicks were assholes not worth my fucking with. But these dudes boldly disrespecting me by hitting on my man, they were the worst.

"It's not funny, James. I'm sick of this shit."

I knew it wasn't my guy's fault that James was blessed eighty inches toward heaven, one hundred and eighty pounds on the ground with a radiant cinnamon-chocolate complexion that attracted men and women.

James opened the door of his electric-blue Tesla Roadster, waited until I was settled in the passenger seat. He got in, then drove west on Ponce de Leon.

As he merged onto the I-85, he said, "Just because you have the right to bear arms, sweetheart, doesn't mean you should. I keep telling you to leave the forty at home," he said laughing. "I'm glad you like my ass."

"Nothing's funny. I don't understand how men hitting on you don't bother you."

"The way you be all up on my ass, what the hell I need a dude for? Soon as you finish your dissertation, I'm signing you up for an anger management course," he said. "You can't keep flashing on men because your father is the ultimate asshole. Let it go, sweetheart."

"That's easy for you to say. Your parents are still happily married. I bet if your dad disowned you, you wouldn't say, 'Let it go.' "

I was still pissed at that waiter. I had to check his ass. I was fed up with dicks disrespecting females. I'd seen my mother give all she had to offer and the only engagement ring ever put on Blake Crystal's finger was the one she'd bought herself.

James held my hand. "You're right, sweetheart. I know how much he's hurt you."

My father, whoever and wherever the fuck he was, was the first male disappointment in my life. Some kids cried because their daddy promised to show up but didn't. Mine never promised. Before I had a first boyfriend, my heart was already shattered into pieces by my dad. Staring out the window, I refused to shed another tear.

Continuing north on Interstate 85, James bypassed exit 86 to my house. "I know how to cheer you up. I'm taking you to Perimeter Mall."

"Thanks, babe," was all I'd said.

I was twenty-six years old and I'd never met my father. My birth certificate listed the father as unknown. Hell yeah, I was angry. My mama didn't fuck herself but in a way she had.

My way of coping with my daddy issues was to not allow any man to penetrate my heart or disrespect me. Every man I dated had to like me more. The second a woman liked a man more than he liked her, she was fucked and screwed.

"Sweetheart, I have a question."

"Don't start that shit with me today, James. Don't go there."

He let go of my hand. "If you answer, I promise, no more questions."

I knew he was lying. He always said that shit and didn't mean it. "What, James?"

"Have you had any other men in your house other than me?"

I could lie. Tell him what he wanted to hear. Or I could tell the truth. Either way it didn't fucking matter! My blood pressure escalated. "I'm not answering that."

He exited the freeway, parked by Maggiano's. "Cool, then I'm not paying your rent this month."

That's why a bitch kept backup.

CHAPTER 1

Blake

A man was supposed to provide for his woman. His wife. His family. What on earth was I thinking having a crocked sixty-year-old man in my house, in my bed, between my legs? His age wasn't a problem. It was his bad attitude I didn't care for. Plus, he'd let himself go. Lost his butt. Gained a gut.

The day we met at an All-White outdoor concert, I was at my VIP table partying with my girlfriend Echo, listening to Keith Sweat charm the crowd with "Make It Last Forever."

"That white dress sho is wearing both of us," he'd said walking up to me. "It's wearing you well but—" He paused, shook his head, then professed, "Um, um, um, it's wearing me out!"

The day I'd met Fortune, I was vulnerable. I was trying to get over a recent breakup with a man I was still in love with. If I'd realized giving Fortune my number would've eventually made me hate him too, I wouldn't have done it. Dating Fortune was supposed to make my ex want me back. That was five years ago.

Rolling my eyes real hard, I heaved. All I wanted to do was scream, *Hurry up and get the hell off of me!* My legs rested in a U position to accommodate Fortune's wide hips. My ass was tilted downward. I'd rather make an impression in the mattress than please him.

The sweat rolling off of his body onto mine used to make me feel sexy. Like all the pumping of his behind was done to satisfy me. Now, each drop made me cringe. I closed my eyes. *Oh my God. Please let him cum,* I prayed, wanting to slither from underneath him.

Hurry the hell up! I yelled at the top of my inner voice. Instantly my nerves throbbed against my temples. *Great. Now, I've given myself a migraine.*

Fortune was the kind of freeloader who thought he looked better than he actually did. Maybe it was his cockiness that made him unattractive. I peeped through the cracks in my lids, then shut my eyes. Nope, he was definitely outside-in, inside-out ugly.

My legs were tiring. I squirmed a little to adjust my inner thighs.

"That's it. Wiggle it for me," he said, humping harder.

I stopped moving, then stared at him.

He believed his regurgitating the news on CNN compensated for his incompetence. He thought his dick was so irresistible that all women wanted him to stroke them. Once upon a time, I craved this man like my favorite Godiva chocolate cheesecake and Cîroc vodka martini. Those days were history.

When did we get to the point of living together and not caring about one another?

"Come on, Blake. Lift your hips, woman."

I squeezed every muscle I could real tight. Why I was still with this man had to be under the definition of insanity.

Opening his mouth, I watched him as he clenched his crooked teeth. His greasy cocoa skin drenched with baby oil slid up and down my body. The first time he ruined my expensive sheets, I downgraded to bargain bedding. As much as I detested cheap linen, I despised him more.

I sighed knowing my anger was self-induced. From my daughters to the men I'd dated, my problem was I sacrificed my happiness to please them. Soon I'd be fifty years old. This was the perfect time to put my desires first and say the hell with everybody else's!

"If you don't cum soon, you're going to have to jack that thing of yours off."

"I'm almost there, woman. Gimme a few more minutes."

When we first met, I loved everything about Fortune. His corniness. Sarcasm. His chronic complaining encouraged me to uplift him with constant praise. I tried helping him find his passion. For each employer that offered him a job, he found an excuse not to accept. Instantly, he fell in love with all I had to give. In turn, I fell for him.

I wanted to smack him upside both of his heads. All the complaining I'd done over the last five years, I was still the only one miserable in this relationship.

What time is it?

As I parted my lips to take a deeper breath, sweat poured from his neck into my mouth. *Damn!* I turned my head sideways, blew the salty slimy liquid onto the pillow. Prickly hairs on the gut he was too lazy to work off at the gym scraped up then down my midsection. Again and again. His three hundred pounds started trembling. His dick slipped out.

I exhaled, "Thank you, Jesus."

"Uh-uh, Blake. Don't say that. You know I'm not done yet."

Damn, did I say that out loud?

He stuffed his dick inside me, then stroked me damn near raw. My pussy was on the verge of forming a new hymen.

I was a smart, successful, financially well off woman living in Roswell, working in Buckhead. Why wasn't I in bed with a desirable, intelligent man?

To get through the rest of this session, I replayed sex scenes from a porn trailer that had gone viral a while ago. I wasn't the type to watch adult movies but my girlfriend Echo had texted me the link. Nikko's big dick was hard, long, and beautiful. It was sad that I had a man on top of me and I was lusting for good dick.

Drool escaped the corner of my mouth as I envisioned Nikko's third eye entering me in search of my G-spot. Pussy juices created by my yearning for a man I'd never met leaked onto Fortune's erection.

"That's it. Work with Daddy," Fortune said, grinding. "I feel you."

Lord, why couldn't I be the lucky one having my vagina rejuvenated by a young man like Nikko? Or where could I find my own handsome, well-endowed, courageous cub in Atlanta? If I found and fucked him, that wouldn't be cheating. That would be restitution.

I sighed. I did not want this old, decrepit-ass man on top of me. Even his thoughts were depressing. Didn't believe in anything unless there was something in it for him.

Thank God for fantasies. Imagining sucking Nikko's dick, I'd lie on my back, lean my neck over the edge of the mattress, tilt my head back far as I could, then part my juicy lips nice and wide.

I'd paint my lips pussy-pink for him. My throat would be elongated to accommodate his amazingly stretched-out shaft. Nikko would slide right in. All the way in. I wouldn't gag. If he'd cum, I'd swallow. In my position I wouldn't have a choice if he didn't pull out. I wouldn't want him . . . to pull out.

"Damn, Blake. Stop tightening up your legs. Let me in," Fortune complained.

If I participated, gyrated a little bit, I'd have time to brew a hot cup of coffee before showering.

Staring at the ceiling fan slowly spiraling above us, I thought about the tasks I needed to complete at work today. My vacation started after I got off tomorrow. Normally, I wouldn't take two weeks for my birthday but God had let me open my eyes for half of a century and that alone was worth celebrating.

Let's see. I had to go over everything with my branch VP, Brandon. He'd be in charge the entire time I was out. I had to follow up on three clients' mortgage refis. Make sure Ms. Stevens's business advantage account was set up and her business line of credit was available. Return calls to corporate . . .

Fortune grunted, reminding me where I was.

"I'm cumming, Blake."

My vaginal muscles snapped in protest. For fifteen seconds, he mustered enough energy to pump his ass. Deep. Fast. Penetrating strokes abruptly slowed to one shallow thrust. His sweat splattered onto my face. I wiped it off.

He collapsed on top of me. I was thankful the second he rolled over onto his back. I sprang out of bed shaking my head, then looked down at him.

"Blake, go get me a hot towel."

I politely said, "The girls want to take me out for my *birthday* tomorrow evening." Standing at the foot of the bed, I waited for a response.

"What girls? Them loose coworkers of yours? Or your daughters? Oh, I saw this nice hat I want you to get me for the jazz concert at Wolf Creek next week. Ask your boy Jeremy Hill for some free VIP tickets. I got my threads picked out. I'ma look good." Pausing, he frowned, then asked, "Why you looking at me with your face all twisted? Didn't I ask you for a hot towel, woman? All this cum is sticking to me."

One thing for certain, all of that cum was from his satisfaction. Not mine. Selfish bastard. My upgrading Fortune was a huge mistake. I should've known I'd made a bad decision when his wife didn't protest his moving out of her house and into mine.

Vanessa's trash had become my garbage.

Staring at Fortune, I lowered my voice then firmly said, "Get up and get out of my house."

CHAPTER 2

Blake

It was time for me to stop falling in love with a feeling.
Starting now. No more convincing myself the dick wasn't bad when
I knew it was horrible. No more accepting his not performing oral
copulation. No more holding him up to my standards to make him
feel better about himself. Never again would I let a man move in,
spend my money, or ejaculate inside of me without his caring about
my needs or intimate desires. And, sex before monogamy definitely
wasn't happening.

Unless, of course, I bumped into Nikko.

Hot water pounded my body, relieving the tension in my shoulders.
I lathered my loofah, scrubbed from the tip of my toes, to my ankle,
leg, thigh, hip, pubic, stomach, navel, breast, shoulder, neck, behind
my ear. I went down the backside, crossed over to the front, and did
the same on the other side.

Grazing my clit, I shivered then resumed cleansing. Determined to
rid my flesh of Fortune's DNA and baby oil for the last time, I
scrubbed harder.

I removed the handheld attachment, rinsed my body with hot
water. I turned the dial to the strongest pulsation, lowered the temperature, then held the showerhead over my vulva.

"Ah, yes. That feels so good."

There wasn't a horizontal bar in my bathroom like the one in the sex video. I wondered if I could hang upside down and thrust my pussy in the air the way Mimi had. Certainly I could stand and hold on with both hands while letting a real man fuck me from behind.

Imagining a strapping jock penetrating me, my mind quickly shifted to Nikko. What would he do if I put my pussy in his face? I directed the water over my breasts then twirled my areola between my fingers. I took a deep breath then pinched my nipple until the pain excited me.

My vagina contracted. I turned the dial to warm, lowered the sputtering water to my pussy, then closed my eyes. I pictured Nikko on his knees in the shower. The tip of his tongue flicked against my engorged clit.

Secretions flowed. My legs trembled. The thrill made my head spin. I closed my eyes, then released the biggest orgasm I'd had in months.

I screamed, "Oh my God yesssss!"

The bathroom door flung open. Fortune reached into the linen closet. "Thanks for getting that towel for me, Blake."

Damn! "You sorry bastard. Get out!"

He'd enjoyed nutting off but thanks to him I didn't get to relish in my afterglow for sixty seconds. I watched him as he wet the towel. He held his stomach, stooped, then slapped his balls side to side. Up and down his thighs he wiped each side, then twirled the towel around his flaccid dick.

"Ah, that sure felt good," he said, then laughed.

Opening the shower door, I told him, "Get dressed and get out. Leave your keys to my house on my dresser. I don't want you under my roof when I turn fifty."

"You're the one that got me kicked out of *my* own house with my wife. Always demanding to see me. If you would've done like I told you to, I'd still be at home with my wife. Vanessa ain't stupid. She—"

"No, I am. Make that, was. You've got to get out of my house too. You're no longer welcomed."

"Where am I supposed to go?"

"You should've thought about that a long time ago! Or at least before you started laughing at me for having the explosive orgasm you've never given me!"

Staring at me through the mirror, he snickered. "I'm sorry but you sounded like you were possessed."

"And you sound like the same inconsiderate son of a bitch you've always been."

This time he looked at me with bulging eyes. "I ain't gon' be too many more of them *b* words, Blake! You should've said you were miserable before I left Vanessa! Why do you hold in *your* problems then when things don't go your way it becomes my problem? Vanessa did the same damn thing. What's wrong with you women? Keep threatening to put me out and one of these times I'm going to pack my bags."

I stared deep into his eyes. If I had the strength, I could drag him outside, gag him, duct-tape him to a tree, and leave him there. I'd beat his behind first.

"Why you looking at me like that?" he asked.

"Hmm," was all I said.

If I left him in the woods, no one would miss him. Especially not Vanessa. I'd seen her out at Twist, the Fox Theater, and Bar One. She had the same fine young specimen escorting her each time. She kept a smile on her face. Not the kind that suggested, *How you like me now, Blake?* No, she had that, he's-pleasing-this-pussy-real-good kind of look plastered on her face. I saw a sexy confidence in the sway of her hips. I was envious at the loving way her man kept his hands on her.

As I stood in front of Fortune, his naked body disgusted me. I stared into his eyes. "I'm serious. When I come home from work, I don't want you here."

"You're serious?"

I didn't blink. Didn't respond. Didn't walk away.

He stepped back. "Baby, let's discuss this when you get home. I'll take you to the concert for your birthday."

The concert that I was supposed to ask my client for free tickets to. I shook my head. Jeremy didn't mind giving me comps. Maybe I'd invite Echo. I hadn't spoken with her in years. I missed my friend.

"I want you out today! Today!"

"Not this shit again." Fortune threw up his hands, exited the bathroom, then slammed the door.

CHAPTER 3

Alexis

"What do you think about the title, 'Barriers to Female Corporate Success: A quantitative study of female post-secondary graduates' ability to attain chief executive officer and chief operating officer positions in Fortune 500 companies in America'?"

My classmate Tréme gave me a slow nod. "I get where you're going. Barriers is your focus but your area of interest is unclear."

"How so?"

"Think about it some more, Alexis. Ability or inability? Is it personal or impersonal? You told me about your mom not getting promoted to the corporate level."

"And?"

Tréme picked up her black tote, placed her laptop inside. Gold fleur de lis symbols covered the front and back. She wasn't into designers or labels the way I was but she was a diehard Saints fan. Her family relocated from New Orleans to Atlanta after Hurricane Katrina.

"If your mom is your only motivation, you're not digging deep enough."

"Maybe you're right." I thought about what James had said to me yesterday about an anger management class. I was too proud to admit that I needed counseling.

Tears filled my eyes. I blinked repeatedly to keep them from falling. Tréme gave me a hug.

I picked up my purse, placed my iPad inside. "Let's go."

Exiting the classroom, Tréme gently interlocked her fingers with mine. "What about focusing your dissertation on a study of women who have their father listed as unknown on their birth certificate. Not knowing your dad haunts your spirit all the time. I can see the pain in your face right now. From what you've told me, your sisters don't seem to care that their fathers are listed as unknown too. But I bet if you had a heart-to-heart with them, you might discover they're hurting just like you. Honey, don't be too prideful to share your pain. My family lost everything we owned to Katrina. Loving, caring, generous strangers donated furniture, gave us a place to live, and paid my tuition in full. I'm indebted to society. So are you. In a way, everyone owes someone something. Letting go of what hurts you is a choice, Alexis. Your opening up can help heal a lot of women starting with yourself."

My heart grew heavier with her every word. I refused to cry. I knew she was right. I had to find my dad or find a way to let my caring about him go. "Thanks, I'll call you later, gurl," I told Tréme, giving her a hug.

She held me close, then went into the restroom. I left the building. Stopping on the curb, I glanced down the aisle where I'd parked.

Please tell me that's not my car.

I stood tall on my Jimmy Choo Lang stilettoes. Slowly, I made my way to the end of the lot. "Get your ass off of my car!"

The female snapped her head in my direction, then stepped aside.

"This is my ride, ma." The guy winked at me then nodded sideways toward the big-booty girl with the small waist standing near him.

Why me? Why today? I didn't care if he was trying to impress this female. His fake New Yorker accent didn't mean shit to me. Sitting on the hood of my convertible was not the right decision. Disrespecting me was worse. I didn't need to pull my hair up in a ponytail or take off my earrings but if he didn't raise up off of the Lexus my man bought me . . .

Dark clouds grew closer together. The warm summer breeze stopped flowing. Class went well this morning. I was in a reflective space, and now this bullshit. I didn't know him and even if I did, I wasn't cosigning on any lies this dude might have told this chick. I inhaled long and deep. The scent of ozone filled my nostrils.

He crisscrossed his ankles, leaned back, smirked at me with an upward nod. Dropping one of my purse straps from my shoulder to my forearm, I opened my bag, took three strides toward this fool, spread my legs, then planted my heels firmly on the ground.

He laughed. "Who you supposed to be, ma? Joseline Hernandez?"

Wait a minute. This bitch rambling like we kin.

The girl eyed me then him. Her glance shifted back and forth.

He slid his hand over his mouth. "Sis, why you trip—"

Smack! Lightning struck as my backhand landed across his jaw.

I watched him slide from the hood then stumble. The girl laughed at him as she held her stomach. The second he raised his hand to hit me, I pulled out my piece.

The girl's eyes grew wide but not larger than his. I gave the area where his ass was a quick once-over to make sure my hood wasn't damaged, then told him, "Don't give me a reason to pop off because I will."

"Damn, I was joking," he said, raising his hands as though he was familiar with surrendering to authorities. "Don't shoot me."

This guy was a waste of my time. As I drove out of the campus parking lot, a call came in from James. Thunder roared. Lightning struck twice. I wasn't sure which came first, the loud boom, or the sudden downpour, but I was accustomed to both.

I answered, "Hey, babe."

"You staying out of trouble?" he asked, then laughed. "I'm in your area, sweetheart. Want some company?"

"Sure. I should be home in twenty minutes."

"Why you sound so uptight? I was just kidding with you. Oh, no. What happened this time?" he asked.

"I'm good. Come by."

"Cool. See you in twenty. I love you, gurl."

"Yeah, I know. Bye, babe."

Huge raindrops splattered against my windshield. I turned down Big Tigger on V-103 to barely audible. I hadn't spoken with my mom in a few days. I dialed her from my list of favorites.

Her voice resonated through my car speakers. "Hey, honey. How was class?"

"It was good. I'll be glad when I'm done."

"You're closer to the end than when you started. You only have a short while to go, then we can officially call you Dr. Crystal. How's James?"

"He's good. He's meeting me at my place in a few. You ready for your big five-O? You should celebrate the entire two weeks," I told her knowing she wouldn't.

"I'm thinking about putting Fortune out."

I kept quiet. She'd lied about that before. She never should've let his broke ass move in. She didn't need to hear my opinion again.

"Hello."

"I'm still here, Mom. Mom?"

"Did you hear me?" she asked with a tone that indicated she was expecting me to comment on her kicking Fortune out.

Instead, I asked, "Who's my dad?"

Now it was her turn. She became quiet, then sighed. "Baby, you turned out well without him. All of you guys are just fine. Leave it alone. Finding out is only going to disappoint you."

She didn't have the right to deny me. The rain stopped as abruptly as it had started. The sun beamed into my windshield. I dug in my purse for my sunglasses and put them on. "I'll see you at dinner tomorrow. Bye, Mom."

Somberly, she said, "Bye, honey."

Lately, I'd been longing more than usual to confront my father. The feeling was more than emotional. The pain in my heart was real. I couldn't understand why my asking my mother about my father annoyed her. I wasn't going to stop pressuring her. I was the one with a birth certificate that read "father unknown."

I was the one suffering. Not her. If she kept refusing to tell me, I'd figure out another way to find his ass.

CHAPTER 4

Alexis

Pulling into the driveway at my complex, I saw that James's car was on the first floor in one of the visitors' spaces. I could've requested an additional pass and remote for him to enter and park wherever he'd like but I didn't want to encourage him to show up at my place unannounced, especially since he only paid my twenty-five-hundred-dollar a month rent sometimes.

I tooted my horn. We waited for the black metal security gate to open. He followed me. I parked on level four. He continued up to the sixth floor where there were posted VISITOR PARKING ONLY signs. Soon as we entered my apartment, I put my purse on the table, checked my hair and makeup in the mirror. My pink lipstick was still fresh. I fluffed my long, dark, wavy strands.

We left our shoes by the door, hugged, then stepped onto the plush white carpet in the living room. I exhaled. Every time I made it across my threshold it felt comforting to be home. James gave me a juicy passionate kiss that lightened my spirit. I sat on my white leather sectional.

"What do you feel like doing tonight, sweetheart?" Lying across my sofa he placed the back of his head on my lap.

This man was in love with me. It wasn't mutual. I cared about him but I'd never been in love. What I appreciated most about James was he accepted me with all my flaws. Others dated me for three months, some longer, but James was the only one that had lasted for three years.

"Why are you so good to me?" I asked him.

James was an excellent protector and a generous provider. In addition to paying for school and my car, he'd whisk me away at least once a month on all-expenses-paid vacations. Occasionally he'd give me money to pay my rent. The sexcapades I gave him in exchange for his kindness were, in my opinion, priceless. I was more than a good lay. I was eye candy. Five-five, a size six, had hazel eyes that sometimes turned green. I thanked my mother for my long, thick, wavy, black, natural hair, full lips, and dark, radiant complexion. Exercising two hours every morning was mandatory to maintain my hour-glass figure.

"You want to catch a movie? Chill here at your place then day after tomorrow we can fly to Miami in the morning. I can book our favorite suite at the Ritz. We can chill poolside, sip on drinks while watching the sunset. You can make your man feel special and we fly back the next day." Pointing the remote at my flat-screen television, he scrolled through the cable guide. Selected a sports channel.

Tenderly I tugged on his ear. He winked then smiled. I mimicked his expression.

"You're awfully quiet, sweetheart. What happened at school?"

Pressing my bottom lip against my top, I told him, "I'm good." That dude that I'd smacked down earlier probably hadn't forgotten me but I was over that situation.

Growing up, half of my friends weren't living in a two-parent household but all of them had daddy stories. I didn't have one memory or photo of my father. What was wrong with me? Why didn't he want to know me? He got my mom pregnant then walked away without offering a minute of his time to be with me. Whatever happened between him and my mom wasn't my fault.

"We can go to my house tonight. Or," he said, nodding, "we can go upstairs and you can give me one of your erotic back rubs."

I shouldn't hate a man I didn't know. Truth was, I didn't know how not to hate my dad. I wasn't some rag doll without feelings. I was human just like him. I was . . . I had to stop myself from revisiting the empty space in my heart. I was not giving up on one day staring that man in his eyes and asking him, "Why?"

"I'm okay with Miami day after tomorrow."

"I hate I'm missing your mom's big day tomorrow but I understand it's daughters only," he said. "I'll tell Blake I'll do something on the side with her before she goes back to work."

They had their own relationship and that was cool with me. I told my babe, "I can definitely give you a massage. Not an hour from now. Right now. Just can't chill with you all night. I've got plans."

Looking at my man, I stroked his smooth cheek. I thanked God for James Wilcox. I knew it was selfish of me to hold on to him with my ulterior motives and deeply rooted problems but I was not letting him go.

Retreating to my loft, we undressed. He got in the shower while I filled my crockpot with water then turned it on high. I placed a plastic bottle filled with sandalwood oil inside the pot then joined my guy. I lathered a towel, scrubbed his lean, muscular body from his shoulders to his ass. After hanging the towel on a rack, I slid my soapy hands up and down his back.

"Lean forward," I said in a commanding tone. That was my alter ego, Dom, kicking in.

Gently inserting my finger halfway into his rectum, I twirled until he felt clean then firmly told him, "Go lay your ass on the bed face down."

Holding open the shower door, he stared at me without blinking. "What?"

"You know what," he retorted. "So you're going to hang out with *her*? Again. Tonight."

If it ain't one thing with my man, it was definitely something. "Go lay your ass down before I change my mind." This was my pussy and I was no longer defending what I did with it.

I closed the shower door. Through the glass, I watched him leave the bathroom. I washed my body, brushed my teeth.

After drizzling hot oil onto his body, I eased the tip of the bottle into his rectum, held it there, gave him a moment to enjoy the warm sensation, then I pulled it out and placed the bottle back in the pot. A few toys were on top of my brown leather chest at the foot of my king-size bed. I picked up my cell to check if I'd missed any calls or messages. Chanel had texted, you coming through. I'd respond to her later. I put my phone back on the chest.

Chanel was my friend. I'd known her for a year. We had crazy chemistry from the moment I'd dropped ten, one-dollar bills between her legs while she was performing onstage at Pin Ups. She had the prettiest pink pussy I'd ever seen. I enjoyed going down on my gurl and going to the club to watch her dance.

Rolling over, James said, "You know when we get married, I don't care if she is your so-called friend. You're not leaving our house to party with her unless I'm with you."

That was the double-standard bullshit that made me hard on men. Why would I let James or any man tell me whom I could or couldn't go out with? I knew a threesome with my gurl had been on his mind for a while but that wasn't happening. I was not sharing Chanel with anyone. Well, maybe my sexing another female with Chanel might be okay long as it was a desirable stud.

Standing at the side of my bed, I rubbed hot oil over James's chest and abs. The more I stared at James my energy shifted. The animosity I harbored toward my father started surfacing. My brows grew close together. My lips tightened.

James said, "I recognize that angry look sweetheart. Let it go, Alexis."

He read me well. If James proposed, if I'd accept, if I'd give birth to this man's baby, would he leave me the way my dad did my mom? I was certain that my father didn't care about me the way I longed for him.

I looked at James while massaging his nipples. James was six years older than I. His lips were slightly darker than the rest of his face. His eyes slanted downward on the insides. His goatee was thin and always neatly trimmed.

I wiped my hands on the sheet, then picked up my cell.

James stared at me. "Really, Alexis?"

Softly, I said, "Alexis isn't here James."

His dick pointed toward the ceiling. I loved his long chocolate thang. "Shut the hell up. Turn your ass over. I want you up on all fours, bitch. Now! Don't make me blindfold your ass."

He obeyed. I replied to Chanel, b there around 10. I locked my phone, tossed it on the chest. It slid onto the floor. I left it there and started playing with my guy's ass. Licking. Teasing. Sucking. I pleasured him from behind. I drizzled hot oil over the crack of his ass then massaged oil onto his dick and balls.

A half hour later I told him, "Lie on your back."

Wiping off the excess oil, I tossed the towel aside. I moaned as I smeared his precum all over my face. I sucked his head while firmly stroking his shaft. I stopped soon as I tasted the tartness oozing through his pores signaling he was on the verge of ejaculating.

"Stop spilling my damn seeds. You're going to cum inside my pussy." Mounting him, I rode his dick reverse cowgirl, held on to his toes until they curled in the palms of my hands.

He screamed, like a bitch. "Alexis, I'm cumming!"

When he stopped yelling, we chilled for a moment then made our way back to the shower.

"What do you see in her?" he asked.

"Who?"

"Her. What do you see in her?" he asked, standing in front of me. "Are you a lesbian?"

"Yes, I am."

"No, you're not," he harshly replied.

"Then why are we having this fucking conversation?"

"Just answer this one question," he said.

I sighed, releasing my frustrations. "No! No!"

"I promise I won't ask again. Has any man penetrated your mouth, ass, or pussy since we've been together."

I became quiet.

He became quiet.

Calmly, I told my guy, "Chanel is a good friend. Nothing more."

"She's your lover, Alexis. Stop hiding behind the friend bullshit and admit it!"

I didn't love Chanel either. Not the way she wanted me to.

I shoved him into the wall. Stared into his eyes. Grabbing the back of his neck, I pulled him to me, thrust my tongue into his mouth, sucked his hard, sprawled my hand over his face, then pushed him away.

He tried but couldn't conceal his smile. "You're sick. I'm out. I'll call you tomorrow to let you know what time I'll pick you up for our Miami getaway." James exited the shower, dressed, then left.

Relieved that my man was out of my space, I went downstairs, played Pandora through my Bluetooth speaker, mixed a mai tai, then lounged naked on my sofa. Maybe one day I'd meet my dad. Get it all out.

I yelled, "You sorry ass son of a bitch!"

Tempted to hurl my glass at the wall, I refrained. No one heard my cry. The worst part was, no one honestly cared.

CHAPTER 5

Blake

"Thank you for overseeing my new account."

As I maintained my professional composure, a half smile parted my lips. "Mr. Sterling, you have been a loyal client for fifteen years. It's my responsibility to ensure your needs are met." I paused, then added, "Banking needs."

He chuckled. "Blake, when are you going to accept my dinner invitation?"

This forty-year-old, single, six-foot-eight, dark and handsome man with light brown eyes and wavy hair made me grin on the inside every time he entered my branch.

The first three buttons on his crisp white shirt were undone. The cuffs were neatly folded above his wrists. Slowly, I inhaled, concentrating on making sure my breasts did not heave. The diamonds in his Rolex flickered each time he gestured with his hand.

I replied, "When you're no longer my client. And don't even think about transferring anything." Why couldn't I meet men like him outside of work?

Picking up my cell, I texted my VP, INU2. That was short for *I need you to rescue me.*

Brandon strolled to my desk. "Hi, Mr. Sterling. I hate to interrupt but I have to borrow Ms. Crystal from you." He looked at me. "Ready to start your two weeks' vacation, birthday girl?"

"Oh, really," Mr. Sterling said. "And you weren't going to tell me, huh?" He smiled. "Dinner is now mandatory."

If I were certain his intentions were strictly business, I'd have lunch with him tomorrow but I sensed they weren't. I knew mine wouldn't be. I was flattered but I was no fool. Going out on a date with a client could be viewed by corporate as unethical.

"I'd love to but I can't accept."

Twice, my bosses had denied my promotion to district manager. First I was told, *You haven't been in your current position long enough.* Then it was, *You don't have enough experience.* Now that my branch was averaging twenty thousand transactions per month, the next time there was an opening, I'd be prepared to challenge them or leave the company. If I resigned, I'd definitely go on a date with Mr. Sterling.

"You have my number. Enjoy your time off. I'll wait for you. And please call me Bing when we're on our date." He stood, nodded at Brandon, then left.

Brandon scanned Bing up and down, waited until he exited the bank, then told me, "You know he's family."

My jaw dropped. "Shut the front door," I said.

"You might as well, honey," Brandon said, walking away.

For a moment I was confused, then I discounted his comment. Brandon suspected all men were bisexual, bi-curious, or gay. I removed my nameplate from my desk, locked it in my drawer, then headed to the break room. My gifts were on the table where I'd left them after lunch. The staff had surprised me with a Godiva cheesecake, catering from prettiplates.com, a bottle of champagne, and a dozen long-stemmed white roses.

"Let me help you to the car," Brandon offered, picking up the roses and gift bags filled with goodies.

A few of my customers gave me cards. One sent a beautiful rubber tree plant. I left it on the credenza behind my desk as a reminder of how people I barely knew cared more about my birthday than the man whom I'd dedicated five years to. Brandon put the gifts in my car, then followed me to the driver's side.

"Thanks," I told him, opening my arms. "Now if you need me, call me."

Brandon held me as he spoke into my ear. "You only turn fifty once,

Blake. You take excellent care of everybody else. Tomorrow, make it all about you, honey. Forget about those grown girls and if you want to, get you some good, young, hung, succulent dick. Be a ho for a day, honey. If you need me to hook you up, I have a few straight friends that would love you."

There was no shortage of dick in this metrosexual vortex. There was also no shortage of new HIV cases. And although there wasn't a cure, Truvada—the HIV and AIDS prevention pill—was giving people a newfound comfort to have unprotected sex. The one thing I could testify to was I'd never contracted anything from Fortune. Not even a cold.

"If you don't want me to find you a man, use the toy I bought you. You don't have to wait until you get home. Pop it in your panties, tune in to Majic 107.5, and toot your horn at every bitch you drive by."

"What in the world did you get me?" I laughed. "Mr. Cutter, you are a hot mess."

A black sparkling Porsche parked next to my car. I redirected my attention to Brandon. He always knew how to make me feel better. He let go, opened my door, waited for me to strap in. Maybe I'd leave his toy in the car and use it tomorrow.

Closing my door, I lowered my window. "Thanks, Brandon. You're a true friend."

I heard a familiar voice say, "Hey, Blake. Glad I caught you." It was Jeremy Hill hurrying toward me. He handed me an envelope with my name on it. "Happy birthday."

My eyes lit up. A wide smile parted my lips. Brandon had stepped aside. His eyes were set in my direction but I knew him well. His peripheral was on Jeremy.

"You remembered. Thanks."

"You thought I'd forget. You're in VIP for Brick, Midnight Star, the S.O.S. Band, and Morris Day. Get there early. I gotta run. Enjoy the show," he said. Getting in the Porsche, he sped off.

Brandon looked into my eyes, then said, "Blake Crystal, you have a lot to be thankful for. You raised four beautiful girls by yourself. You have a gorgeous home in Roswell that *you* paid off. You're sitting in this all-white Mercedes-Benz sedan that's paid for. You have a red Ferrari in your garage that you seldom crank up. Drive that bitch tomorrow, Blake. You worked your way up to president of this branch. Don't worry. You'll get the next DM position. You're the best supervisor I've ever worked for, honey. And I'ma stop there, bitch, 'cause I'm getting emotional."

"Thanks. I needed to hear that." I was grateful for my accomplishments but I'd never celebrated them or myself. Starting now, I was making myself a priority.

"If it's any consolation, honey, most people are in messed up relationships. Either they ain't fucking at all, the sex is mediocre at best, or they're cheating. Men are acting like women. The women want to be men. Do like me. I just fuck my way in and out of my problems. Having a good orgasm makes you feel better about everything, not everybody, honey. Bye, bitch."

I watched Brandon strut into the bank. His broad shoulders complemented his slender muscular frame. His clothes were designed by one person; tailored by another. Neon-lime was his favorite color. His radiant glowing skin, high butt cheeks and cheekbones, made women take a second look. Brandon's nails were always manicured to perfection. Hair never looked like it needed to be cut. He was a you-only-live-once kind of guy.

Brandon was right. Out of all the couples I knew, only a few seemed truly in love. I wanted to be in that minority. I wanted a man who sincerely loved me. I exhaled.

Was promiscuity the new normal nowadays?

CHAPTER 6

Blake

Not ready to go home to an empty house, I stopped in Buckhead at Posh Nails for a manicure by my favorite technician, Amy. While she pampered my hands, Anna massaged my legs and feet with hot stones. After they were done, I sat in the plush tan leather chair checking my Facebook and Instagram pages.

Sandara, my youngest daughter, had posted a video. She was holding up a pair of shoes. *Lawd, I'd better connect my Bluetooth before listening to this.* I tapped my screen and heard, "Raymond, these are too small! While you rollin' in yo' new ride, your son needs a new pair of shoes, ho. Size ten, ho!" She flashed five fingers twice.

I shook my head at how she'd handled the situation but she was right. Early birthday wishes were posted on my page from my siblings. Ruby, Carol, Peter, Walter, Teresa, Kevin, and Kim stated they wished they could be with me tomorrow. I became sad. Growing up, no matter how much we argued, we loved one another. I missed them. We'd all moved from our hometown of Charlotte but I was the only one living in Atlanta.

I started to open my work e-mail account. I locked my cell, dropped it in my purse. "Thanks, guys. See you in two weeks."

Getting in my car I unwrapped Brandon's gift. OMG! A pink Rock-Chick? One end was a G-spot stimulator. The opposite tip was a clit stimulator. Each time I pressed the button the buzzing got stronger. I touched it again and the toy started pulsating.

"This thing can't be safe to use while driving," I said, continuously pressing the button. "Lawd, how many speeds does this thing have? I can see myself crashing while having an orgasm." *How do I turn it off?* Forget it. I tossed it in my purse, then talked a text message to Brandon. LOL Thank You!

I circled Lenox Square Mall and Phipps Plaza several times until I was tired, then I headed home. The black BMW 750i was in my driveway. When I opened the front door, his cheap cologne greeted me. He didn't.

Fortune was lounging on my sofa, drinking a beer, watching the game. "You ask Jeremy for those tickets? You know I want to take you to the Affordable Old School concert at Wolf Creek."

My stomach churned making me want to vomit. I picked up the remote, turned off the television. Staring at Fortune, softly I said, "Get off of my sofa and get the hell out of my house." Then I yelled, "Now!"

He stood, opened his mouth. I held up my hand, shook my head, then told him, "I'll have your clothes delivered wherever you'd like. But right now, you need to leave. And *never* come back."

"Blake—"

"I'm serious. Get out of my house."

He went upstairs, returned with his keys. Slowly, he removed my house key, handed it to me.

I shook my head. "I don't need it." I dialed a locksmith. "Can you send someone to rekey my entire house right now?" I paused, then replied, "Great," giving them my address.

Fortune stared at me. He took baby steps toward the door, placed his hand on the knob. His eyes drooped, then his head hung as he opened the door. Hesitantly, he crossed the threshold. He stared at me, closed the door. I watched the latch turn as he locked it with his key.

The first thing I did was go to the kitchen, get a metal bucket, and put my champagne on ice. Next, I went upstairs, changed the cotton linen on my king-size bed to a new set of white satin sheets, pillowcases, and Euro shams. I stuffed the white duvet with a white down feather comforter, then opened two bags of clean cotton potpourri. I spritzed my bathroom with the calming fragrance of home sweet home.

The doorbell rang. Trotting downstairs, I welcomed in the lock-smith, gave him instructions on rekeying every lock throughout my home. While he did his job, I sat on my sofa. Soon as he left, I lit a few candles, drew my bathwater, undressed, stepped into my sunken tub, leaned back, and relaxed.

For Blake Crystal, a self-centered, unapologetic lifestyle was start-ing right now.

CHAPTER 7

Alexis

The parking lot at Pin Ups strip club was packed.

A dozen premiere reserve spots were on the first row. Twenty dollars to occupy a space in the front. Ten in the back behind the building. Either way everybody had to park their own shit. Big Z moved one of the orange cones. I zoomed in my convertible, raised the top. Getting out of my car, I grabbed my pink Michael Kors bag, then gave Big Z a hug.

"What's up, Alexis? You looking fresh as always. When you gonna make that happen?" Big Z asked, holding my hand.

He'd been trying four months to get Chanel and me to double-dip on his dick. I couldn't blame him for wanting to taste my chocolate-cherry-colored punany. He'd have to fall in a line that extended down the block and round the corner. Long as he kept giving me VIP for free, I'd keep stringing his anxious ass along. Walking toward the flashing sign with the club's name in neon lights, I told Z, "I got you."

"Yeah, but when?"

I blew him a kiss. "When the time is right. I have to get my gurl to say yes." Opening the door, the cashier motioned for me to enter the club. She'd stopped hitting me up for the ten-dollar cover after I started dating Chanel.

The pool table room on the other side of black metal bars facing the entrance had a few guys hitting balls. There were female dancers grinding on the laps of men and women for twenty dollars a song. I never lingered in there mainly because no one inside that area could see any parts of the stage.

I made my way to the bar, stood at the end watching two performers. The girls here were not lazy like some I'd seen at Magic City or laid back like the ones at Strokers. The Pin Ups were in full effect every night.

"Here you go, sweetheart," the mixologist said, handing me a mai tai. Peaches didn't need to ask if I wanted my usual. I never deviated from this drink at this club.

"Thanks." The tab was eight but I gave her a twenty to include my next cocktail, then I strolled to VIP where the round black tables and vinyl chairs were dining height.

The stage was eye level, which meant the higher the girls climbed the poles the more I had to tilt my head back to see them. This VIP setup was intended to accommodate lap dances during the show.

I sat at my usual corner table next to the stairway the dancers used to enter and exit the stage. In case some dumb shit jumped off I was in position to snatch my gurl and get out.

The identical twins, Kandy and Karmella, were cleaning the gold poles in preparation for their routine. They tossed the rags to the back of the stage. Soon as the first beats to "Turn Down for What" came on, one quickly ascended a pole to the lateral bar near the ceiling, tossed one ankle over the bar, kept the other leg around the pole, then started rubbing her pussy as though she were masturbating.

"Hey, Alexis. What's up?" the security guy asked. "You looking tasty in pink tonight."

"Thanks, Big Norm. I see you got your sexy on," I said, adjusting my halter a little lower.

"When you gon' call me, woman?" he said, scanning the room.

"Grad school taking up all my extra," I lied.

"I'ma let you have that. Hit me up though. For real. I wanna take you out," he said, walking away.

Bam! The other twin hit the floor with a full split, bounced, flipped onto her back, twirled her legs in the air, spun, spread her thighs, then held her pussy lips apart. Dudes gathered at the platform, stood there until the song ended. Some of 'em never drizzled dough on her. I shook my head. Cheap bastards should've bought a two-piece chicken special, went home, popped in a DVD, and jacked off.

I chilled until my gurl made her way center stage. Entertainment was cool but Chanel was an entrepreneur. From the first beat to the last, she focused on making the customer farthest from her stop whatever they were doing, come up to the stage, and drop them dollars. It worked on me.

The DJ pumped up the crowd announcing, "You don't want to miss this, people. If you've never witnessed a squirter in action, here's your chance. Lady Waterfall is about to gush. You gon' need a raincoat and I ain't talkin' 'bout no condom, fellas."

"Here you go, Alexis," Peaches said, sitting a fresh drink on my table.

Dudes and chicks flocked to the stage. The DJ teased the crowd with a few more songs before Chanel did her thing. She sat in front of guy number one, opened her legs, placed her knees behind her shoulders, gazed into his eyes, then rocked on her back.

His mouth hung open like he was thirsty. He stared at my gurl's pussy. Twenty seconds later the only thing in his hand was the dick inside his pants. Lady Waterfall politely slithered to the opposite end of the stage. She did the same move for a different dude. He made it rain so heavy I thought my gurl was gonna gush for him. Dude number one could hold out for the next female to flash his cheap ass but I knew Chanel well. She was not spreading for him again. She worked every side of the stage until the stage was covered with paper.

The DJ said, "Who wants to marry this pussy? I think she'll say yes to the guy that drops the most cash," then he played "Throw This Money on You" by R. Kelly.

Chanel climbed the gold pole nice and slow. She hung upside down, slowly descended head first toward the floor. Ascending midway up the pole she spun sideways. Lady Waterfall made her way to the top, placed one foot over the bar. Her other leg was on the pole, then she gave the crowd what they'd come for.

Lady Waterfall gushed like a river bursting through a dam.

Men shook their heads real slow. Several had that glossy I'm-in-love look in their eyes. Married or single, Chanel could have any one of these guys, females included. After the song ended, it took her five minutes to gather our wet dough into a large bag. Another ten minutes was needed for two guys to sanitize the stage and poles for the next performers.

No one knew Chanel as well as I did. Offstage, my gurl was submissive. To make certain she didn't stray, I had to keep Chanel in check.

I didn't want to be hard on her. I had to.

CHAPTER 8

Blake

"Happy fiftieth, Blake Crystal. I love you." Untying my leopard robe, I let it drop to the floor.

I stood face-to-face with my naked reflection. I saw a beautiful, dark-skinned African-American woman. I was strong. Successful. I scanned myself head to toe. I was far from perfect. My breasts hung lower, stomach protruded a tad. Those were things I could fix with cosmetic surgery. The ass God blessed me with still sat high enough for a pencil to fall if placed underneath my cheek.

"Starting today, I am going to concentrate on me."

The little girl inside of me cried for my mother. My lip quivered. "I miss and love you, Mommy." I dried my tears. My feelings for my father weren't the same. It wasn't that I didn't love him. The paternal love I had was different. Outside of being told that I was his daughter, I didn't know him very well. Not wanting to be sad on my birthday, I went into my bedroom.

Fortune's name had registered on my caller ID seventeen times. Make that eighteen. I declined, switched my cell to silent, tossed it on my comforter. I picked up the open bottle of champagne. The ice from last night had melted. Cool water dripped into the bucket. I refilled my flute then headed downstairs.

Sliding open my door, I stepped onto my patio. The fresh mid-afternoon humid breeze filled my lungs. I took in as much as I could, sat my flute on the table, then stood at the edge of my pool. Eighty-five degrees of sunshine heated my body.

I inhaled, stretched my arms wide, then softly exhaled, "Thank you, Jesus."

All that I had, I owed to Him. I placed my palms together, closed my eyes, then I dove into the deep end. The cold water felt exhilarating.

I opened my eyes.

Midway, I came up for air. Treading the blue chlorinated water, all that I saw, I owned. The twelve blue lawn chairs with yellow cushions. The barbecue grill, round tables with umbrellas, and the outdoor fireplace were mine. Two acres of backyard covered with trees. Mine.

I swam to the side, got out, relaxed on a lounge chair. Raising my glass to the blue sky scattered with white clouds, I said, "A toast, to Blake Crystal." I slid on my sunglasses.

The sound of my breathing was peaceful. I rubbed sunblock on my skin, reclined, and enjoyed my "me time." I couldn't recall the last time there was no Fortune, no Mercedes, Devereaux, Alexis, Sandara, or some man living under my roof. In this moment, I felt good.

I thought about my dad, wondering if our casual acquaintance made it easy for me to bond with men I barely knew. My memories transitioned to my daughter. While I felt she still needed my protection, Alexis deserved to know her dad. All of my children did. It was time for me to let my baby judge Conner Rogers for herself. After she walked across the stage, I'd give her his number.

The sweet melody of the saxophone penetrated my soul. I loved my *Hidden Beach Unwrapped* music collection. I reflected on my life. It wasn't perfect but it was good, and I was grateful.

I'd better get up and get dressed for dinner.

Picking up my glass, I strolled through my place naked. I thrust my hips side to side. The room I entered off of the living area used to be Mercedes's. The other girls were jealous my eldest, Devereaux, had the largest bedroom next to mine and that Mercedes had a Jacuzzi in her bathroom. Now that I was alone, I had the freedom to do whatever, whomever, wherever, in my house. The whomever included me doing myself and that was exactly what I was getting ready to do.

I filled the tub, stepped down two times, then pressed my lower back into the strong stream of bubbles. I sat directly on top of a jet that pumped cool water into my vagina. Today was all about me!

I squeezed my vaginal muscles to stop the flow of water entering me. "Yes!" I held my hands high. She still had it. I relaxed. Sipped champagne.

Thirty-four years had gone by since my sweet sixteenth birthday. I remembered 1980 well. Junior year my skirts were shorter; my legs had grown longer. My firm breasts were larger and my nipples stood out. They still did that. The skin-tight yellow, pink, blue, and green Gloria Vanderbilt jeans I loved to wear made boys and men stare at my ass.

Mama couldn't buy me the clothes I wanted. I refused to accept hand-me-downs from my older sisters Ruby and Carol so I kept a part-time job babysitting until I got a work permit.

Damn, Blake. You've worked thirty-six years.

Soaking in the tub made me restless. I no longer felt like masturbating. Getting out of the Jacuzzi, I stepped into the shower, washed my hair. I dried off with a plush towel, then I massaged lotion all over my body.

I applied my favorite Lash Love Front Row eyelashes with the rhinestones, then eased into my fitted mid-thigh, red halter designer dress. I smoothed my hair into a bun, slid Tom Ford Slander red lipstick across my mouth.

Locking my door, I dropped my new keys in my red Lady Dior bag. Firing up the engine of my Ferrari, I listened to R. Kelly's *Genius,* while cruising south on I-85.

The valet attendant opened my door. He reached for my hand. I gave him my key and a tip at the same time. I strutted inside the Cheesecake Factory at Lenox Square, sat at the bar, dangled my red stiletto on the tip of my toes, then ordered a drink.

"I need to see your ID," the bartender said.

Smiling, I handed it over.

He looked at my driver's license, then at me, then at my license, back at me, then said, "No way."

I had to admit. Right now, I was feeling myself.

CHAPTER 9

Blake

"You chill?" the bartender asked.

I nodded.

"If you need anything else," he paused, tapped the bar twice, then said, "I got you."

"Thanks," I said, stirring my vodka martini with the three olives that were aligned on a plastic pick.

He was cute. I stared into my glass. Waiting for my girls to arrive, I thought about Brandon's comment that most relationships were messed up. He was right. I recalled the families that lived on my block when I was a teenager.

Where were they now?

If God were gracious to say, Blake Crystal, I'm going to let you go back to being sweet sixteen, what would I do differently?

Not have lost my virginity in the back seat of a Camaro? Not have had sex with more than one guy in the same day? Have all of my kids by the same man? Been a hundred percent sure who the fathers of my children were? Marry before starting a family? Not allow some of the men I dated to move into my home? I wasn't proud of my past but I wasn't ashamed of it either. I'd done well on my own.

He tapped twice, then asked, "You chill?"

This time I looked at him and smiled. I hadn't noticed his sexy undertone the first time he'd asked. "Yes, I'm chill."

My gaze lingered. I shook my head as though I was trying to awaken from a dream. This mixologist had a lot of sexual energy resonating from his mannerisms.

"If you need anything—"

I interrupted, "Yes, I know. You got me."

A young lady wearing a white sleeveless maxi dress and high heels, said, "Is this seat taken, ma'am?"

Looking at her, I replied, "Only if you sit in it."

"Cool beans," she said, pulling out the vanilla-colored wicker stool.

She was shaped like most of the twentysomethings in Atlanta. Big breasts. Bigger butt. Small waist. She could've placed her purse in the chair next to me and sat one seat over. She did the opposite. "You look real nice, ma'am."

"Thanks," was all I said.

A text came in from Echo. Happy birthday my bff Blake Crystal. I love you.

I smiled on the inside. Echo was going to be excited when I gave her the news about ending my relationship with Fortune. Finally, I could reunite with my best friend.

"What's your pleasure, beautiful?" my waiter asked the young lady next to me.

"I'll have a lemon drop and I'd like a menu, handsome."

Observing them from my peripheral, had I forgotten how to flirt? I ate two of my olives.

More texts chimed in from my siblings. Peter, Walter, Teresa, Kevin, and Kim. I didn't want any of them to think I was clinging to my cell on my fiftieth. Nor did I want the bartender to detect my hint of jealousy. I'd respond to my family's texts tomorrow.

Sipping my drink, I let my tongue marinate in vodka. *What was the purpose of my life?* At some point it would end. In the meantime . . . heaving, I almost swallowed the third olive whole when I'd gotten a glimpse of the waiter's dick imprint. Quickly, I took another sip, placed my cocktail on the counter.

"You okay, ma'am?"

This time, I narrowed my eyes. Softly, I hissed, "Please, stop calling me ma'am."

"Cool beans," she said, then scrolled through her cell phone.

Exhaling, I took another swig, placed my glass in front of me.

When I was sixteen, the dad who lived next door to us desperately wanted to see his children. I recalled how that man spent his time and money in court fighting for joint custody because the mother of his children was pissed that he was remarried to a much younger wife. She wasn't prettier though. Not in my opinion. Eventually, he won his case. But what would've become of his children if he'd conceded to his ex, moved on, and never fought for his parental rights?

The guy who lived on the other side of him—we called him Mr. E— could see his children anytime he wanted, but Mr. E never did. Every weekend there were men coming and going in and out of his house. Sometimes different ones visited in the same day. None stayed more than two days. Religiously washing his luxury cars every Sunday morning seemed more important than his being a dad.

Setting a lemon drop by the young lady next to me, he tapped the bar twice in front of me. "You chill?"

This time my smile was tighter. I gave him a firm, "Yes."

"Excuse me, handsome, may I tell you what I'd like?" the young lady said.

"I'm all yours," he replied, taking one step sideways to his left.

I waited for him to take her order, then said, "I'd like another."

He stood in front of me. Gazed into my eyes. I swore the temperature between my legs rose six degrees.

"I can't allow you to stack drinks but . . ." He gave me a closed-lip smile.

"Excuse me, handsome, but, can you put my order in? If I don't get something to eat soon, I'm going to have to eat you. I'm hungry."

Frowning, I looked at her.

"Oh, I'm sorry, ma'am. No disrespect," she said.

He didn't move. He replied to her, "I'm on it," then he tapped the bar twice and told me, "When you're ready." He paused, then said, "I want you." Then he walked away.

Okay, it's been a while since I've dressed like this and sat at the bar alone. I hope he doesn't think I'm an escort.

I downed my drink, turned the glass upside down. He picked it up, cleaned the counter, made me another, then placed it in front of me without saying a word.

I texted Brandon, This young bartender is hot. I like him. I'm pretty sure he's flirting with me. Should I take him seriously?

He replied, Send me a selfie of you and sneak a pic of him.

Looking into my camera phone, I pretended I was capturing myself. I clicked the side button, got the bartender's photo. Then, I took one of myself and sent both to Brandon.

Sipping my drink, I read Brandon's reply. Is that his dick! Bitch pull up your dress and bend your ass over the bar! Fuck him! Seriously, he wants you to ride that dick. Do it bitch!

I laughed.

By the age of sixteen, I was certain that a man who didn't want much was worse than a man who didn't have much. At least this young man had a job and I believed he wanted me. If only for one night, I definitely wanted him.

Growing up my mother had told me to keep my legs closed. That worked for a while. Until I turned sixteen and met the most beautiful boy I'd seen in my life.

Billy Blackstone was tall, dark, had nice white teeth, huge biceps, thick thighs, and drove an orange 1975 Camaro his father had given him. His Afro was cut short and always neatly trimmed. I didn't care much for basketball but I enjoyed watching him run up and down the court.

My eyes trailed the bartender. I didn't care if he saw me.

I couldn't stay a virgin forever and the truth was I'd held on to mine longer than any of my girlfriends, including Echo. Billy was my first lover. First and only love, too. Maybe that was because I didn't know what love was. The thing I appreciated most was before we did it, Billy made me cum by licking my pussy.

I hoped the mixologist was great at performing oral sex. Drinking made me start lusting for the bartender. My pussy was overdue for some good dick. I finished my cocktail, turned my glass upside down.

"Now, you need to chill for real." He placed a large glass of water in front of me. "When you done with this, I've got something for you."

Dressed in a long-sleeved black button-down shirt and black slacks, he was about six-two, broad shoulders, firm ass, and had a slender waist. I imagined he had that definition that started at the base of a man's waistline then dipped inward toward his inner thighs.

I watched him wrap his long fingers around the silver shaker. Each time he shook, his shoulder-length locks jerked back and forth. *I bet his hair grazing my clit would make me cum. I could bend over this barstool and let him spank my ass until cream saturated my inner and outer labia but I was not pulling up my dress.*

Sometimes I liked it rough. Then there were times I wanted the dick slow and easy. As he poured, I became wet. I swallowed the ice-cold water, then set the glass down.

Fortune called again. I pressed decline.

"Good job. Drink a little more. If you need anything, I'm your man," he said with confidence. Then he slid one step to the left.

"Excuse me, bartender."

He smiled, flashing the most perfect large white teeth. "Yes," he said as if he were willing to do anything I'd ask of him. He could start by kissing me with those full sexy lips.

"How old are you, young man?"

A closed-lip smile accompanied the lifting of his brows. Right before he opened his mouth, he stood in front of me. For the first time I noticed his beautiful light brown eyes. He placed his elbow on the bar, leaned toward me, and whispered.

"Legal," was all he said, then he backed away. "By the way, those lashes." He nodded at me real slow.

Maintaining eye contact, I extended my tongue, then pressed my lips to the edge of my water glass. He sure looked as though he could fuck for hours.

I glanced down, then coughed. "Aw, damn!" His dick imprint was huge.

He smiled. "Think about what you want next," he said, then stepped to the left. "You good?" he asked the young lady.

"The best," she answered. "I'll have one more drop, handsome."

"I got you," he told her.

I felt him looking at me. I refused to give him eye contact. I was not secretly going to compete for his attention. I'd convinced myself all men were flawed. They all suffered from, as Brandon would say, ADDD—Attention Dick Deficit Disorder.

I gave birth to four girls, each one was older than the young lady next to me. Devereaux, Mercedes, Alexis, and Sandara entered the bar at the same time carrying bags and balloons.

In unison, they shouted, "Happy birthday, Mommy!"

The sexy mixologist came from behind the bar, placed a small folded piece of paper in my hand, then said, "Happy birthday, Mommy." Those raised brows and that closed-lip smile turned away after he winked. I recalled how happy Fortune's wife, Vanessa, looked every time I saw her with her younger guy.

Greeting my girls, I thought, *I've pushed four babies out of this vagina. It's still tight and I've still got it.* I hugged, kissed, and thanked each one of my daughters.

As a single mother I may have gotten some things wrong, but my children were all right. Well, perhaps. Depending on how one viewed their situations.

CHAPTER 10

Alexis

I scaled the chick sitting next to my mom. Twenty-two, maybe three. She gave me a head-to-toe once-over. Her gaze into my eyes steadied for three seconds, then she smiled. Just like the guys, we had our unspoken signals to express interest. I gave her a small upward nod. No smile. She was cute but there was only one opening in my entourage for a feline and Chanel had that on pause.

An alpha female—cheetah in nature—was more devious than an alpha male. The difference was women were more manipulative when it came to getting our way. Couple deception with determination and a real woman was dangerous . . . potentially lethal.

"I like your dress, Mama," I said, touching her outfit. I smoothed her fly away in with the rest of her strands, tried to uncurl her fingers to see what dude gave her. The larger-than-average print in his pants, I did not miss it. Instantly, I created a vacancy for his dick on my team.

My mom moved her hand. "Oh, no you don't," she protested.

"You know you're not going to use it. You've got Fortune, Mama."

"And you've got James, Chanel, and God only knows who else."

Didn't matter that the chick next to my mom redirected her attention from her phone to me. I could do her tonight if I wanted but I didn't play games. I had game. There was a major difference.

Mercedes exhaled. "Sandara, go ask the hostess to hurry up and seat us please." She dragged the last word out of her mouth.

My baby sister got her strut on like she was on a runway. I wished she'd discover her God-given modeling talent and get paid for being beautiful instead of comping her coochie to the lames. One more kid slide out of that womb and Sandara's baby count would be tied at four with our mom's.

Dude tapped twice on the bar. My mom turned as though he was her man. I stared at him.

"You chill?" he asked, picking up my mom's water glass.

Her eyes lit up. She smiled then nodded.

"Birthday beautiful. This one is on me." He set a martini with three olives in front of her. "Remember what I told you."

Aw, hell no. Game recognized. I started to whistle at him and command, down boy. Tapping? Really? That shit wasn't cool. I'd lose points if I reacted. I'd let it go for now. My wanting to ask about my dad and getting whatever my mom was holding on to in her hand would wait for now. This was her day.

While he was standing there, I leaned, hugged my mom, pushed my butt out a little so he could see the curves of my ass. Mercedes tugged the hem of my mocha minidress. She'd better be happy I didn't adjust my thong for an added visual. I ignored my sister.

I made sure my mom was facing the flirtatious bartender. This was the gorgeous mother who used to get all dolled up on weekends. The woman who had taught us how to keep it sexy almost had it all together. She could've done a better hairdo. The pulled-back look was too uptight for that slammin' fitted halter. I would've gone over the top, added in extra pieces of hair, and created big wavy curls that bounced right above ass.

I whispered, "I love you, Mommy." Despite her not telling me who my dad was, regardless of my being the one who'd challenge her the most, my mom was everything to me.

"I love you too, Alexis."

Admiring my mother, I shook my head. She was the bomb and didn't realize it. *What made her lay with lames?* Not only that, long as I remembered she'd taken up residence in that putting-a-man-first lifestyle. I shouldn't think poorly of Sandara for having three kids. She got that mental from our mom.

"They said another ten minutes at the most," Sandara reported.

"Move, Alexis," Devereaux said. "She's my mom too. Happy birthday, Mother, you look stunning," she said, taking my space.

Southern hospitality was out there in abundance but love was unavailable to the woman who'd put her heart first. And Blake always put her heart on a limb before she knew if the guy was legit. I'd seen where that had gotten her. That's why I had to stay on top of my game and my bitches.

To me, men were bitches too.

Dude behind the bar was probably in search of a sponsor. Whatever his intentions were, he was not going to use my mother. I could dismiss his note as innocent but the seductive expression on his face said he wanted to stick his dick inside my mom's pussy.

No apology, Mom. I was definitely running interference. I was going to ride his dick while letting him suck mine. If he thought he was going to use my mom, I was going to make him *my* next bitch.

Life was all about a challenge. I could take a lot of people's money but I wanted them to give me a reason to steal their heart. If everybody's happy, somebody got fucked. I made sure men were held accountable for every dickcision they made.

A text came in from Chanel. Call me boo

She was twenty-five going on eighteen. The dollars she earned from stripping paid the rent on my Buckhead loft apartment whenever James didn't give me the money. I refused to let her move in. Hadn't given her the key she kept asking for.

I was a Georgia peach but I owned Apple everything! The iPhone, iPad, iPod, MacBook Air and Pro, I had it all but hadn't paid for any of it. Some of my electronics were still in the box.

I knew my not responding to Chanel's text made her anxious. Rejection made her want me more. Chanel's jealousy of my going out with men had been a constant concern throughout our relationship. For her. I loved dick more than I enjoyed pussy.

My mom stood, picked up her drink. I took it from her, set it on the bar. "Leave it," I said, eyeing the bartender. "I got you."

Trailing my mom to our table, I read my girl's next text. You need to choose, Alexis. You want me? Or you want James? I love you but you can't have both.

I could. I did. And I was about to add one more to my team. I glanced over my shoulder at the bartender. He smiled. I winked to let him know I was interested.

Mercedes was behind me. She cleared her throat. "Let it go, Alexis."

My mother had Fortune's old tired ass at home. I was doing our mom a favor. While flirting with a much younger man may have made Mom feel good, she wasn't experienced enough to let that youngster stick his dick in any hole he wanted.

But I was.

CHAPTER 11

Spencer

"**M**other? Daughter?" I pointed them out to my boy, LB, then repeated, "Mother? Daughter?"

"Definitely the mother," he said, watching me pour a glass of merlot. "I saw you double-tap that at least a half dozen times."

We'd come up with our own Morse code for women. Two taps meant we wanted an exclusive op to hit it. One tap signified first to get it could have it. Sometimes we'd both do a customer if she were open. No tap. No interest.

I laughed. "Bruh, you must have eyes in the back of your cranium. How you waiting tables and spying me?"

LB was my boy. I'd gotten him on here bartending six months after I'd started two years ago. Derrick, our manager, was short-staffed on servers tonight. LB didn't mind filling in. He could do damn near everything except cook. LB was the only dude I hung with. Only one I trusted with knowing the real me. There was one thing I hadn't and probably never would share with him. Didn't want my friend looking at me sideways.

"If you think there's a man in here that didn't see that fine-ass woman in red walk through those double doors, you'd better do that or I might beat you to it, bruh."

I shook my head. "That's mine. You can have the daughter. When I get to first base with Mom, I'll arrange that for you."

"Might not need you, man. You see where they're seated though?" LB strolled away.

He was three inches shorter than me. Five-eleven was decent but he told females he was six feet. My double tap was seated at his table, but I paused. Damn, I didn't know the lady in red's name. How could I have forgotten to introduce myself?

A familiar voice said, "Check, handsome."

I stepped to the computer, closed her out. Soon as I turned, I thought, damn! My used-to-be side, now my main, was in the seat where her potential replacement was a few minutes ago.

Handing the customer her bill, I looked at my gurl. "What's up, Charlotte?"

"Why the fuck she calling you handsome like she all familiar? Give me a JW."

I loved my AfJam. She was half Nigerian, part Jamaican, and one hundred crazy turnt up twenty-fo. But sometimes I wished she'd give me a drama-free day.

I leaned over the bar. "Boo, I need you to do me a favor. I forgot to pick up my dry cleaning." I handed her a hundred. "Get it for me."

"Forgot my ass. Where the ticket at? Huh?"

My manager, Derrick, crept up behind me. "Ask her to leave or you leave. I'm not tolerating her disruptions again."

I told my gurl, "I'll stop by your place after I get off. What you want me to bring you, boo?"

Charlotte took the cash. I know my calling her boo in front of the girl sitting next to her helped my gurl turn down. Charlotte eyed my shit. "Bring me my dick," she said, then left.

Not tonight. My dick had intentions on making plans with the lady in red. I'd deal with my gurl's repercussions tomorrow.

Why did I always attract the crazy ones? This foolishness never happened to LB.

CHAPTER 12

Blake

"Mama, that bartender is delicious," Devereaux said, nibbling her bottom lip.

I sat on the end of the vinyl booth beside Devereaux. Just in case he came my way. Didn't want the bartender to have to reach over any of my daughters to get to me, especially Alexis who'd sat on the opposite end facing me. Not that he'd come over, but from my seat, I had a complete view of the bar.

"You like him?" Devereaux asked.

Devereaux was twenty-eight and a new mom of my two-year-old granddaughter, Nya. My child's deep brown eyes were the same color as the thick flat-ironed hair that hung below her shoulders. She stared at Alexis, then narrowed her eyes. "Don't say a word. I asked Mom, not you."

"He's cute," was my answer.

The heart-shaped engagement ring on Devereaux's finger had been there since she'd graduated from Clark-Atlanta four years ago. I tried to tell her not to let Phoenix move in with her after Nya was born but . . . she adamantly wanted them to be a family. Didn't want her daughter to grow up without her dad around.

"You're too old for him, Mama, give me that number," Alexis exclaimed. Stretching her long arm across the table, she wiggled her fingers in my direction.

"I knew it was coming," Devereaux said, shaking her head. "Contrary to what's in that brain of yours, every man does not want you. He's attracted to Mama."

Confidently, Alexis stated, "But they all want to do me."

Rolling my eyes at Alexis, I shook my head. I shouldn't be annoyed but couldn't she let me enjoy his flattery? As sexually free as she was, Alexis was my only child who didn't have a baby. I was grateful she'd made it to twenty-six without ever being pregnant and I prayed she'd wait until she had a husband. Hopefully she'd choose her on-again off-again guy. I liked James Wilcox. Not because he bought Alexis expensive gifts. Upgraded her from the Lexus 300 I'd bought her to a new convertible. My respect for James was based on the countless times I'd seen him protect my baby even when we knew she was dead wrong.

James, like the others Alexis dated, loved her craziness. I could learn some things from the way Alexis never hesitated to tell people what she thought. I didn't understand her reasoning of dating both males and females but she was my Leo child. Eventually, Alexis always got her way.

Curling my fingers into a fist, playfully I shook the paper at her. Hopefully the bartender had given me his contact. I was too mature to entertain chasing behind a man who looked young enough to be my son. My child's hand was still open and facing me.

Sandara swatted Alexis's hand. "Mama, you keep his number and use it. It's not like you're trying to marry him. You only turn fifty once. Get yourself some young, hard, good stuff."

Good stuff got my youngest child three babies and no husband. Got me four. Having casual sex made me think about CNN's ranking by city of reported HIV cases, as it appeared online at rollingout.com. Atlanta wasn't first or second but we were definitely in the top ten. Miami and Baton Rouge were numbers one and two.

Sandara and Devereaux favored one another the most except Sandara didn't press her hair. She had that long gorgeous wash-and-go that became real curly when she conditioned it. My youngest and oldest both had caramel complexions, long noses, large almond-shaped eyes, and naturally reddish lips.

Alexis could've been a supermodel if she weren't five-foot-five and

a size six. The platform stilettoes she wore all the time gave her runway attitude. All the dresses she wore barely covered her ass. I think if
it weren't against the law, that child would never put on clothes.

"Don't encourage Mother to be unfaithful," Mercedes interjected.

Her mention made me wonder where Fortune was. I checked my
cell. No new missed calls or text messages from him.

Sandara fired back, "Mama should do the bartender. Maybe it'll
give Fortune an incentive to go back to his wife and leave our mama
the hell alone."

"Did Raymond get your son those shoes?" Mercedes asked.

My brows raised. Sandara's lips tightened. *Please, Lord Jesus. Not
today.*

"Of course not. He probably came over with forty dollars. Fucked
you, then left with sixty," Mercedes said.

Sandara angrily replied, "Raymond is not broke."

Sarcastically, Mercedes asked, "And you're on welfare because?"

Sandara's eyes were in the left corners when she closed them and
in the right when she opened them. Next to Alexis, my youngest had
the worst temper. What made my babies quick to anger?

Mercedes was a perfect size eight. Her light brown hair, bunched in
clusters at the edges, framed her pale face. Barely touching her shoulders, her super eight-inch Afro flopped over her ears. Today, she had
in her green contacts. She'd blinked several times. I would offer her
my drops but that one didn't share anything.

"That's enough, you two," I insisted.

Sandara should've stayed in college and dated men who were at
Baylor University. The end of her sophomore year, she'd said, "It's too
hard, Mama. I quit." For whatever reason, the men she chose to bed
never took her seriously.

Mercedes commented, "Mama, I'm not asking, I'm telling you.
He's beneath you. He's a bartender, for goodness' sake. He probably
gives his number out all day long. All he wants is sex. I bet he doesn't
even have decent health coverage."

Mercedes's five-year-old twins, Brandy and Brandon, were in the
most expensive private school in Roswell. Whatever Mercedes needed,
her husband, Benjamin, provided. Benjamin was no pushover. He had
that quietness about himself. He loved his family and provided for

them. At twenty-seven Mercedes had it all together. I just wished she'd realize her sisters didn't.

The waiter approached our table. "Happy birthday to?" he asked, pausing.

"It's our mother's fiftieth," Mercedes said loud, looking in the direction of the bar.

Our waiter smiled. "I can't tell. You all look alike to me. I thought you were sisters. Well, I'll start with the beautiful birthday *young* lady," he said, staring at me. "My name is LB. That's short for Lawrence Bennett. May I take your drink order?"

He didn't have finesse like the one heading my way.

"Don't push up on my gurl," my bartender guy said. He placed a martini in front of me and continued his stroll.

I had to smile. It felt good having a man whatever his age was flirting with me. Opening the piece of paper, I saw his name, then read, *I want to blow the candles on your cake. Tonight. Spencer Domino.*

Mercedes opened her hand. "Give it to me, Mama. Now."

I stuffed the paper with his number on it in my purse. "Order your drink, child."

Giving me a gift bag, Devereaux politely said, "*Happy* birthday, Mama."

Mercedes requested a cabernet. Alexis ordered a mai tai. Devereaux wanted a JW Lemonade and Sandara asked for the same with a shot of vodka chilled on the side.

Opening the bag, I removed the tissue. I laughed. I knew exactly where the pink envelope was from. "Thank you, baby." Inside was a fifty-dollar gift card to Victoria's Secret. I flashed it in front of Mercedes.

She heaved, then said, "Fine, you might as well have this one too." Mercedes placed her bag on the table in front of me.

Rummaging through the tissue, I held up a five-hundred-dollar gift card to Bloomingdale's. Alexis's gift was a fifty-dollar card from Sephora. Sandara handed me a twenty-dollar card for The Body Shop.

The waiter returned with the drinks and we placed our food orders. Sandara handed him her cell. "Take a picture of us, LB."

He snapped several photos, then handed the phone back. Before Sandara had her cell in hand, Spencer intercepted it, leaned close to me, held the phone in front of us, clicked the side button twice. He said, "Here you go, beautiful," then placed the cell in my hand.

"Her name is Blake," Mercedes retorted. "Mother, he doesn't even know your name."

I gave the phone to Sandara.

Sandara said, "I just texted you the pics, Mom, and I posted them on my Instagram, Facebook, and Twitter."

"You put too much of your business on social media, lil girl. That's why you're always feuding with your welfare-rich-and-fameless friends," Mercedes said.

Sandara fired back, "At least I have friends."

I held my finger up to Mercedes. "Stop it. I mean it."

Raising my girls by myself, I felt my heart ache for my youngest child. The hardship for me wasn't monetary. It was being a solo parent even when a man was living in our home. I didn't want to stop financially supporting Sandara. I had to figure out a way to help her become responsible for her kids the way I'd done for mine.

"I've decided to combine my cards and do a total makeover."

Mercedes started tapping on her cell. Her phone dinged twice. "Let's do it tomorrow! I booked you a hair appointment with Marcus Darlin! He's fitting you in so we have to be there at six sharp."

"Hush!" Devereaux said, then she started texting. "He told me I had to wait until he got back from a hair show in Dallas."

Mercedes snatched Devereaux's cell. "Don't ruin it for Mother. He's doing this as a favor to me."

I glanced toward the bar, then back at my girls. "I want the sexiest style that takes ten years off of my fifty."

"See what you've started, Mercedes," Alexis said. "You're the one encouraging Mama to get her feelings hurt."

Sandara chimed in, "Alexis, don't mess up Mama's birthday."

Mercedes stared at Sandara, then said, "You mean the way you messed up your life by having three kids by three different men and none of them are around."

Sandara circled her finger along the rim of her glass. Tears filled her eyes as she mumbled, "If this bitch say one more thing to me, I swear she's going to wear this drink." Increasing her tone, she said, "You're not better than me."

"By what standards. *My* twins have a great father." Mercedes dragged out the *f* word like it were a knife slowly slicing my baby girl's heart in two.

"Really, Mercedes?" Devereaux commented.

Mercedes rolled her eyes at Devereaux. "You don't want me to go in on you, trust me."

The base of Sandara's glass was still on the table. Quietly, I exhaled, "Thank you, Jesus."

"I don't have baby daddies. I have a husband. That's because I am smarter than both of you," Mercedes said. "Devereaux, Phoenix is never going to marry you. Never."

Holding my breath, I watched Sandara pick up her glass. I shook my head. "Please, Sandara. Not today."

Mercedes's eyes narrowed as she stared at Sandara.

"Speaking of smart," Alexis interrupted, then stood. "I have to work on my dissertation, about how having my father listed as unknown really impacted my life. As part of my research I'm going to find him mother."

A bitter taste emerged in my mouth as I scolded her. "You will do no such thing young lady. I forbid you."

Mercedes tugged on the hem of Alexis's dress. "You're creating a scene. Sit."

Alexis stood taller, stared down into my eyes. "No apology, Mom. I've made up my mind. I believe the reason we're all messed up is because we don't know our fathers. You'd rather take it to your grave than to do the right thing. If you want to talk about this, I'm willing to discuss it with you later." She strutted away, stomping one foot in front of the other.

Did she have to go there? Now each of my daughters was frowning. Attempting to regroup from the unexpected, I insisted, "Mercedes, apologize to your sisters."

"For what? Why do I always have to be the one to say I'm sorry? I'm telling them the truth."

"Because you are pathetic," Devereaux said. "You always lash out at Sandara. You know she admires you. Stop beating her down all the damn time. So she made a mistake."

Mercedes stood. "And you didn't? When a mistake is repeated more than once"—she paused, and stared at Sandara—"it's stupidity.

Maybe Alexis is right. I'm out. Mama, I'll call you later. And we're still on for tomorrow morning."

"Morning? I thought you meant six in the evening."

Mercedes looked at me. "I'll meet you there in the morning. "She told Devereaux, "Since you rode here with me, you can catch a ride from Mom." Mercedes picked up her designer purse, eased it onto her shoulder, and left.

"I've lost my appetite. I'ma catch up to Mercedes. Plus, I need to get home to Nya . . ." Devereaux paused, then stared toward the bar. "Alexis doesn't know when to quit. Let me go get that girl. Happy birthday, Mama."

I stood. I did not want to be responsible for getting anyone anywhere. "Go catch your sister."

Devereaux slid out of the booth. "I'll meet you guys at the salon."

Gazing toward Spencer, I noticed him smiling at Alexis. For a moment, I was jealous. My daughter was decades closer to that young man's age than I. Devereaux pulled Alexis away and I saw Spencer's eyes follow Alexis's jiggling behind until she was out the door.

LB returned with five orders but only two of us remained.

I looked at Sandara. "You can go, baby. It's okay."

My child stared at the food, then at me.

I told LB, "Please, package everything to go."

Sandara sat next to me, and leaned her head on my shoulder. I held her face with one hand as she cried.

"Why does Mercedes hate me, Mama?"

"She loves you. Baby, each of you are like me just in different ways. Mercedes has my high maternal standards. Alexis got my drive for college education. Devereaux desperately wants a family so she'll hold on to Phoenix until he lets her go. And you choose to have sex with men who don't do anything for you or your children."

LB placed a large to-go bag on the table. "Can I get you anything else?"

"The check," I said, drying my baby's tears.

"It's already taken care of. Courtesy of Spencer Domino," he said, nodding toward the bar.

Raising my brows, I was impressed. I'd thank Spencer later. Focusing on my child, Sandara was in a trance.

"It's just so hard for me. I give all my love to my children. Mama, I need someone to make me feel like a woman. I love my babies but why don't their daddies love me anymore? They don't even try to help us out."

I told my daughter, "It's hard for a man to fall in love with a woman who never gives him a reason." Those were the exact words my mother had spoken to me when I was twenty-five.

Sandara cried aloud.

I wish I had all the answers. God knew I didn't want any of my children to end up like me but with four girls the odds weren't in my favor.

"Hush, honey. God doesn't give us any more than we can handle. Just make sure your new boyfriend doesn't eat before you feed my grandbabies."

"Yes, ma'am."

"And, I'll see you at church Sunday with my grands."

"Yes, ma'am," my baby said, picking up the bag.

I watched her walk away. Praying I could save her, I knew I couldn't. Sunday couldn't come fast enough but I was going to enjoy the night.

Church didn't make me a saint. God didn't make me a sinner. The pastor couldn't save me from the devil. And Alexis was not taking Spencer from me.

CHAPTER 13

Spencer

Dang!!!! How much longer you gonna be? Charlotte texted.

Just closed out boo. Waiting on your food then I'm in motion. I had to lie to my gurl or she'd hop in her ride, jet over here, and give me drama.

I slipped my cell in my pocket. Focused on Blake sitting at the table alone. She stared into her half-full glass, stirred the olives repeatedly. The way her daughters bailed one at a time I was sure that wasn't how she expected her evening to end when she got here. Sensing her loneliness increased my odds of making Blake my sexual conquest tonight.

"Still figuring it out, huh, playa?" LB said, picking up his customers' cocktails. "She looks V to me, Spence. Go for it."

We used the first letter for words like *vulnerable, booshie, freak, desperate.* We dismissed spittin' *THOT* (that ho over there), *ho,* and *bitch,* although there were times when I seriously came close to calling Charlotte a bitch.

The six highboy tables aligned in the center of the bar area were full. Same was on the real for the booths in my section. There was a crowd of people near the door.

Derrick approached me. "Spencer, you want to close? I could use you."

Shaking my head, normally I'd take the extra. My time out was official in ten minutes and a brotha had to be avail for his intentions.

Firmly, I replied, "No can do. Not tonight, man."

I couldn't let Blake soak on her birthday. If we were going to hang, she had to perk up. I was not slinging dick for a depressed broad. A customer paid their tab. I placed a martini at the spot as they were leaving, covered it with a napkin. "Sorry, this seat is reserved," I told the next person.

Walking up to Blake, I picked up her cocktail. "Come chill at the bar for a sec," I said, reaching for her hand. I noticed en route she staggered a notch or two.

Pulling out the same stool she sat in earlier, I told her, "Relax. I got you."

A ten-thousand-dollar fine and incarceration was not the way I wanted this beautiful woman to end her night. If she got a DUI, that was exactly what would happen in Georgia. I drained both of her drinks. Gave her a tall glass of cold water.

"And who else you got?" she replied. "My daughter?"

Whoa. Don't tell me fifty is on one too like Charlotte.

"I'm just trying to make sure you're okay. That's all." That wasn't completely true but it would be if she threw tude my way again. I had enough problems with my gurl.

"I apologize," she said. "Why are you being considerate of me?"

Could be considerate of her daughter, too, but that Alexis was certifiable on some Mars dominating-type shit. Couldn't lie, Alexis had my attention. I did not sense Blake had low self-esteem. Maybe the big five-O had kicked in making her feel some type of way about her daughter.

"Why not?" I told her. "You don't believe you deserve to be treated nice for no reason? You're gorgeous."

Her lips curved.

"That's what I'm talking 'bout. Chill here for a few while I close out my shift."

"I'm going to shop. Maybe that'll cheer me up."

And sober her up. I dug into my pocket, folded two C-notes, placed them in her palm. "Buy us something. I gotta make a run. I'll get back in an hour. You'll get off for two. I promise."

She was quiet. At fifty, she should be grown up to answer direct. I needed a response or I could go to Charlotte's and chill.

"Here you go, bruh," LB said, handing me a to-go bag with my food. He patted me on the back.

The order was originally for Charlotte. Now it was mine. I needed the sixty minutes to go home, shower, change, and meet Blake back here. Hopefully the menu selects would be ours if Blake opened her mouth.

"Thanks, man. I'm out in a sec." I looked at Blake. Her eyes were glossy, lids were midway. "Meet me outside of Sprinkles at eight-fifteen."

"In an hour?" she asked, then nodded.

Good. She was paying attention.

I confirmed, "In exactly one hour."

CHAPTER 14

Alexis

Spencer offered his number. I declined. Never gave him mine. The charade added a layer of mystique to fuckable-azz Mr. Domino. His sexual energy sparked heat from my Good Good. Not many individuals could do that. I was positive my mom wouldn't spread for him.

I squashed females who laid claim to what wasn't theirs just to prove my point. The way I saw it, everything was fair game. But if a bitch didn't have game, they'd already tapped out. If I changed my mind and took Domino up on his offer to hit this pussy, I knew where he worked.

Mom was probably back home with Fortune watching television. I had no regrets for what I'd said to her earlier about my dad, I just wished I'd waited another day. Mercedes was known for being condescending. I had bad timing and a worse temper. My upside was I didn't hold grudges. Devereaux was passive-aggressive. Sandara was quick to splash her drink, easily charmed by lames, and cared too much about what others thought of her.

I didn't give a fuck about an opinion rendered!

I texted my mom, Enjoy the rest of your birthday. 2mrw will b tons of fun! Can't wait for your makeover. Love you!

An apology might've sent mixed messages. I'd continue the convo when I saw her. Parking outside my gurl's apartment building at Atlantic Station, I texted Chanel, I'm downstairs.

Waiting for her, I texted James, Meet me at my place in two hours.

Flirting with Domino made me juicy and put me in the mood for my guy's dick. I didn't step out on James because he wasn't great in bed, I diversified because I wanted to. Men cheated remorse-free and so did I. Chanel had to work tonight. Taking her on a dinner date before she clocked in, plus seeing her after I was done doing James, would make her happy. I didn't regret leaving my food at the Cheesecake but I felt famished for more than fish.

"You look sweet, C," I told her soon as she got in the car. "Where you want to eat?"

She had on jewel-beaded flat sandals and a green, orange, and yellow tropical dress. Without shoes, C was five-six, one inch taller than I. Her maxi was sleeveless and she was braless. The seatbelt separated her breasts. I noticed her nipples were hard.

I leaned sideways, gestured for a kiss. Her chocolate lipstick mixed with my red. "Suite Food Lounge or Stats is cool," she suggested, then said, "You think about what I asked?"

"Suite it is," I decided, driving south.

Chanel loved the lemon pepper wings drenched in lemon juice, smothered in black pepper, and the hot ones were my favorite. I talked a text to Al the manager, "You at work, question mark. My girl and I are coming through period."

William Alfred Williams replied, The usual table, drinks, and food?

"You got me set?"

4sho but don't start no shit tonight Alexis. Cool?

"Cool."

Halfway there, Chanel asked again, "You think about what I asked you?"

I waited for the signal light to turn green, then I made a U-turn, and headed back toward her place to drop that bitch off.

"Fine, Alexis. I won't ask again," she said.

Making another U-turn we were silent until I valet-parked at Suite. I knew she was feeling some type of way but better for her to be salty than me.

We sat at our usual table for two in front of the projection screen. I avoided the hookah side of the lounge. The setup over there was nice but the people smoking were amped. I didn't need any influences in my system outside of my mai tai.

After we settled in for five minutes, our food and drinks arrived. C gazed at me with sad eyes then looked away.

"What is it?" I asked.

"I want us to have a baby," she said.

Unexpectedly, my drink spritzed in her direction. I wiped my mouth. "No, C. Where is this coming from?"

"I'm starting to get tired of dancing. We can adopt."

"How are we supposed to support a kid? Nah, you haven't thought this through."

I'd lost my appetite. She nibbled on her wings and sweet potato fries. There was no way I was leaving James for C. I knew that's where the baby idea came from. She'd have to work to support us. I'd become a stay-at-home mom.

"You love me, Alexis?"

"C, you know I do."

"Then say it."

Shaking my head, I told my gurl, "Eat up. I gotta go."

CHAPTER 15

Blake

Was Spencer flirting to bait me in, or was he sincerely attracted to me?

My cell rang. I sat on a bench outside the Cheesecake Factory. It was the man I'd put out yesterday. I pressed the button on my Bluetooth, then answered, "What?"

Switching from checking out athletic gear in the window, I began people-watching.

"Where are you?" Fortune demanded.

Though the day was almost over and he'd blown up my phone earlier, filled up my voice-mail box, now that I answered there was no "happy birthday." No "how are you doing?" No "I apologize." Nothing. There was no remorse in Fortune's voice.

"Com'on, Blake. I can't take this. I'm tired of being in my car. How long you gon' be?"

My jaw dropped. "I don't have to answer to you and you'd better not be at my house."

"Where else am I supposed to be?"

Spencer approached me. "You chill?" he asked.

I nodded, smiled. I clenched the cash he'd given me in my hand. "I'm good. See you shortly."

"Who was that I heard? What you mean you'll see him shortly? You'd better not be giving away my stuff."

Looking at the time on my cell, calmly I replied, "I'm busy, Fortune. Good-bye."

"Hurry home," he said, ending the call as if we were still together.

From now on what I did with my pussy was my business. Maybe treating myself to some dick would cheer me up. Admiring Spencer until he was out of view, I could be a damn fool, an old fool, or just plain stupid if I allowed this young man to seduce me any further. Or he could become my inspiration to try new things. Walking through the Nike store, I entered the mall. Opening my hand, what felt like two bills, was. I figured they were twenties. They were hundreds. The new, crisp, colorful ones.

What I needed to do with this cash was give it back. Didn't want to feel obligated. Spencer hadn't done anything to make me feel sex was all he wanted but my spending his hard-earned money didn't seem right.

I texted Brandon for advice letting him know, He gave me $200 to buy us something.

Brandon texted back, Make sure it's sexy bitch! Cute shit is for little girls!

Walking into The Body Shop, I sampled a fragrance, then thought about Sandara. I handed the cashier my gift card, took a picture of my two items, then texted the pic to my baby.

Spencer didn't ask for my number. He gave me the option to contact him. Didn't act as though he'd be upset if he never saw me again. I strolled past a few stores then entered Aldo's. Tried on a few pair of red high heels. Bought the sexiest open-toe pair then went to Victoria's Secret. Bought a black lace nightie and a red thong.

Glancing at my watch, I saw it was eight-thirty. I grabbed my bag and receipt then hurried toward the cupcake store praying I hadn't missed him. Was I supposed to wait inside the mall, the store, or out front? I stood still for a moment then exited through the turnabout. I looked right toward the Cheesecake Factory, scanned the parking lot across the street, then glanced to my left.

"Would you like me to get your car?" the valet asked.

I'd almost forgotten I'd given him my keys. "Yes. Please," I said, handing him my ticket. When he drove up, people started taking pictures of my car. I'd probably had one too many drinks because why else would I be frantically in search of a stranger?

What I wanted right this minute was what I needed. My own Nikko. The man I'd gotten rid of was toxic. I refused to spend another day living for . . . him.

My cell rang. It was my unwanted ex. Just when I motioned to press my Bluetooth and tell Fortune to leave me the hell alone, I heard, "Don't answer that."

Turning around, I looked up and directly into his eyes. I'm not shy and don't know why I looked down but there was his dick imprint.

Yeah, he was hung.

Spencer took my bags, then spoke with authority. "Let's go, birthday woman. I've got plans for you."

Softly, I said, "My car is right here."

His eyes widened. His closed-lip smile slowly grew larger. "If you don't mind my spinning your wheels, I can come back and get my car tomorrow."

Dropping my keys into his hand, I said, "Let's go."

CHAPTER 16

Blake

The garage door opened to his apartment building. I couldn't breathe.

"This is where you live?" I asked as he drove past the fourth floor where Alexis usually parked. I didn't see her car. She was probably at the strip club.

I wanted to switch seats, drop him off where he'd left his car, then pray I'd never see him again. He drove over one familiar speed bump then another until we were six stories high. Spencer backed my Ferrari into a space marked VISITOR PARKING ONLY. I'd been here before. I waited for him to open my door. He reached for my hand. Taking a deep breath, I was here now.

"What's wrong?" he asked, leading me to an entrance I'd walked through a week ago on my own.

I didn't answer.

The elevator opened. At least he lived in a different building and we weren't on the same floor as my daughter. Spencer did not need to know that Alexis lived in building four on the fourth floor and he was in number two on the fifth. Or maybe he was already aware but hadn't mentioned it. Perhaps that was why they were friendly when she left the restaurant. I decided not to inquire. Not tonight. Maybe tomorrow. Maybe.

"It might seem difficult to get into the building but it's not. If a person's timing is impeccable, they can follow another car into the garage, then wait for someone leaving or entering the building then walk right in." He stared at me. "You chill?"

"I'm fine," was all I'd said. I knew what he'd said was true. Wasn't sure why he'd told me. Hoped he wasn't the kind that encouraged women to stalk him.

There were almost four hundred apartments here. I barely saw Alexis's next-door neighbors. Truth was, I knew my child well and I didn't want them two friends or friendly.

Spencer slid his hand in his pocket, pulled out a black ring with a Falcons emblem. A lot of keys dangled but there was only one lock on his door. I wondered if any of those keys fit the home of any females he was sleeping with. I noticed how his fingers danced in a rhythmic motion until he found the one to unlock his front door.

"Welcome to my haven." He unarmed the alarm, then sat my packages on a royal blue velvet bench at the entrance. "Get comfortable, sexy."

I stood near the door. The chocolate hardwood floors, high ceilings, and stainless appliances were the same as Alexis's. His layout was different. There wasn't a loft; his living/dining area was more spacious. Most things in the room and on the walls were indigo-blue or black. A bookshelf was near the front door. The titles I scanned were all nonfiction.

"Oh, that's what I call my sexology department top one hundred. I've learned shit they didn't teach a brotha in college, like a woman's clit have legs underneath the hood." Confidently, he said, "Yeah, I wanna make you walk and talk at the same damn time."

What? My morals said, *I should exit.* My desires dictated me to stay. As I watched him stand at the kitchen counter preparing two vodka martinis, my heart rate increased. Two barstools faced him. I opted to sit on the black leather sofa. It was firm, yet soft. Spencer handed me a drink, then sat beside me.

"A toast. To a beautiful sexy *woman*. You make fifty fabulous. That's what I'm going to call you. Fabulous."

No man had given me that nickname. "I like it."

"I like you," he replied, taking a swig from his martini. He set his drink on a mirrored coaster on the black coffee table with silver mirrored trim. His hand traveled under my red dress, caressed my inner thigh, then slid down to my calf.

"Lay back. Relax."

As he propped a black-and-blue pillow behind my back, I held on to my cocktail.

Spencer removed one of my shoes then the other. I let him. He scooted over, lifted my foot, placed it in his lap. My heel touched his dick. Opening a drawer under the coffee table, he retrieved a small bottle of baby oil, greased his palms. His strong hands massaged my ankle, arch, and toes.

I smiled.

"I know what you're thinking," he said.

"What?"

"Yes, it's a warming drawer. I like to keep my oil heated at all times."

He'd answered my thought. *Lawd, please don't let this man connect with my daughter.* This was a first. No man who I'd met had pampered me like this. Not this soon. This youngster might know more about sex than I imagined.

"So what's your story?" I asked. "Why aren't you attracted to women your age?"

Soon as I'd said that, I wished I hadn't. *Blake Crystal you sure know how to mess up a good mood.*

He changed his voice. "It ain't cool being no jive turkey so close to Thanksgiving."

I frowned. "What?"

He stopped rubbing my toes. "Please do not tell me you haven't seen *Trading Places*. Please."

"Actually, I haven't." Was I wrong for that?

"Don't make me have to put you out," he said jokingly. Resuming my massage, Spencer shook his head. "Never said I wasn't attracted to women my age. It's just that I'm not usually fascinated by anyone." Looking into my eyes, he continued, "But we have sick chemistry that's undeniable. Do you know the major difference between mature and younger women?" he asked.

The olive in my mouth tasted like the fried chicken I loved at the Cheesecake Bistro at Atlantic Station. I was starving but food could wait. I had plans of feasting on this gorgeous young man. He was right. I couldn't deny my sexual attraction.

I heard the chiming sound of a text message registering on my phone. I dug into my purse, got my cell.

Sandara's text read, Ty mama 4 always taking care of us.

A picture of my three grandbabies was attached. They were seated at the dining table. Each made an X with their chopsticks. Their plates were filled with chow mein, salt-n-pepper prawns, spare ribs, salmon, and broccoli beef. I showed Spencer the photo. "These are my grandbabies."

Frowning, he asked, "They all have the same mom?"

"Yes."

"Which one of your daughters? The dark one that looks exactly like you?"

He seemed a bit too concerned for my liking. The only one who had my complexion was Alexis and why was he pretending not to know her name.

"No," was all I said.

"That's what's up. Family first. I like that."

I wanted to say, "I like you and your ass had better not go there with my daughter." Instead I replied, "You have any kids?"

Shaking his head, he said, "Not ready for that level."

I tried to shift mental gears from dwelling on if he liked Alexis more.

Spencer stared into my eyes. "The world won't miss us for a few hours." Taking my cell, he placed it on the coffee table. "Live in this moment with me, Fabulous."

I let him take my phone because I enjoyed the way he took the initiative. I should've skipped drink number four. Even if my count wasn't right this younger man was what I needed. I convinced myself if I sipped slowly, I'd be done in an hour with both my martini and this gorgeous man. My pussy twitched causing me to shiver.

"Everything chill?" he asked.

"So what's the difference?" I was curious.

"Why don't I show you in the shower."

Maybe he did expect something for his two hundred dollars since he hadn't inquired as to what I'd bought. I closed my eyes. There was no denying I wanted this man sexually but to give myself to someone probably two decades my junior was out of character for me. His mother could be my age. She could be my customer. I was the president of a bank. Regardless of where a person opened an account, all of our customers were considered mine.

My cell rang. His picture appeared. It was Fortune. Again. Maybe his calling was my awakening to take my fifty-year-old ass home.

And do what? Sit on the sofa by myself and watch the housewives? Let Fortune back in and listen to him talk to me as though he knew everything and I knew nothing?

This time Spencer picked up my cell, powered it off, then placed it in my hand. "I'll start. You decide if you want to join me. We can do this now. Or we can do this later. But you know I'm going to make love to you," he said, exiting the living room.

CHAPTER 17

Blake

Leave his apartment or stay? Sit on the sofa until he comes back? Take a shower with him?

I tossed my phone in my purse, untied my halter, removed my dress and panties. Placed them one on top of the other on the back of his couch. Exhaling, I picked up my drink, swallowed a mouthful of vodka, placed the empty glass on the mirrored coaster, then entered his bedroom.

Standing in the doorway of his bathroom, seeing the silhouette of his body made my heart race with lust. His ass sat high. His dick hung low. Spencer opened the glass door and extended his hand.

"Wow. You are so beautiful . . . to me," he said.

His words made me feel desirable.

Spencer said, "Younger women want to fuck to impress. Mature women want to be sexed . . . real good. All women want to be loved." He paused, then continued, "I got you, Fabulous."

Sometimes all a woman needed was a man who cared enough to take his time, treat her like an angel, and Spencer was on point with me when he said, "Mature women want to be sexed . . . real good."

That was what I'd come here for.

CHAPTER 18

Spencer

"Fabulous," I whispered. "Don't do anything you don't want. But if we're going to make love"—I paused, tilted her chin upward, stared into her eyes, then continued—"I want you here with me. It'll feel better. Can you do that? For us."

Nodding, she cried, covered her face, then turned her back to me. She let the shower wash away her tears.

"Why are you crying?" I asked.

Her voice trembled. "I, I barely know you."

I could dismiss her emotions as her being on that premenopausal flotation or she might be one of those females longing for a man to show her some love. What I was feeling wasn't that deep but I knew how to romance a woman with my sexy tone.

"You want this dick?"

Giving her a moment to respond, I soaped my hands with body wash, then squeezed her shoulders. My shit pointed straight up. I stepped closer. She shivered when my hard dick touched her spine. My six-two frame had a solid seven inches over her.

Fabulous was what I wanted. Maybe just for this moment. Maybe not. Depended on how the night went. I bet that Alexis would've taken charge. I liked a woman that took control like Charlotte. Make that a need. Passive chicks were cool but they couldn't hold my attention.

She whispered, "Yes," but didn't move. Seemed as though she was mentally on some other page.

Repositioning myself in front of her, I said, "Let's see if this can help you to stay focused." I squatted, parted that sweet labia majora, closed my eyes. I teased her shaft. The tip of my tongue flicked on her clit.

She cupped her breasts. "Oh, my, God," she said, grabbing my head.

That was chill. I stared up at her. "I knew you'd taste good but you have no idea how delicious your pussy is. Happy birthday, Blake."

Standing before her, I penetrated her with my finger, then stroked her G-spot. Removing my finger, I slipped it into her mouth. What the water didn't wash away, I asked her to, "Swallow," then softly said, "Told you."

Squatting again, I smothered her lips one kiss after another.

"Ohhhh!" she screamed when I gently clamped her clit between my teeth.

She pushed my head away. It probably hurt a little but if we were going to have great sex, I had to challenge Fabulous outside of her comfort zone.

I stood, turned off the water, then told her, "Come with me." Escorting her, I motioned for her to sit on the edge of my king-size bed.

Fabulous stared at my dick, then waited for . . . I had no idea why my dick wasn't in her mouth. Okay, chill. I took charge.

Walking to my oversize black leather chair in the corner, I nodded toward the seat. "Over here, bitch, right now."

She frowned.

"Don't make me come get your ass."

Slowly, she approached. Firmly, I grabbed her hips, faced her toward the chair, pushed between her shoulder blades.

"On your knees, bitch," I said in a commanding tone. "You gon' take this birthday dick. All of it."

I thought about the chocolate cheesecake in my fridge. I could get it and spread it all over her pussy, drizzle hot oil on her back, and eat her ass out from behind. She probably never had a dude do that.

She leaned back. I shoved her forward. Slapped her ass with this dick. "I said, on your fucking knees, bitch. Don't make me ask again."

If she were offended, she would've left by now, but I knew what she wanted. Kneeling on the chair, she braced her forearms on the top. Her titties leaned against the leather.

Sternly, I told her, "Back this sweet pussy up, place your knees on the edge."

Fabulous wasn't moving fast enough. I snatched her hips in my direction, shoved the crown of her head into the seat. She didn't protest when her chin parted her breasts.

"That's my gurl."

I spread her cheeks. Let my tongue glide against her tight asshole. The tip of my tongue stretched to her clit, then to the inner left side of her pussy lips where most women had that sensitive spot. I revisited that asshole.

Smack! I slapped her ass. "Say something, bitch, you too quiet."

"I have to make it to church to repent for this or I'm going straight to hell. I'm sure of it."

"On second thought. Shut the fuck up!"

CHAPTER 19

Blake

Going from an old man who wasn't comfortable saying the word *pussy* to a youngster calling me a bitch was a major turn-on.

I felt his finger penetrate my pussy. Pressing down, he circled my G-spot. Alternating the pressure against my now-plump tissue, his other hand played with my clit. He massaged my engorged shaft.

"Relax. You familiar with Lamaze?" he asked.

What in the hell? I said, "Yes."

"Then breathe like you're giving birth to my baby."

I started doing quick, sharp breaths in and out of my mouth. Instantly, I got a pleasure rush all over my body. Rotating my hips, I began riding his finger like it was his dick. I felt my pussy throbbing.

"Fuck me!" I yelled. "Faster!"

Lightly touching my lower back, Spencer said, "Fabulous. Relax. Let me do my job. I'm not letting up and I'm not letting you up but you need to chill."

I slowed my breathing. I was so wet I wanted to slam him to the floor, take control.

He rubbed his dick on my pussy, put the head in, then quickly pulled out. In. Out. Slow. In. Out. Fast. All I felt was the head. I thrust my hips toward him while he placed his hand on my ass.

"Fabulous," he whispered. "I told you. I got you. Let me make the sweetest love to you."

Now I wanted to cry. My pussy was on the verge of exploding. Containing myself in the heat of the moment heightened my internal awareness.

What he'd done next made me pause. My ears perked. I lifted my head. Doggie-style never felt this damn amazing.

Whispering in my ear, he said, "Yeah, I just made your pussy whistle," then he lowered the top of my head back toward the leather cushion. "Bitch, move again without my permission and I'm going to put this dick in your ass."

Short, shallow breaths in and out my nose as though I was sniffling accompanied a desire for him to put it in my ass. Did I want a dick in my ass? Or not? His eargasm made my pussy juices flow. I moved my head side to side about an inch in opposite directions. *Damn!* Best to keep still.

Spencer's finger massaged my G-spot. Removing his finger, he slid his dick all the way in. Out. Back in with his finger, massaging my G-spot. I knew I should've insisted on a condom but I didn't have one. The pleasure of his flesh inside of mine made me crave all of him. Bare. But there were reasons to be responsible.

Spencer whispered, "The world can wait, Fabulous. Don't make my shit go soft."

His finger eased out of my vagina and his dick traded places. He pulled my back to his chest. Slowly. Gradually. He gave me more and more of himself until his head was so deep inside of me it couldn't go any deeper.

His right hand cupped my breasts, then he pinched my nipples. His left played with my clit. At first it was gentle. Then he started applying pressure to the point of pain.

I covered his hands with mine. "Ease up, please."

"Lamaze," he insisted, not relinquishing the intensity.

Short, shallow, in and out my mouth. "I can't take any more."

He ignored me. Fucked me fast and hard with dick jabs like he was going straight for the knockout, not the technical.

"Damn, Fabulous. Your pussy is the shit. I'm about to go into the zone," he said as he started twirling my clit hard.

"Ow!" I didn't know which one hurt more, my nipple or my clit but his dick-head jabs gave me excruciating pleasure. Back and forth deeper and deeper he thrust. A minute later he pulled out fast and let go of my tit and clit at the same time.

What in the hell! Instinctively, I pushed like I was giving birth to his baby. My pussy juices splashed against his leather chair like I was pissing on myself. I screamed, "Oh, my, God."

"Push harder, Fabulous. That's a good girl. Push it all out." Spencer held me until my fluids finished flowing. I knew what squirting was but this was my first time. Not sure if I can handle a second, I collapsed in his arms.

"Good job, Fabulous," he said, kissing the nape of my neck. He escorted me to his bed. "Lay down while I clean this up."

I eased into bed, laid my head on his pillow. He raised covers to my shoulders. I couldn't tell how much time had passed but I was sure I couldn't make it to the living room where I'd left my clothes and shoes.

After cleaning up the chair and his hardwood floor, Spencer lowered the sheets, wiped a warm towel between my thighs, then covered me back up. He tossed the wet rag onto his end table.

Getting into bed, he pressed his chest to my back. This time the head and shaft weren't firm. I felt his breath on the nape of my neck.

"Happy birthday, Fabulous," he said, hugging my waist.

I covered Spencer's hand with mine, then I closed my eyes.

CHAPTER 20

Blake

Growing up in a five-bedroom home I had to share a room with my sister, Teresa. She was a year younger than I. My two brothers shared a room and my other four sisters did the same, two to each room. Mama's room was the only bedroom on the first floor. She seldom slept alone. Her gentlemen friends came and went without our seeing them. Sometimes I wondered if my dad was down there. The moaning and grunting, much like what I'd done with Spencer, was what I'd heard through the vents somewhere between midnight and six a.m.

I stared at Spencer's ceiling. His snoring turned me on. It was a light fluttering sound with a pause between breaths. My head was on his chest; his arm was around my back. I felt amazing. I wished I could wake up to this each morning.

Being the older middle child of a large family, I used to be an introvert. I stayed in my room a lot. At first studying was my excuse but when the As started flooding my report cards, I liked being called "the smart girl."

Somewhere along my way, that Billy Blackstone . . . where was he? After I lost my virginity to him, I felt as though I'd shared myself with the right guy. My feelings of having sex the first night with Spencer were the same. He was the best I'd had and that included Billy.

Daybreak greeted me good morning as rays beamed through the

blinds. I heard birds chirping outside his window. I kissed Spencer's chest. He stopped snoring. There wasn't much time before I had to leave but a quickie would be nice. Peeling back the cover, I saw his dick was hard. My breathing became heavy.

A churning in the pit of my stomach growled. Air moved in short waves then stopped. Squeezing my cheeks, I quietly planted my feet on the floor.

Spencer's hand gripped mine. "Where're you going, Fabulous?"

I replayed our sex scenes in my head, thrilled that I'd squirted for the first time. I wondered if he could make me do that again. Would we do *it* again?

The pain in my abdomen subsided. Bubbles rippled in the opposite direction but eventually this gas had to escape and I refused to embarrass myself. Pressing the button on his cell to check the time, I saw he had ten text messages and fifteen missed calls from someone named Charlotte.

"I have to shower and go. My daughter scheduled a hair appointment for me."

His cheek pressed against the pillow. I fingered his earlobe. Spencer's voice trailed off. "This early?"

Letting go of his hand, I answered, "Yes. It's for six."

Sleepily, he asked, "What time is?"

"Five o'clock."

"I'ma check out the inside of my lids for a sec. You wore me out." He faintly smiled. "Wake me so I can make sure you get to your car safely. Don't want anything happening to my new lady."

No time to respond. I hurried to the bathroom, locked the door, turned on the vent, sat on the toilet, and released a lot more than trapped air. A painting of a woman holding a little boy's hand hung on the wall facing me. Their eyes sparkled. Their smiles were joyful. The little boy in a white shirt, tie, pants, and loafers was Spencer. The woman in an all-white dress and shoes was presumably his mom. It was just the two of them. His hand seemed to disappear in the woman's grip. All that showed was his thumb.

I stared in the mirror and smiled. For a second my eyes beamed, not wanting my connection with Spencer to end. Suddenly, I noticed the short lines gathered beside my eyes, bags sagging below. Maybe I should get NeuBelle and have my teeth whitened. My lips uncurled. The lines and bags vanished. Perhaps I hadn't noticed the wrinkles before because I hadn't had a reason to smile ear-to-ear. I was genuinely happy.

Turning away from the mirror, I unlocked the door, then stepped into the shower. Water splashing against my naked body brought that kind of inside-out pleasure I hadn't sensed in years. I wanted to exhale my excitement with a loud sound of satisfaction. Instead I contained it.

I hoped I'd see Spencer again. It was unrealistic to expect a relationship commitment with Spencer. With all the missed messages from Charlotte, seems like he had a situation similar to mine. In ten years I'd be sixty. He'd be? I laughed at the fact that I didn't know the answer. All he'd said was, legal.

I washed my arms, neck, and breasts. Tears of joy emerged. Was Spencer sincere when he called me his new lady? I stopped crying. I'd heard quite a few lines in my time. Men claimed they cared, then they'd cut off communication unexpectedly. Spencer was the change I welcomed but I'd let him take the next step.

The bathroom door opened. "Your birthday is officially over but I still have a present for you," Spencer said. Joining me under the water, he pointed the showerhead toward the wall.

He squatted then spread my thighs. Looking down at Spencer, he was staring up at me. His lips pressed to mine. Spencer inserted his finger inside my pussy. My body shivered with pleasure. I gasped repeatedly. If I had this every day, could I handle him?

I'd heard that dicks have muscle memory. Would his dick become bored with me? Was that why men enjoyed sexing different women? Who was this Charlotte woman and what did she mean to him?

Spencer stood. "You're not here with me, Fabulous."

Maneuvering behind me, he pressed his stiff dick between my butt cheeks. I felt the tip of his head thrust against my asshole. "We have to work on your ADHD, Fabulous. We haven't explored what's behind door number two," he said, grinding. "I bet that'll hold your attention."

I faced him. "I've had the most amazing time but I have to go or I'll miss my appointment."

"Stop by the restaurant later. I want to see you and your new do." He stepped out of the shower as though he wasn't asking.

I dried myself off, put on my dress, my heels. He eased into a pair of black sweatpants and a gray T-shirt. "You can leave your goodies here if you'd like. We can do a Groundhog's Day." Pressing his lips together, he smiled.

Why not, I thought. I had two weeks off from work. I blurted, "Let's go to Vegas for the weekend."

"I'll get the tickets today, Fabulous. Text me your info."

Wait. What just happened? "I wasn't serious."

"Fabulous, you worry too much. You have to learn how to live in the moment."

His hand cupped the nape of my neck. He pressed his lips to mine, opened his mouth, then slid his tongue past my teeth. I swallowed his sweet breaths and his saliva. Softly, at first we exchanged back and forth. Hungrily, he began to devour me and I did the same.

Gently, placing my hand on his chest, I pushed him back. "I'll drop the money off to you by noon for my ticket."

Spencer shook his head. "It's your birthday. You're my treat. I got you."

I left my bags on the royal blue bench by the door to have a reason to come back to his place tonight. He escorted me to my car.

The last kiss before I drove off was the best.

CHAPTER 21

Blake

Powering on my cell, I saw I had twenty missed calls. Three from Mercedes. Two from Devereaux. The rest were from Fortune.

Starting my Ferrari, I doubted I'd run into Alexis. Her late nights at the strip club with Chanel usually meant awakenings closer to noon. I drove past my daughter's Lexus on the fourth level and kept going.

Happy that I no longer had to regret what it was like to live alone, I was excited that I was a single detached woman. I'd had sex with Spencer first so I knew Alexis wouldn't come behind me. Just like the both of them I could entertain whomever, whenever I wanted.

I exited his garage, turned east onto Pharr Road. The joy of solitude while sitting on my sofa, I was looking forward to that. I could not wait to swim naked in my pool, chill in my Jacuzzi, hell, control the remote to my own television.

I called Brandon.

He answered, "Bitch, if you did not ride that dick I'm hanging up."

I laughed. "He made me squirt."

Silence followed.

"Hello?"

"Bitch, I just died and came back. I can't hear this over the phone. Face-to-face. Where are you?"

My cheeks hurt from smiling. "I'm headed to see Marcus Darlin."

"Bitch, stop! How did you get on his calendar? I'ma headed over there right now. Good-bye."

Brandon really ended our call. I kept laughing, not remembering when was the last time I had a juicy sexcapade to tell anyone about. Sharing my body with Spencer was easy. He'd made it that way.

I stared at the photo Spencer had taken of us together, then made it my screen saver. He was so sexy. Those eyes. His closed smile. The thought of his lips between my legs a few minutes ago made me moist.

Honk! Honk!

Turning onto Piedmont, I merged into the middle lane. The woman behind me needed to relax. Get laid. Stop blowing her horn and blow a man. Damn. I hadn't sucked his dick. Didn't even kiss it. Should I apologize? He didn't seem to care. Glancing at my cell, I tapped my message app, then Spencer's name.

A call came in from Mercedes as the person behind me skidded around my car at the Sidney Marcus Boulevard intersection. I stopped at the red light by Chick-fil-A to give her time to move on.

I answered, "Hey, honey."

"Don't hey-honey me. Where are you?" she demanded.

"On my way to the salon. I'll be there shortly."

"Mother, why haven't you an—"

I ended the call, blasted Beyoncé's "Drunk in Love," playing on 107.5, then shouted, "Oh, baby!" in my most raspy tone. All the way to the salon, I replayed the scene with my knees on his oversize chair.

As I turned onto Edgewood Avenue, thoughts of Spencer's big dick inside my pussy filled me up. Gushing all over his smooth black leather chair made me shout, "Oh, baby!" I whipped my sports car into a space next to Mercedes's car.

Marcus Darlin opened the door. "Blake, get your behind in here! If it weren't for Mercedes begging me to stay, you'd be off my schedule."

I was only fifteen minutes behind schedule. I rushed inside. Mercedes was in a stylist chair with her legs crossed. Her foot swayed back and forth.

Marcus Darlin pointed at his chair. "Sit."

Fingering my hair, he commented, "No need to ask what you've been doing. What style do you have in mind?"

"Give her something elegant and age-appropriate. And trim those edges," Mercedes said, thumbing through the recent issue of *Hair* magazine.

"Honey, too late for that. Her edges have already been trimmed," Marcus Darlin said, then added, "Real good."

Mercedes eyed my attire. "Mama, why did you still have that on?"

"Have what on?" Devereaux asked, entering the salon. She stopped. Stared. "Mama, you could've changed your clothes. Do you have on the same underwear?"

"Blake, plead the fifth," Marcus Darlin said. "That's why I never wear any." He took my cell out of my hand and placed it in his drawer.

I laughed. I was in a great mood. "I'm clean. That's all that matters," I said.

Suddenly, I remembered Spencer's car was at his job.

"Mercedes, Devereaux, out!" Marcus Darlin, shouted. "Come back in three hours to pick up Ms. Blake."

"I need my phone, Marcus Darlin," I told him.

My girls walked out. Brandon entered.

Marcus said, "You too. Out! Come back in three hours. And Ms. Blake, no. You are not getting your phone until I'm done."

Spencer seemed resourceful. He'd get to his car. His seeing my new do would make him happy. I was actually relieved Marcus Darlin had put everyone out. That way I could get the style I wanted without their input.

CHAPTER 22

Spencer

Rolling over, I snagged my cell from the nightstand, ignored the messages from Charlotte, then texted Fabulous, miss you already

Lying on my back, I spread my thighs to let my nuts breathe. I did twelve dick curls. Had six more to go. Had to keep my foundation strong. Got the next half dozen out of the way, then moved on to my pull-and-resist exercise. Squeezing my shaft, I tugged my dick away from my body then I used my PC muscles to bring my dick toward me. I went back and forth until I'd done twenty. I did that every morning.

I'd read in one of my books that a hard dick drove women wild. That shit was true. Females didn't care which hole my piece was in. They were fascinated that this motherfucka felt like steel. Glad I learned early on that fucking wasn't the same as exercising. Pumping didn't account for much if after busting loose I couldn't get my shit right back up.

Damn, I didn't know which was hotter, that blazin' Ferrari, or Fabulous in that tight red halter dress with all that cleavage facing me while a brotha was trying to serve up cocktails last night. Her virgin asshole turned me on too. If she gave me the green light, I was breakin' that all the way in. The right way. A little at a time. Vegas was the perfect spot.

Damn, I never asked Fabulous what she did to earn her keep. It didn't matter. I knew it was legit. I could tell she wasn't random like that daughter of hers. The one who'd tooted her ass in my direction. I hadn't missed that. She knew I was interested in her mom. The way she moved let me know she was trouble with a capital *T.* Conversing with Alexis right before she left the restaurant, I'd gotten an erection. A man would never put on his drawers if he tried to get all the available pussy in the ATL but I couldn't lie. I wanted to hit that. I'd be a fool to do so since I'd done her mom. Alexis was a different kind of crazy. *Freak* might be a better word.

Mother and daughter. I hadn't done that at the same time before. Wondered if LB was still interested in Alexis. I shot him a text, Ole gurl gave it up last nite. You still want in on her offspring?

I knew Blake wasn't lying about her age. She could though. If she'd told me she was forty-five, I'd believe her. Forty. Not so much. I knew she had to have men of all ages trying to get with that the same way I was on it with a quickness. Atlanta was that spot. A lot of sexual interactions happened in less than twenty-fo of saying hello.

Soon as LB's text, give her my digs to give to her daughter, came in, my doorbell rang. That wasn't happening until I made up my mind about Alexis.

Eagerly climbing out of bed, I smiled, rinsed my mouth with wash, then rushed to the living room. Maybe she remembered what I'd mentioned about getting into the building. Maybe she came back to ride me before giving me a ride to my car.

I opened the door, and my smile disappeared. It wasn't Fabulous.

It was Charlotte.

Leaving the door open, the first thing I noticed was she didn't have my clothes. I went to the kitchen. Poured a shot of vodka, downed it, then refilled my shot glass. Downed that one, too, then refilled again.

"What's up?" I asked her.

I used to cater to Charlotte until she cheated on me. Apparently one man wasn't enough for her lil hot ass. Yeah, I probably deserved that shit now but before she'd stepped out, I was one hundred faithful.

My ego was more of a bitch than any female. But on the real, I hated the fucking drama.

"Where my . . ." Charlotte paused. Stared at the bag on the bench.

Damn! Before I got to the bag, she snatched it.

"Who's this shit for?" she asked, thumbing through Fabulous's things.

I told her, "You. Take it with you on your way out."

"You're a damn liar, Spencer!" Charlotte stood inches from me. Looked up at my face. She did not blink once.

I went to the kitchen counter, picked up the glass, tossed back the shot. Refueled. This woman literally drove me to drink whenever she was on. Our relay wasn't always this amplified.

"What bitch did you fuck last night? She ate my food, too?"

Walking around her, I answered, "Not today." I went to my bedroom.

Charlotte was so close on me I felt her breasts nudge my back.

"I said! Not today!"

"Oh, I see y'all had a good time! You give that bitch my Charlotte special?" She rubbed her fingertips on my black leather chair. "Uh-huh. Fuck you, Spencer!"

She tapped her shoe on the floor in front of the chair. "You bastard! You made her squirt! I taught you that shit!"

What difference did that make? She got the info from reading one of my books. Charlotte and no other woman I'd bedded had a monopoly on sexual techniques and positions. Hell, I expected to learn something from every woman I sexed. Otherwise what was the point? Fabulous would teach me some things eventually.

Tossing the cover back, Charlotte said, "That's why your sheets are scrambled like your eggs? Huh, motherfucka?"

No use in denying or admitting the truth. This woman should've been a forensic scientist, police, or a dominatrix. Charlotte wasn't a control freak. She was straight crazy.

"Charlotte. Please, leave. I'm asking you nicely to . . ." My voice trailed off, then escalated, "Get the fuck out of my house!"

She stormed out of the bedroom. Slammed the door. The next sounds I heard were shattering. I ran into the living area.

"I'm tired of you fucking up my shit every time you get pissed off! Where's your other nigga! Go fuck up his shit!" I opened my front door. "Get out!"

No one would understand if I'd beat her ass. Why did she provoke me? Exhaling, I pictured the photo hanging in my bathroom of my mom and me. We were so happy back that Easter Sunday. Why did she have to leave me? Life wasn't the same without her. Nobody understood how close we were. No one was there for me now. Not even

Charlotte. I was supposed to be tough and shit but I was weak when it came to missing my mom. That was my main gurl. After the funeral everyone who'd said, "I'm here for you," retreated to their world.

I wished I could put a time frame on grieving. Seem like my pain was never going to end. When my mom stopped breathing, a part of me stopped caring until I'd met Charlotte. Then my gurl shattered my ego.

So what if I did give Blake the "Spencer," not "Charlotte" special. Charlotte didn't have a dick. Everybody deserved to feel good and the next breath wasn't promised to me or anyone else.

Charlotte's father was killed a year ago. She was no longer Daddy's girl. An accident, a couple fighting while driving, ran him into an embankment on I-85 South near the Williams exit. Maybe that was why she started seeing the other guy. After she lost her dad, I believed she was in search of the nurturing her father gave her.

I gave her attention but knew that wasn't the same. She couldn't give me what moms did. I couldn't replace her old man. I had no idea how to keep her happy anymore but I knew for sure that I hated this shit!

Charlotte started crying. "I don't want him. I made a mistake. If you don't want to be with me just say so. And you'll never have to say it twice."

She knew I had a weak spot in my heart for her. I hugged her close to my chest. The tears I cried were for my mom. I wondered what hers were for? Why were we destroying one another? I loved this woman. But there were times when she drove me fucking nuts.

I wasn't cool with the fact that my gurl had opened her legs for another man. But I wanted to get to know Fabulous better. People fascinated me. What was Fabulous's story? She had a bittersweet kind of vibe. She wasn't on sabbatical from sex like some of the other older women I'd met. I imagined someone was getting that on a regular.

A woman who hadn't had sex in over a year tasted like a new car smelled, fresh. Not that Fabulous smelled bad. She just didn't have that just-off-the-assembly-line odor. Neither did her Ferrari. She'd had those wheels for a minute.

I placed my hand on the doorknob. "Give me a few days to cool off," I said, not wanting to put a time limit on it.

I was definitely keeping my commitment to Fabulous about our trip to Las Vegas. After the vacay, I'd stay with Charlotte, or let her go.

"I'ma clean your mess up, again," I said, pointing to the glass in my kitchen area. "Seriously, this time, Charlotte. Think about what you want. I'll do the same. When we—"

Charlotte yanked down my sweats, kneeled before me, then started licking and sucking my dick like it was an ice cream pop. Since Fabulous hadn't gotten or jacked me off, I closed my front door.

This was why I had the hardest time letting Charlotte go. Her mouth never got tired. Thank God, I had seven hours before I had to be at work.

CHAPTER 23

Blake

Sitting in the chair at Sephora, in less than twenty-four hours I found myself back at Lenox Square Mall in the same clothes. In any other city shoppers might look at me sideways being scantily dressed this early in the morning. I wasn't the only one. Hot pants that could dub as boy shorts hugged the butt implants of several women passing by. I knew all of them weren't born with asses that big and round.

Handing my cell to Mercedes, I told her, "Take a few before pictures of me but don't put them on social media." I wanted Spencer to see me in person first.

"I'm not the one you need to tell that to, Mother," Mercedes said.

The picture Sandara posted yesterday, the one Spencer had selfied of us, I was glad Mercedes made her take it down. I understood my youngest meant no harm. Initially I wasn't concerned since I was in birthday mode.

Mercedes didn't want corporate to have a reason to deny promoting me or for my clients to have a reason to file a complaint if they saw me with a much younger man. Once upon a time my personal life was private but social media changed that for a lot of career individuals.

Out of all my girls, Mercedes understood my struggle the most. Tired of proving she was worthy of being the chief operating officer and the mastermind behind her company's success, she launched her own business, Crystal's Clear Consulting.

"I can't remember the last time I was this spoiled!" I had to admit. The way Spencer sexed me last night had a lot to do with my new attitude.

"You deserve it, " Devereaux said.

Mercedes had video-journaled parts of this already amazing day. Why was it that one man made me feel like a queen and the other disgusted me?

"Mom, you look ten years younger already. Your new hair is growing on me," Mercedes commented, giving me a lingering hug.

Marcus Darlin gave me a versatile style then taught me how to create several looks in a matter of minutes. Gathering it up top really made me appear my daughters' ages. I felt like a schoolgirl when he put it in a ponytail on top of my head. Pulling it back, twisting it into sections, then wrapping one section over the other into a pretzel was more professional. Letting it hang below my shoulders the way it was now was my favorite.

Devereaux stretched her arms around both of us. "I love you guys. Mom, you're stunning." She whispered, "I'm glad you got some."

"I heard that," Mercedes said. "You don't have to announce it. We can all tell."

I stared in the ceiling-to-floor mirror beside the makeup booth. My hair went from above my shoulders to halfway down my back. I didn't think jet-black would complement my toffee complexion. Thought darker hair would age me but Marcus Darlin said to trust him. He was right. I'd worn a part on the side for years, now it was down the middle. My straight hair wasn't flat. It was silky, fluffy, and fluttered whenever I moved my head. No one could tell where my hair ended or where my extensions were rooted.

Damn! I'm sexy as hell. Normally, I wouldn't compliment myself but it was true. I hadn't felt this beautiful in I couldn't remember how long.

My cell rang. Mercedes answered, "We're spoiling our mother today, Fortune. All day."

Moving my cell from her ear, Mercedes switched to speaker. I could hear my ex-man pleading for me to come home but I wasn't done admiring myself.

"Blake, where were you last night?" he shouted.

"She was at my house," Devereaux lied, but she didn't know she didn't have to.

"Who else were you with, Blake? Who was the dude in the pic that was on Sandara's Facebook, Instagram, and Twitter pages? Did he spend the night at your house too, Devereaux? I'm not stupid."

Wow, all of a sudden Fortune was social media savvy. I laughed to myself.

"Yes, you are stupid, Fortune." Soon as I'd said that I wished I hadn't. But that was my honest thought. "Any man in his right mind would worship me. Hey, the makeup artist is standing here. I have to go."

Mercedes ended the call.

I insisted, "If he calls back, nobody answer."

Stepping away from the mirror, settling into the high chair, I was ready to let my face become a canvas. Soon as she was done, I wanted to go to Spencer's place. That feel-good sensation his dick gave me danced inside my pussy.

I took my phone from Mercedes and texted, You want some company before you go to work?

The makeup artist swept my hair away from my face, then slid hair clips on both sides. She draped my yesterday's wardrobe with a black cape. "I'm going to have fun with you. Your skin is flawless," she said. She applied a moist layer of something, then wiped it off.

"I'll set aside all the products I use and you can choose what you'd like to purchase after I'm done. We simply ask that you spend at least fifty dollars since the makeup session is complimentary. But there's no obligation."

I waved my gift card. "I'm ready! I can do all the basics except eye shadow. Never learned how to apply it right. And I don't like the press-on shadows."

She told me she'd explain the process when she got to that part. I didn't bother telling her I'd taken a few classes at M.A.C. Still couldn't get it right. I felt eye shadow, foundation, and blush were nice but not necessary. Maybe since I had a younger man interested in me I should rethink wearing makeup.

"Bloomingdale's when we're done," Mercedes said.

"Bebe's. It's closer and they have a sexier selection," Alexis said, entering the store. She wedged herself between Mercedes and Devereaux. "This is our, not your, makeover for Mom. You are not taking charge." Alexis gasped, "Oh, Mommy! I love this hair!"

She fingered my strands then let them float to my back. The silkiness touching my skin felt sensual.

"Thanks, baby. I'm glad you made it in time to see my transformation."

"Mother wasn't the only one who got some," Devereaux said. "I saw how you strutted in here. Out with it, Ms. Alexis."

Alexis cut her eyes toward Devereaux, then shook her head. "You know I'm not giving details. Soon as I tell y'all what happened, y'all have too many questions about how it's done."

"Look who's growing up," Mercedes said.

Alexis sarcastically said, "I been grown, Mrs. I-Only-Do-It-In-The-Missionary-And-I-Don't-Suck-My-Husband's-Dick."

"Really? Really. And you would know that because?" Mercedes questioned.

"Quick. When was the last time you had sex outside of your bedroom?" Alexis asked.

"I have two children, Ms. Freaky-Freelancer-Screw-Anything-With-A-Hole-Between-Their—"

Frowning, I interjected, "That's enough, you two." Glancing at my phone, I noticed Spencer hadn't responded.

I looked at Mercedes, wondering if she enjoyed making love to her husband or did she feel sex was a part of her wifely duties?

The makeup artist said, "Close your eyes."

I pictured relaxing on my sofa with Spencer. He could fuck me on my satin sheets. Afterward, we could listen to jazz, sip martinis, then he could make me squirt in whatever room we desired. Peeping, I checked my cell. He still hadn't responded to my text.

"Don't open your eyes yet," the makeup artist said.

Closing them, I exhaled.

"Where's Sandara?" Alexis asked.

"Probably ass up, legs wide open for that trifling dude she just posted a pic with online," Mercedes said.

Devereaux replied, "This time of the morning."

"Not every guy she meets is trifling," Alexis said.

"Really? Really. I was trying to wait until she got here but . . ." Mercedes paused.

I pictured Mercedes's lips drawn in as she stared at Alexis through tight eyes.

"My husband," Mercedes said, dragging out the *h* word, "is taking the twins to Disneyland for two days so we can have a mother-daughters weekend at my house. That way Sandara can keep her pussy to herself for forty-eight hours."

Wait. Not this weekend. I didn't want to miss the opportunity with my girls but I hadn't been on vacation with a fine-ass man in forever. It had also been too long since I was with all my daughters for more than a few hours. Hoping the sleepover at Mercedes's lasted more than forty-eight minutes, I prayed Spencer hadn't bought our tickets to Vegas. If so, I could reimburse him.

Opening my eyes, I said, "Let me see if I can cancel my plans." Actually, Mercedes had given me a reason to do what I'd wanted since sitting in this chair. Call Spencer.

"What plans?" Mercedes asked. She placed her hand on her hip.

Not wanting to smear my makeup, I dialed Spencer's number and placed the call on speaker.

"Hey, Fabulous."

Slowly, I sang, "Hi, Spencer."

Mercedes rolled her eyes. Devereaux smiled. Alexis's brows rose high.

"You done already?" he asked.

"Almost. I just need to—"

"What you need to do, bitch, is stop fucking my man. Spencer, tell her she's done!" some woman shouted. "I can't believe you answered her call and I just finished sucking your dick! Bye, bitch! Get your own man!"

If I weren't in shock, I would've ended the call.

"Are you Charlotte?" I asked.

"How that bitch know me?!"

"Fabulous, we're still on for Vegas. I'll explain later. Let me hit you back," he said, before ending the call.

I didn't know if I should feel embarrassed or stupid. I was wise enough to know everyone in Atlanta had a woman, a man, or both somewhere, even if they didn't mention it. Charlotte screaming wasn't my problem. What bothered me was I'd left his place five hours ago and he'd already had sex with someone else. Had he done to her what he'd done to me? If so, I understood why she was angry.

Everyone at our station was speechless, including myself.

Sandara entered the store. Looked at our faces, then asked, "What happened?"

CHAPTER 24

Spencer

"You can dish it out but you can't deal. Now you know how I feel about you doing another dude. You think I want to hit your pussy raw after him? What if he gave you something?"

I hadn't used a condom with Fabulous but the odds of someone her age having HIV were less than Charlotte's. "Are you still fucking dude?"

"But you answered the damn phone," Charlotte said, sitting on my dick, "while you're inside of me. You lucky I'm not done." She folded her arms across her titties.

"What's his name?"

"Fuck you, Spencer!"

No, what was fucked up was Charlotte's perception of monogamy. I swear I wanted to push her ass off of me. I could have Charlotte, Blake, and Alexis if I wanted. Placing my cell on the nightstand, I looked up at her. Damn, was the other dude sexing my gurl better than I was putting it down? Was he old school, new? Better looking? What did she see in him that she didn't see in me?

"You make me sick to my stomach. Seriously," I told her. Staring into her eyes, I wanted to make her cry.

Once she did dude, she released the beast in me. The way I was treating her was her fault. She had no idea how many females hit on my ass every day. At least fifteen to twenty. All that "men can't be trusted" talk she'd done when we started kicking it and she ended up being the one to creep first. What we had was special. Not no more.

I had doggish tendencies but she made me dog her. For the guys that were cold toward women, I bet they had a Charlotte story similar to mine. Maybe I deserved this shit. Wasn't like I hadn't intentionally misled a few females in order to get my stroke on.

I hit my gurl's pussy hard! I started thrusting deep into her belly the way she liked it. Charlotte bounced up and down. More so from my determination to make her unfold her arms and cum on this dick. Breaking her grip, I clamped her breasts, then pinched her nipples hard.

"You gon' stop fucking dude." I wasn't asking. "Or you gon'." I paused, pushed her back onto this big dick, restricted her hips from moving, then shoved my shit up in her again. I held her there.

She stared into my eyes, wrapped her pussy muscles tight around my shaft, then asked, "Dude, who?"

At times my girl had more game than me but I refused to let her know that. She stroked her clit. "You know this is your pussy." She squeezed. "Stop." Squeezed again. "Trippin'." The continuous pulsation let me know she was cumming. I knew her body well. I kept still.

I wanted to say, "I love you, boo." That was the truth. But my sentiments could change before she finished climaxing if I pictured her riding that other nigga.

Charlotte's eyes rolled toward her forehead. Quickly, she got off of me, then out of bed. Hands on her hips, she said, "That bitch isn't more fabulous than me. What's her real name?"

That's what I got for holding out. My shit was straight up in the air. "I know you're kidding, right? Get back on this dick."

Charlotte stormed into the kitchen. Scrambling to my feet, I followed her this time. She opened my cabinet. I slammed it.

"Don't touch my shit! I'm serious. What the fuck is wrong with you!"

She opened a different cabinet, swept four small plates off the shelf. "Now what?"

I swear I wanted to hit her. There was my answer. Charlotte had to go. For real this time.

"So do you love her ass?"

"Who are you talking about?"

"Don't act like you didn't just say in front of me that you're taking her to Vegas. All these thirsty bitches around here, it's probably more like she's taking you."

Staring down at Charlotte's face, I shifted my eyes to the side. My lips pressed together. Not in anger. Out of sadness.

Why couldn't we make our thing work?

I wasn't going to cry like a bitch but my eyes filled with tears of frustration. Whatever attracted me to this crazy-ass woman was slowly killing me. One day she might push me too far. Make me pull out my forty. Then what? I'd sit behind bars while her people bury her. Or while dude sit at her bedside waiting for another opp to do her. Fuck that!

She yelled up at me, "I asked you a question?"

"I'm not asking, Charlotte. Leave my damn house. We can't keep doing this. You can't keep going off." I pointed at the ceramic. "I can't keep forgiving you for breaking my heart and my shit."

Laughing, she said, "Me? Me? Own up to your shit, Spencer!"

Calmly, I told her, "I can't keep this up. It's over between us," trying to convince myself.

Before the call from Fabulous, Charlotte and I had just taken a breather from the best makeup sex we'd had in a month. I'd apologized for standing her up last night. Charlotte's hair was intertwined in my fingers as I penetrated her from behind. Other positions were cool but doggie-style was my favorite. The feel of my balls slapping against her creamy pussy took me to a new orgasmic plateau. I loved each time she'd reached between my thighs then held on to my balls real firm.

I'd pulled out, came all over her ass before penetrating that sweet asshole again. She'd screamed with pleasure, then grunted, "I love you so fucking much, Spencer. I hate you!"

I'd told her, "Same here, boo." I'd meant that shit.

The tightness of her asshole gripping my shaft drove me insane. I eased out. Came again. My body was exhausted. She'd removed the condom, cleaned me up. Sucked my head. Rolled her tongue in circles around my corona until she got him back up, then squatted on my dick.

My head was pointing north right now and I wanted another nut. Just one more. That wasn't happening. At least not with Charlotte. Maybe Fabulous could come take care of this before I had to leave for work.

"Spencer, do you love me?"

What's love got to do with this bullshit?

Charlotte was fucking crazy. Her glossy eyes were real scary right now. She gave me that possessed look.

We had a lot of chill things in common. We were both twenty-seven. We liked the same movies, places, video games, and hobbies. Maybe it was time for me to let all that go and date a mature woman like Fabulous. The older women I'd encountered were rational. But irrational females kept me on my game.

I turned away. Tiptoed over the chunks of broken ceramic. Suddenly I felt the piercing of fingernails in my back. Layers of my flesh burned.

"Damn!" Instinctively, I swung my fist at her.

She ducked. My aim went well above her head. If I had hit her ass, she'd be knocked out. I was glad I didn't connect. Dropping my arms to my side, I shook my head. I'd never been incarcerated. Planned on keeping it that way.

"Show her that!" Charlotte said. She stormed into my bedroom crying.

Forget the pussy. My dick was flaccid. I wasn't falling for it this time. I sat on my sofa, stared at the broken glass. A few minutes later she came out dressed, stomped by me, then left my place. She'd slammed the door so hard the walls shook.

I was relieved that she was fucking gone.

The first thing I'd done was lock my door. Second, call Fabulous.

"Hey, Spencer. You okay?" she asked.

"I apologize for my lil situation earlier."

"No need. Just wished you would've told me you were in a rela—"

"It's over," I said, trying to convince myself again. "We still on for Vegas?"

Silence filled the space between our ears. What did I expect? I deserved that.

"If you text me your info, I'll take that as a yes. I'll make reservations for us to leave in the morning and come back Sunday. And don't text me a pic of your makeover. Stop by the bar anytime after five and show me. Please, Fabulous. I need to see you."

Honestly, I wanted her to come now and lighten the heavy load in my nuts. But I also needed to know she wanted me for more than my bedroom skills.

"I know that's not Spencer on the phone, Mother. Hang up," an angry female voice exclaimed.

The call ended. I wasn't sure who terminated our conversation but I hoped it wasn't Fabulous. I turned off my cell. What I needed was a cold shower.

After I got out of the shower, I turned on my cell. Nodding with a smile, I'd received a text message with Blake Crystal's information. I went online, purchased two round-trip tickets to Las Vegas. Made a reservation at Bellagio. My salary wasn't that great. Thirty thou' a year plus twenty Gs or so in tips. The trust my mother left me didn't require me to have a nine-to-five but I wasn't the type of dude that found comfort in doing nothing all day. Bartending was a great way to meet interesting people.

The free-and-clear apartment building in Buckhead brought in ten grand a month. My new all-black Range Rover was paid for. I was smart enough not to let Charlotte or any woman know my net worth. A female's expectations escalated when she knew a man had three things—lots of money, love for her, and a big dick.

How many more potential acquaintances was I going to let Charlotte ruin before I did what needed to be done?

Fabulous was going to help me to let go of Charlotte so I could get next to Alexis.

CHAPTER 25

Blake

Spencer is taking me to Vegas I texted Brandon while I was in the dressing room.

My decision to go with Spencer to Las Vegas wasn't about doing what Mercedes believed was best. Spencer had a situation. I had one, too, two days ago. If Mercedes's husband, Benjamin, were home the next two days would've been about them, not me. Texting Spencer my information was all about what I wanted to do for my birthday.

Brandon replied, Bitch you'd better go to LV & suck that young dick like you trying to swallow it whole!!! If you need a personal assistant, you know my bags stay packed.

The form-fitting green, blue, and black pattern midthigh dress at Bebe's was my favorite. I hung it on the right, tried on the cotton candy pink maxi dress. It flattered my figure. The red dress, long-sleeved on one side, neck, arm, and shoulder exposed on the other side, stopped above my knee. A definite no. I hung it on the left. The petite white and black skirts were a yes.

According to Alexis, all the clothes in my suitcase should be pussy accessible. I planned on being a complete whore the entire time I was vacationing in Sin City. I needed freak tips from Brandon.

I texted him, 5 o'clock Ocean Prime on Piedmont?, then slipped into a pair of gold open-toe platforms and felt like a giant.

"Mama, what's taking you so long? Come out so we can see," Alexis said.

Spencer texted, Reservations, done! Can't wait 2CU later today Fabulous! Anytime after 5. Don't give me a heads up just show up.

I loved a man who did what he'd promised. One last look in the mirror. I fluffed my hair. My shimmering chocolate lips, smoky eyes, dramatic lashes made me fall in love with myself.

Brandon confirmed dinner with me. I strutted out of the dressing room wearing a sleeveless minidress with a cutaway that highlighted my cleavage.

Devereaux gasped, then covered her mouth. Tears streamed down Sandara's face. Alexis hugged me.

Mercedes said, "Wow. You are extremely attractive, Mother. Red is your best color but that purple is hot on you. You've been hiding all that sexiness since you got with Fortune. Keep all of that on."

"I'll get your things," Sandara said, heading toward the dressing room.

Mercedes charged everything to her credit card. "Now what?"

"I have to go home next," I answered. "I'm having dinner with Brandon, then I'll meet you guys at Mercedes's by eight tonight and in the morning," I said, hugging and thanking each of my babies, then told them, "I am going to Las Vegas with Spencer."

Seven hours would give me enough time to pack my bags, dine and have a couple of drinks, swing back to the mall to let Spencer see me, then make it to Mercedes's for a sleepover with my girls.

As I strutted to the valet with lots of shopping bags, I thought this truly was the best weekend I'd had since before I'd met Fortune. I turned heads all the way to my Ferrari until I drove off.

Cruising to Roswell, I wished marriage would've come before Devereaux had Nya but the license wouldn't have guaranteed her a healthier relationship with Phoenix.

Parking next to my Benz, I was glad Fortune's car was not in my driveway. I pressed the remote to open my garage, gathered my bags, then entered my house through the kitchen door. I went upstairs to the master bedroom, dropped my purse and shopping bags on my chaise, emptied my dirty laundry into the hamper in my closet.

I admired myself in the mirror. Twirled. Smiled. Took a few selfies.

"You look nice," Fortune said, staring at me.

"Ah!" My heartbeat pounded in my throat. Breathing heavily, I asked Fortune, "What the hell are you doing here? Do not start stalking me. Get the hell out!"

I should've closed my garage. Locked my door but I'd planned on putting on panties and heading right back out.

"You dressed up for him?" he asked.

"What difference does it make who I'm dressed up for? It's over between us. You did not do anything for me, not even wish me a happy birthday. I'm tired of supporting you. Go home to your wife. Go live with your other woman. I don't care about you anymore. Just get the hell out of my house! I hate you!"

"So you're serious this time?" he asked. His eyes weren't droopy. They were glossy.

Shaking my head, I didn't answer. His hatred for me was in his eyes. I saw it. I felt it. I moved closer to my nightstand, where my gun was.

"Your house?" He leaned his head back, laughed, then yelled, "Don't act like I didn't fix things around here!" Picking up my Bebe's bag, he flung my clothes, shoes. He opened the Sephora bag. Tossed my makeup in the air.

I ignored him, I admired myself in the mirror, ran my fingers through my fluffy fluttering hair, then told him, "Your priorities are screwed up. I figured out why you're so miserable. You've never invested in a woman. That's why no woman wants your trifling ass. And even the times that I've taken you back it was never because I wanted you. I was afraid to be alone. But I'm not anymore. You still don't have the decency to wish me a happy birthday."

Standing by the drawer of my nightstand, I checked my messages. One percent battery life remained. My phone powered off but not before I saw Spencer's message.

He'd texted, I want to get to know all about you this weekend. I'm going to spoil you Fabulous.

Fortune stood by me. I opened my drawer. He closed it. I eyed the man in front of me. He was pathetic. My disgust for him had to have shown on my face.

Fortune's eyes focused on my cleavage, lowered to my hips. He stared at my mouth. He didn't look into my eyes when he said, "I'm sorry. You're right. Happy birthday, Blake. You look amazing." He placed his hands on my hips.

Firmly, I grabbed his wrists. "Please, don't touch me."

"Don't deny me, Blake. Give me some of this," he said, sliding his hand under my dress and between my legs.

I pushed him away.

His eyes grew large. "You naked under there?"

What difference did that make? He didn't deserve to know but I told him, "I'm spending the night at Mercedes's house with my girls. You need to get out. For real."

He didn't have anything to offer me. Even if he did, I didn't want it. This time I was one hundred percent sure. The smell and sight of him disgusted me.

He shook his head. "Stop lying to me! You're going to be with another man."

"Even if I were lying, it wouldn't matter. I don't owe you anything. Not even an explanation. For the last time, get the hell—"

Whack! Fortune backhand-slapped me so hard my hair hit the bed first.

I scrambled to get up. He shoved me down, unfastened his pants, pulled out his dick, then pinned my wrists above my head using one hand.

I jabbed my knee into his dick, and he grunted. "Bitch!" His fist charged toward my face. I moved my head enough for him to miss my eye, but his knuckles slid down to my ear. "Knee me again."

He didn't have to ask for what was already coming! I gave my best effort to put his dick out of commission permanently this time.

"Ow! You trying to take away my manhood," he yelled. His fist bashed my face several times. Felt as though my head was going to separate from my body.

Everything went mute. I struggled to free myself. He spread my thighs. "Don't deny me, Blake. I want what you gave whoever you let fuck my pussy last night." He stuck his finger inside me, then sniffed it. "You think I can't smell him on you. I know you. You—"

I spat in his face. I froze when I saw my blood on his lips. Then I realized my hands were free. I tried to scratch his eyes out.

"Ow!" Fortune ripped my dress, snatched my hair toward the mattress.

What the fuck was he fighting me for? "This is *my* pussy you nasty son of a bitch!"

Fortune fought me like I was a man. When I gave up, he held my wrists with one hand, shoved himself inside of me. I threw up bile and blood. I hadn't eaten all day.

That bastard shoved, thrust, and grunted with anger until he came. I looked at my nightstand. He started at me.

Fortune said, "If you put your finger on the trigger, Blake, you'd better pull it."

CHAPTER 26

Spencer

It was six o'clock. I'd hoped Blake would've dropped by the restaurant by now. I was excited as hell to see her. Fifty smashed on her in the best way. Nice titties. Tight enough ass. Whatever lucky guy was smashing that on a regular wasn't treating her righteous. Not the way she came on my dick.

Bank president. Had to Google for that info. House in Roswell. You go, Fabulous. All of her girls were beautiful and seemed to have their stuff together. That was a testament. I wanted to know more about Blake Crystal. Not sure yet if I wanted her full or part-time though. It was way too soon to get serious. Decided to hold off on AC, but her daughter was tempting.

Filling a martini glass with a margarita, my coworker LB said, "Dude, you're doing it again."

Damn! This was the third drink I'd overpoured. I'd washed away the salt rim. Again. "Thanks, man."

Emptying the glass, I started over. This time I stayed focused long enough to get it right. I placed the martini glass in front of the customer.

LB stood beside me. "What's up, Spence? What's on your mind? You're starting to attract Derrick's attention, dude."

I placed two wineglasses in front of me, reached for the cabernet, scoped out my manager through my peripheral. He was at the opposite end of the bar. I came straight with LB. I spoke in a low tone. "You remember I told you I put it down on her yesterday."

"Yeah, the older broad?" His brows hiked. "The one who looked liked she could be her daughters' sister. Not the daughter, right?"

Nodding, I told him, "She's coming by to see me tonight. I don't know why I'm so damn nervous. She was supposed to be a conquest but I'm taking her to Vegas tomorrow."

LB tapped on the computer screen, entered an order, redirected his attention to me. "Taking or going with?"

"You heard me right. Taking."

Didn't want Fabulous to have that crazy rep like she was an easy lay. Lots of females in the ATL had a rotation of men. Fabulous didn't seem the type. I cared about her. *Cared* might be too strong a word. I liked her. Might have to pass on Alexis.

"Real shit, dude? Sin City? On your dime?"

"Damn, nigga. It's the US. You trippin' like I said I was taking Fabulous to the French Riviera."

"Fabulous?"

"Fabulous," I repeated.

LB shook the shaker, flipped over a glass, then poured a JW Lemonade over ice. I filled the wineglasses a third of the way. Answered him, "Real shit."

We placed the drinks in front of the customers. LB tapped the bar twice in front of this beautiful babe. I told him, "I gotcha, bruh."

While he punched in another order, I continued, "Crazy, huh?"

"Nah, what's crazy is who just walked in."

Excited to see Fabulous, I quickly glanced toward the entrance. "Aw, fuck."

LB said, "You got that right. Derrick is headed this way. I'ma give yo' ass space, Spence. I'll handle the incoming orders. You, handle her," he said, walking away.

Charlotte sat on a stool in the center of the bar, then pushed the adjacent chair over enough to squeeze in her four-roller, too-large-to-carry-on suitcase.

"Good to see you're still in town. I'm hungry. Get me an order of fried zucchini with extra ranch. What time is *our* trip to Vegas?"

Derrick said, "Spencer, let me speak with you for a moment."

"Sure," I said, following my manager to the opposite end of the bar. I ducked under the opening, stepped out onto the patio area.

He stared me square in my eyes. "You're spilling more alcohol than you're serving. Your customers are complaining their orders are taking too long. Notice their body language when you walk back in. You need more than a few days off? I can give you two weeks. The only reason I'm not firing you is because I like your work ethic."

I shook my head. "I don't need extra days off. I got this."

"I don't think you do. I'll let you know by the end of your shift. You know my rules. You have to pay attention to everything in the restaurant to service our customers well. I'm watching you," he said, walking away.

The policy was straight. Every customer was every employee's responsibility. I got that. I loved that. Was starting to feel more for Fabulous, less for Charlotte. If every woman I'd sexed was my responsibility, I'd be a lifetime patient at a mental institution. Outside of riding my dick, I was starting to believe that women didn't know what they wanted either. Charlotte was a good example. One day it was me, then she slept with dude. Now she's hounding me. But she probably still in good with dude.

I didn't like being checked but Derrick was right. I went behind the bar. Wanted to ignore Charlotte but she was a customer.

LB whispered, "Yo' girl refused to let me serve her. She wants you."

Politely, I asked Charlotte, "Can I get you something to drink?"

She damn near shouted, "What you can give me is a public apology for fucking that Fabulous bitch! She staying her ass right here. You taking me to Vegas!"

Derrick swiftly approached. Stood in front of Charlotte. "I'm telling you to leave my restaurant and don't ever come back."

"Unless your name is Cheesecake, this ain't your damn restaurant!"

Actually it was. Derrick was an operating manager. My lips tightened. Charlotte's selfish ass thought this shit was funny. Bet it wouldn't be so cute if I showed up on her job at the car dealership acting a damn fool. If she lost commission on selling one of those used vehicles, she'd be pissed off for months.

Derrick turned to me, then said, "You need to leave now and take her with you."

LB brushed by me, whispered, "You know what you need to do. Cut her loose," then said, "I'll holla at you later, Spence. Don't forget about my hookup with the daughter."

Embarrassed as fuck, I strolled toward the front door. Charlotte grabbed her suitcase, followed me to the parking lot. Tossing her luggage in the back of her car, she followed me all the way to my apartment building. When the garage gate opened, she tailed me until she was inside. I didn't care. By the time she got to the sixth floor and parked in a visitor's space, I'd be inside.

She parked next to me knowing they might boot her car. I was not giving her seventy-five dollars to have it removed. I checked my cell. No missed texts or calls from Blake. I sent a message, Something came up. I have to rain check you on Vegas.

I sent that moreso because I was pissed. Getting out of my car, I refused to say a word to Charlotte. I unlocked my door, left it opened. She entered behind me.

"Spencer, I'm sorry. I hope I didn't make you lose your job."

Turning on my shower, I took off my clothes, and stepped in. The water was hot as I could stand. I yelled at her, "What the fuck is wrong with you!"

That could've gone either way. For Charlotte's crazy ass jeopardizing my job. Or for my dumb ass dealing with that bitch!

CHAPTER 27

Blake

He deserved to die!

I contemplated picking up my gun, pointing it at his head, then pulling the trigger but I was in shock. I sat on the side of the bed, slid the straps of my gold platform heels off my feet, then let them drop one at a time to the floor. Easing out of bed, I saw that the hem of my purple dress was unraveled. Threads hung to my ankles.

Lowering my ass, I flopped on my chaise. My arms dangled as I stared at my red polished toenails. My hair hung like I was a rag doll. Thirty years ago I was in great shape. Now I weighed more and was less motivated to work out. If I had been stronger, I could've fought my way out of being raped by that filthy jealous bastard.

Never again would I leave my home accessible under the pretense that I lived in a safe neighborhood. I used to run a 5K in fifteen minutes. If I were faster, I could've escaped, run out the house, and screamed for help. I wished my neighbor across the street would've heard me. Tom would've killed Fortune.

Short breaths. Small steps. My sleeve fell to my bicep. I pulled the torn material over my shoulder then cupped my aching breasts. My side was sore to the touch. Quietly I inhaled, then held my breath as I paused at the foot of the bed to stare down at Fortune.

His mouth wide open, drool seeped from between his lips and slid down his chin onto my white satin pillowcase. He turned onto his side then snorted. His back was to me. That was the way we'd slept most nights. Facing away from each other.

I entered my spacious bathroom, stood in front of the full-length mirror trimmed in glittering gold. The image before me was nearly unrecognizable.

One eye that matched the color of my dress was nearly shut. My other eyeball bulged so far out that my eyelid couldn't move. I blinked but couldn't close either of my eyes.

Softly, I sang, "Happy birthday to . . . me." Well, I was beautiful for almost a whole day. If Spencer could see me now. My body jerked but there were no tears, on the outside.

Sitting at my vanity, I soaked a cotton ball with witch hazel, then gently stroked my swollen jaw. I flinched.

I'd come home after the best day of my life to this bullshit. *This is bullshit!* Why the fuck did he come back here?

My girls must've given up on my coming over by now. No one had called. Suddenly I remembered my phone had died. Better for my daughters and Spencer to be mad at me for being a no-show than for me to show up looking like this.

Dropping the cotton ball into the trash, I exited the bathroom, got my phone off the bed. I placed it on the charger in the bathroom, then went to my walk-in closet, closed the door, turned on the light. I scanned everything I'd bought but had never worn. Dresses. Skirts. Jackets. High heels. Anne Klein. Donna Karan. Jimmy Choo. Red bottoms. All beautiful clothes too sexy to wear to work or church. But there were a few things appropriate for a funeral.

I'd worked my ass off to buy the finest house. Seven cars—one for Fortune, one for each of my daughters as their graduation gifts. The most expensive luxury sedan was my Benz. The red Ferrari was simply a gift to myself because I could afford it. I was on the verge of being genuinely happy. If I'd invested in a man who loved himself, this would've never happened.

I didn't believe any man would love me unconditionally but I'd never been beat down. Maybe it was best I let things between Spencer and me end. He may have been intrigued by me but he'd never fall in love with me.

Don't deny me. Fortune's words echoed in my head as I searched for the perfect dress. Suddenly, my body's temperature was too hot, the memories were chilling. Hours ago that motherfucker had the audacity to force himself on me like he owned me!

I returned to the bathroom. Soaked another cotton ball. I hurled the bottle of witch hazel into the wall. "That motherfucker deserves to die tonight."

My cell started chiming with incoming texts and missed calls. I picked up my phone, silenced the tone. Instead of returning calls my trembling fingers texted Mercedes, I can't make it. Thanks for a beautiful day. I love you. XOXO

As I put my phone down, my vision became blurry. I squeezed a few drops in each eye, then read Spencer's text. I replied, Something unexpected came up. Can't do Vegas. I wanted to add, "rain check," but that wasn't what I was feeling. Plus, I was tired of struggling to see the keyboard.

The voice in my head spoke softly: *Definitely the black dress.*

I returned to my closet. Too sore to raise my arms over my head, one leg at time, as though putting on the pants I'd worn for the last time, I stepped into my dress. The side zipper remained undone.

I went downstairs to the kitchen. Opened the cabinet. I gripped the handle of the longest knife, sharpened the blade. One long stroke after another I repeatedly slid the edge in one direction.

I picked up a piece of paper, rubbed the edged of the blade along the side. It tore halfway then stopped. I continued sharpening. The next time the paper effortlessly divided.

What I was about to do was premeditated. There'd be no need to plead temporary insanity or guilty. I wasn't crazy and this was not my fault. I dropped the sharpener to the floor.

There was one more thing I had to do before going upstairs. Reaching for a pen and a fresh piece of paper, I wrote, *I love you, Devereaux. Take care of your sisters.*

In a separate note, I wrote, *I love you, Mercedes. Take care of your sisters.* I'd done the same with Alexis and Sandara, then left the notes on the countertop.

Quietly walking toward the bedroom, I heard him snorting. He was lying on his back. I clutched the handle so tight that my red polished fingernails cut into my palms. I steadied the razor-sharp knife directly above his heart.

I knew if there were a God, there was forgiveness.

CHAPTER 28

Spencer

Sitting in the center seat on the plane next to Charlotte, I stared out the window.

Being with her wasn't as much of a problem as how I'd gotten here. She spilled drama from the moment she stepped into the restaurant until the second I'd agreed to let her come.

If I wanted to take her, I would've invited her. Charlotte was a straight trip. I shook my head, kept watching what was happening on the ground.

Charlotte leaned on me. "I love you, Spencer."

Her hair was loose, flowing down her back, pressed against my chest. It felt good in a soothing kind of way. I inhaled Gucci Guilty. Charlotte had this thing where she'd spritz perfume in her palms then run her fingers through her hair. Whenever I inhaled or a breeze blew, I wanted to grab her long blond strands and hold them under my nose. I hugged her tighter.

"I love you too, boo." Truth was, I needed her to hold me. The sizzle reel in my head of the last twenty-fo highlighted the good, the bad, and the ugly.

I'd taken Charlotte on a few weekend road trips to Augusta, Savannah, and Macon. Was reluctant to drive with her to New York, New Orleans, or Miami. Didn't want to cross the state line of Georgia with her by my side. This trip on a plane was about to be a first for us. Our first experiences—the day we met, kissed, had sex, made love—were memorable in a good way.

Out-of-state getaways were reserved for my boy, LB. I wasn't a fan of traveling in groups. Hated hearing Charlotte whine before we left, then again when we returned. What the hell was she bitching about? I mean we could have a perfect day and she'd find that fucking needle in a haystack and poke me with it.

"Let's get married in Vegas," Charlotte said without facing me.

I ain't gon' lie, though. I had a tightness in my chest for Charlotte. The kind that made it hard to breathe at times but getting married was out. Right now, I was in excruciating emotional pain. If I were a "I don't give a fuck about females" kinda bruh, long as I get mine, I would've cashed in Blake's ticket, invited my boy, LB, on this trip, and let Charlotte sit this one out in the ATL with her other dude.

"Let's figure out if we honestly want this relay, boo."

Casually, she answered with an "Okay."

I recalled my first kiss with Fabulous while we stood by her Ferrari yesterday morning. I was upset with Fabulous, too. She'd changed her mind about traveling with me but I went out of my way to celebrate *her* birthday. My ego told her ass not to worry about the trip hoping she'd plead her case. Her not having the decency to call was foul to the tenth power. Recalling her text message, *Something unexpectedly came up. Can't do Vegas.* I balled my fist, placed it on my knee, tucked my lips, clenched my teeth, then shook my head. *Oh, she could've done Vegas.* It was more like, Won't? Don't want to do Vegas? Do me? Both? Nigga fuck you, Fabulous!

"Miss, I need to take your purse and put it in the overhead compartment," the flight attendant said.

Charlotte's head snapped toward the aisle. "I know you're not talking to me."

We were in bulkhead. Charlotte refused to hand her purse to the attendant. We'd both checked in our luggage. Hers at ticket check-in. Mine at the gate.

"Give it to me, boo." I put her purse under the last seat in first class so we could see it the entire flight.

Charlotte said, "Thanks," then leaned the back of her head on my chest.

I inhaled slow and deep, filling my lungs with the scent of my woman.

The attendant announced, "When we close the door, you'll have to switch your cell phones to airplane mode or power them off."

Taking my cell out of my pocket, I took the opportunity to check my phone for messages. Anxiously, I wanted Fabulous to have sent a text or left a voice mail apologizing.

Clenching my teeth, I powered off my cell. *Fuck that whore!* With every passing second I became angrier. I couldn't lie. I felt like a fool.

Heaving, I tried to calm down. On the upside, at least twenty-four hours hadn't passed since I'd paid for Blake's ticket so I'd gotten a full refund from the airline back to my credit card. I could've cancelled my ticket, too, but Charlotte had become "get back at Fabulous." But what good was a get-back if the person I was trying to make trip was clueless about my being pissed the hell off?!

"The world can wait," Charlotte said without looking at me. "I love you, Spencer. Stop thinking about her. I promise I'll never break anything in your house ever again."

"Why do you lie to me? You've said that way too many times. You know I don't believe you." Just like I didn't believe she'd stopped fucking dude. "From now on, I'm coming to your crib. No more kicking it at my spot."

"That's fair," she said, glancing over her shoulder. She looked up into my eyes. "Your not having your mom. Me not having my dad. That's why I'm so messed up, you know. Baby, maybe we should consider getting counseling together."

My dick instantly got hard when she said, "Baby." The way she looked at me with those sexy eyes. She had the sweetest voice even when she was mad.

"Tell the truth. Did you fuck dude when you left my place yesterday? Don't lie." I tried to lock eye contact with her.

Charlotte turned away, answered, "No," then looked at me. "Let's get married when we get to Vegas. Maybe being married and living together will help us grow closer together."

What? She didn't think I could tell she was lying and trying to change the subject. Marrying Charlotte wasn't happening. Not this or any other trip. No amount of counseling could change her crazy ass.

I wanted to push her off of me! Best for me not to respond.

Maybe the way I'd sexed Fabulous scared her off. That shit was unforgettable. My hard dick wanted Fabulous seated next to me. I wanted to lick her asshole. Make her squirt again. Nah, I wanted to give her this dick nice and slow missionary style. Stare into her eyes, make her cry the kind of tears that would make her say, "I love you," while holding me in her arms.

I told Charlotte, "I've gotta take a piss before takeoff." Facing the person next to me, I said, "Excuse me."

Standing in the aisle, I looked at Charlotte for the last time. Bypassing the flight attendant, I exited the plane onto the Jetway.

"Dude, I have an emergency." Handing him my claim ticket, I asked, "Can you get my bag? Or is it too late?"

"Let me see," he said, hurrying down the stairway.

The stewardess looked at me, opened her mouth. I pressed my finger to my lips, then shook my head. She closed the door. Instantly I felt relieved when the guy said, "Here you go, man."

I offered him a tip, but he refused. "Go take care of your business. I'll pray for you, brotha."

Exiting the concourse, I headed to the MARTA station, hopped on the train. I might regret having memorized Fabulous's address when I checked her ID at the bar. My destination was to get to my car in Buckhead then head north to Roswell.

CHAPTER 29

Blake

"Nine-one-one operator," she answered.

Matching her tone, calmly I said, "I need an ambulance to . . ." Giving her my address, I adjusted my Bluetooth deeper into my ear.

She questioned, "Is this an emergency?"

My pointing finger glided from the handle, along the dull side, to the tip. I stared at the knife, then at him. Softly, I answered, "Depends on how you look at it. Please. Send an ambulance. No, wait. Send the coroner." I ended the call. Cleaned my face best as I could.

Fortune wasn't man enough to stay gone after I'd put him out. Brought his disgusting-had-no-place-to-stay black ass back up in *my* house. Without *my* permission! Acted as though he had the right to go upside my head, then fall asleep in my bed as though nothing bad had happened.

He didn't love me. He never loved me. This could've ended differently if he'd stayed gone.

Four hours ago I stood over him, watched him exhale his last breath. That was my first time watching a person die. I wasn't sad. I was numb. Couldn't stand to look at myself with all these bruises.

Softly, I said, "Do unto others." He'd gotten what he deserved.

I'd waited to dial for assistance. Wanted to make sure there was no chance of the paramedics reviving him. One less trifling man in the world would save a few women from being abused.

The blaring sounds of sirens got louder and louder. I stuck my finger in my left ear. Entering my closet, I removed a pair of pink shoes from my Prada box, dropped the knife inside, then replaced the top. I changed from my black dress to a long pink silk robe. Quickly, I changed my robe from pink to white. White would make me appear as though I was the victim. Well, I was. Had two black eyes and a busted lip to prove it.

One last stare at that no-good rapist. The sirens stopped. I said, "There is God." I spat in Fortune's face, then I headed barefoot downstairs to my living room.

Opening my front door, the paramedics stared at me. One of them asked, "What happened, miss?" Immediately, the other one opened his first aid case, then said, "Have a seat. Let me check you out."

I shook my head to the sound of more sirens. "I got my ass beat but I didn't lose the fight. I'm not the one you came for." Stepping aside, I pointed, then told them, "He's up there." I was at peace with what had happened to Fortune.

The paramedics rushed up the stairs. At the same time, a police car parked beside the ambulance in my driveway.

Oh, shit! Racing into the kitchen, I ripped the notes to my daughters into tiny pieces then sprinkled them in the trashcan. I hadn't realized blood was in the palms of my hands from gripping the knife. Quickly, I washed my hands, dried them with a paper towel, then tossed it in the trash. As I returned to my living room, two cops entered my home. I pointed upstairs.

Mercedes's car pulled up. All of my daughters got out. Hurried to me. This was the first time that I needed each of my children more than any one of them needed me.

"All hell no!" Devereaux shouted. She started crying.

My girls talked over one another asking me questions at the same time. I heard, "Mama, what happened." "We can see what the fuck happened!" "Where's that bitch at?!" "I can't believe this." "Oh, my, God."

I was relieved my girls were here. I opened my arms to all of them praying nothing like this would ever happen to any of them. No woman deserved this.

Mercedes stepped back from the group hug. "Fortune! Bring your trifling ass down here right now!" she shouted.

"I hope you cut his nuts off," Sandara said, bouncing up and down. She threw a few jabs to the empty space in front of her face.

I nodded, then shook my head fast. Sounded as though they were speaking underwater. *Lord, please don't let me lose the hearing in my left ear.*

"Fuck that bitch! If he won't come down, I'm going up!" Tears streamed down Alexis's cheeks. She pulled her gun from her purse, wrapped both hands around the handle, pulled the firearm to her right shoulder, pointed the barrel toward the ceiling, then headed toward the staircase. "If he's not dead, I'm going to make that bitch wish he were, Mama."

Mercedes yelled, "Get back here, girl! And put that away. It doesn't have a safety."

Alexis said, "I'm the fucking safety."

Devereaux chimed in, "Let the police do their job."

A police officer appeared at the top of the stairs. "Ma'am, she's right." He drew his weapon toward Alexis, deepened his voice, then spoke with authority. "Put your gun away, now!"

Alexis placed the gun in the side compartment of her purse.

The officer said, "Everyone stay downstairs. No one leave." He disappeared from the hallway.

I think the only time Alexis didn't have a piece on her was when she was in church. Shaking my head, I wasn't sure about that.

My girls knew a lot about guns. I did too. In Georgia, guns were allowed in the home. The car was an extension of the home. Possessing a firearm outside of the home or car required a license that all of us had.

I heard footsteps approaching my doorway. I wiggled my finger in my left ear. Assuming it was more policemen, I pointed toward the staircase.

"Fabulous, what's going on?"

The voice and nickname were unmistakable. I turned and faced Spencer. "How'd you get my address?"

With all the commotion, I hadn't noticed the black Range Rover in my driveway. It must've been his.

"Aw, hell nah!" he said, covering then uncovering his face. He hunched his shoulders, shook his head at the same time. "Fabulous, all I need to know is, where that motherfucka at?"

Two more officers entered my living room. They stared at me. Then one questioned Spencer, "Who's responsible for this dispute?"

Yep, I'd lost some degree of hearing in my left ear. I could understand but the words were slightly muffled.

An officer standing above by the railing said, "Guys. Up here!"

One of the policemen eyed Spencer, then said, "Don't you leave. Nobody leave." Then, both officers headed to the second floor.

Spencer looked at me then shook his head. "You should've told me you had a situation at home. Now I feel bad for keeping you out all night. It's my fault."

"No, it's not." Spencer obviously felt bad about what happened to me but the only person I blamed was dead.

Mercedes objected. "Yes. It is his fault, Mother. If he would've remained professional and not taken advantage of you, you would've made it home that night. Instead, thanks to Spencer Can't-Keep-His-Dick-To-Himself Domino, you had on the same red halter dress the next day. And no panties, may I add!"

Spencer's eyes widened as he slowly said, "Wow."

Devereaux commented, "Keep it down, Mercedes. We don't want the cops to think Spencer did this."

"How do you know his last name, Mercedes?" I asked, then told Spencer, "It's not your fault."

Spencer came closer to me. "I can leave if you want me to. I was pissed that you stood me up so"—he paused then hunched his shoulders—"I was stopping by." He paused again, then asked, "You okay?"

Sandara answered this time. "What you think, lover boy?"

Mercedes told Sandara, "I know you're not talking."

Just as I opened my mouth to speak, a paramedic came into the living room and confirmed what I already knew. He said, "I'm sorry, ma'am. He's dead. We'll do an autopsy to confirm his cause of death but it appears he suffered a heart attack. The coroner will be here shortly. We'll wait upstairs until they arrive."

Tom, my neighbor from across the street, rushed into my house. Stared at my face. "Oh, my Heavenly Father. Who did this to you, Blake? Was it that sum-of-a-bitch Fortune? Where is he?"

I nodded, then said, "Dead."

"Good," Tom said. "I should go get my rifle and kill that sum-of-a-bitch again."

Alexis swayed side to side. Patted her purse. "I'm with you, Tom. I say we do this!"

One of the police officers stood at the top of the staircase, then said, "Tom, is it?"

"Yes sir, officer. I'm Blake's neighbor."

The police trotted down the stairs. "Unless you're involved in this situation, Tom, I'm going to have to ask you to leave. Ms. Blake, we're going to have to take a report from you and everyone who was here at the time of death. We can do it here or at the station."

"If you need me, call me and I'll come a-runnin'. You hear me, Blake," Tom said, heading toward the door. "Good-bye, officer. You have a nice day."

Mercedes said, "Officer, please. Take our mother's statement here. She was the only one present at the time."

"All of these are your children, ma'am?" the officer asked.

Alexis responded, "These are my sisters. He," she said, pointing at Spencer, "is my boyfriend."

Looking at Spencer, I was relieved that Alexis had taken the spotlight off of him.

CHAPTER 30

Spencer

Waiting for Fabulous to finish giving her statement inside the house, I sat in a rocking chair on her front porch. Didn't need to know the specifics. There was zero justification for a dude laying fists to any woman's face.

The afternoon sunshine disappeared behind a layer of dark clouds. From what I'd heard, not much drama happened in the city of Roswell. If Fabulous became my new woman or my side gurl, this place could become a real chill zone for me. I liked how Fabulous's house was tucked away from the congestion I was accustomed to in Buckhead.

She had the seventy-inch-screen television, surround sound speakers, all the shit a man liked. Showing up to curse out Fabulous for standing me up, I felt bad when I saw her black eyes and busted lip.

That fucked up shit brought back memories of what my dad had done to my mom. Guilt crept in on how I'd abandoned Charlotte. A lot of shit was competing in my head for attention. If it were true that everything happened for a reason, my being here with Fabulous was where I was meant to be. I missed my mom, and a few tears rolled down a brotha's face.

A soft voice said, "Hey, Spencer. You okay?" Alexis sat in the rocker beside me, then held my hand. "I'm glad you came."

This female was bold, straight trouble, and one hundred percent sexy. Alexis dried my tears. Instantly my dick got hard.

"I'm not that sentimental brotha that cry all the time," I told her, toughening up.

"Then what's got you flowing?"

Trouble with a capital *T.* I volunteered to share my story for two reasons. One, to take my mind off of fucking her. Two, I wanted to let her know I understood how she might be feeling about her mom.

"When I was ten I saw my dad beat my mom. It wasn't the first time but it was the worst I'd witnessed." My high school drama days kicked in. I added serious facial expressions as I continued. "That day it was so bad I thought, if he hits her one more time, my mother is going to die."

Alexis leaned closer.

"This shit is real. I was so angry. I wanted to blow his brains out. Scared as a rat might be crossing a starving cat's path to get to a piece of cheese, I didn't care what would happen to me." I paused, stuck out my chest, squeezed her hand, then proudly said, "I became brave that day. I'd gone to the garage, grabbed the shotgun. Boldly, I aimed the barrel at my father's head. He'd taught me how to shoot to kill. Two shots to the chest. One to the head. My ten-year-old hands started trembling, uncontrollably. His—"

Alexis interrupted. "Spencer, is this a true story?" Her hand glided up and down my bicep.

Sucking in my lips, I glanced toward the front door. "Yes. It is."

"Don't worry about anyone coming out here. You're my boyfriend, remember? Tell me the rest of your story," she said. Letting go of my hand, she removed her cell from her halter, tapped on a few keys. "I'm listening."

My phone was in my pocket. I pulled it out, scanned my messages.

Alexis touched my hand. "Let's not do this. I'll put away my phone. I'm all yours."

Did she just one-up me? I put my cell away and continued. "My dad told me if you ever put your finger on the trigger, pull it."

Alexis nodded slowly.

She flinched when I said, "Pow! I'd done as he'd instructed, except I'd fired once. Not three times."

She shook her head. "Do I need to take you to the shooting range?"

I waved my hand, then continued. "My mom screamed, 'Jesus!' That first shot gave me courage to shout, 'Leave my mama alone or

I'm gonna shoot you in your heart for real this time.' " I lowered my voice. "I'd meant it. Going to juvenile detention would've been worth it knowing he'd never beat my mother again."

Blinking, I looked up at the sky, rocked back and forth.

"Is that the end?" Alexis asked.

I shook my head, told her, "I'd never forget how my dad rushed toward me, took the gun. That day my father fought me like a man and told me, 'If you ever come between me and your mother again, I'll kill you, you lil sissy.' That's the end," I lied. When my dad called me a sissy, I assumed he knew his brother had molested me.

"I have daddy issues too," she said. "Maybe one day I'll tell you mine."

I was battling demons. My heart was hurting. I wanted someone to love me the way my mother loved me. It was one thing not having my dad. Fuck that nigga! I didn't care if he was dead or alive. But moms . . . Moms, man. I still questioned God about His decision to take her from me. He knew she was my world.

The thought choked me. I swallowed. I wanted, make that needed, a woman to truly care for me. Maybe Fabulous was that person.

Alexis asked, "You have kids?"

I shook my head.

"I'd never forget what my mom told me the next day. On our way home from Piedmont Hospital, she said, 'Baby, I'm so sorry.' When we got home to our apartment, my father was gone. Probably afraid he'd get arrested again. Punk. He was always running from his responsibilities as a man, as a father. His doing time for beating my mom was always somehow my mother's fault."

Alexis sniffled. I stared into her eyes. "It's okay to cry," I said, rubbing the back of her hand. Damn, her skin was like silk.

"I'm tired of crying over my dad," she said.

"Never take your mom for granted," I said. "That day was the last time I saw my father. My mother held me in her arms. Rocked me for what must have been hours. She'd said, 'I'm grown, baby. I can take the abuse. But I'll kill your father if he ever puts his hands on you again. It's just you and me now, Spence. We're all we've got.' "

I became quiet like Alexis.

My mom apologized all that night. Honestly, I didn't believe her. I thought she was going to let him back in. But I watched how strong she became afterward. Whatever she told him, he never came back. Not even to get his things.

There was a strange sense of comfort that came over me while holding Alexis's hand. Being with her released the tightness in my chest. Maybe I simply needed a woman who cared enough to listen to my story.

"I hate that that happened to your mom," she said.

"And I swear I didn't know your mom was married."

"She's not. He is. Or should I say, was. Honestly, Fortune should've been gone a long a time ago. I don't know why my mom let him move in with her but she makes irrational decisions."

I wondered where Charlotte was.

Alexis and I rocked in unison.

"Now what?" she asked.

"I'm not sure. I like your mom."

"You like Charlotte, too," she said, then asked, "You have any brothers? Cousins? Friends, that are nice like you?" Alexis interlocked her fingers with mine in a sensuous way.

I looked at her. A ray of sunlight broke through the darkness and beamed on her sweet chocolate radiant skin as though she was in the spotlight. Alexis's full cocoa lips had a dimple right in the middle of her bottom lip. I wanted to kiss her.

"My boy, LB. He's a good dude. If you're serious, I can introduce you."

A closed-lip smile brightened her face. My facial expression mimicked hers. Alexis nodded. "He's hot enough but I want you," she said, staring at my dick.

I took a deep breath, then exhaled.

"You're a good guy, Spencer. Stay that way." Alexis patted my hand, let go, then stood. Her pussy was a fraction of an inch from my face. The breeze blew her short dress high enough for me to see her orange lace thong. If I stuck my tongue out, I could lick her clit.

Planting my feet firmly on the porch, I made sure I did not rock forward.

CHAPTER 31

Alexis

I texted, **Hey LB.**
He texted me back. Hi Alexis. What's kosher?

I replied, Depends on what you're working with. You tell me.

He hit me with, Ladies first.

Sighing heavily, I was ready to put this bitch on block. There was no third text from me. If a man (or woman) didn't call me after two texts from me, I moved on. If LB had taken me out on a first date, that'd be different. After having sex with someone, they were officially in my roundup. That's when texting without a call was cool.

My cell rang, it was my on-again, off-again. "Hey, babe."

"Hey, sweetheart, what's up?" James asked.

"Missing you."

"Same here," he said. "You want to grab something to eat, then chill at my place?"

I told my guy, "I'd like that."

"Be there in thirty, sweetheart."

"I'll be ready in twenty."

Softly, he said, "You're in a good mood. Stay that way. I love you."

I ended the call with a huge smile on my face. I'd already taken a shower. Decided to take another one. Removing my black minidress, I slipped on a shower cap, freshened up all over, then stepped out. Lotion. Makeup. Perfume. My emerald strapless minidress with rhinestones that were aligned with the crack of my juicy booty was the ideal selection. James liked easy access to my breasts and my pussy. Chanel did too. After seeing my mother's face, I appreciated James more. He'd get upset sometimes but he'd never put his hands on me in an aggressive way, not even when we were making love.

My cell registered a call from the garage box. I pressed the number nine to open the gate. A text registered from James, I'm parked on your level. Take your time sweetheart.

I put on my gold stilettoes, checked my firearm. Placed my gun in my purse, then trotted down the hallway and out the door.

James extended his arms. "As usual," he said, drawing me close to him. "You look and smell amazing.

I lay my head on his chest. He held me. I mouthed, "I love you." Wasn't ready to say it aloud. Had to maintain my position of letting my guy love me more.

The way the coroners carried Fortune's body out in that black bag, not being able to get the image of my mom's face out of my mind, hearing Domino's story about his mother, I had many reasons to be grateful. None of those things changed my mind about meeting my dad.

"I've decided to take Tréme's recommendation for my dissertation. That means, soon I'll have to question my mother about my father."

He stepped back and smiled at me. "Sweetheart, that's great. I'm proud of you for making that decision. Whatever I can do to assist, let me know."

Settling into my guy's white Porsche, I fastened my seatbelt. A text came in from Chanel. You coming tonight?

I replied, Of course baby. See you around midnight.

I still want us to have a baby, she replied.

Texting back, maybe, I dropped my cell in my purse.

Driving east on Pharr Road, James turned left onto Piedmont. In five minutes we were at valet at Ocean Prime. Two hours to eat. Four to have sex then chill at my place, was my plan. Hopefully, we wouldn't have to argue about his not spending the night. Sitting in a booth by the bar, I kissed the back of his hand then interlocked my fingers with his.

James was the most beautiful black man. His flawless cinnamon-chocolate bald head, those dark succulent lips, gorgeous teeth, and thick black brows turned me on. The whiteness of his eyes when he looked my way made my pussy tingle.

He smiled at me. Shook his head. "Alexis, when are you going to stop running around and settle down with me?"

"We've been together three years. I'm not going anywhere. We can discuss becoming a family and starting one over drinks."

For a moment he was speechless until the bartender came. James ordered. "The lady will have a mai tai and a vodka and cran for me."

Chanel wanted a baby but she couldn't make one. James would love for me to have his child. I was almost done with college. I wasn't planning on getting pregnant right away but conceiving his child before graduation would give me financial and emotional stability. I'd worry about how to handle my sexual freedom later. James still hadn't said anything.

"You okay?" I asked.

We were seated on the couch by the fireplace near the pianist. This was one of our favorite places.

The server placed our drinks on the table. "May I take your food order?"

"You can take back the drinks," James said. "Let us have a bottle of champagne."

"Are we celebrating a special occasion?" the server asked.

"Depends on how my lady is feeling." James rubbed my thigh and my pussy got wet. I felt moisture between my thighs.

Another reason why I wore short dresses was to avoid perspiration stains on my clothes. That was just nasty.

"Does our being a family include Chanel?"

"Here we go." Leaning back, I slouched a little then straightened my spine. Poor posture was for the lazy. *It's complicated.* I looked into his amazing brown eyes. "I love you." There, I'd said it. Felt strange.

Didn't want to say it this early but this fine black man adored me. If he owned the world, I knew for a fact he'd give it to me. I swallowed the lump in my throat. I wondered if my mom had ever let a good man get away.

The waiter placed the ice bucket on the table, filled two glasses, then asked, "Are you ready to order?"

"Give us a moment," James said.

Exhaling, I said, "I'm not sure if I want to stay in Atlanta after I complete grad school next year."

Leaning back against the couch, he spread his legs. His cream-colored pants bulged at the zipper. "Why?"

I closed then opened my eyes. Imagined his long, thick, pretty dick. He had that mouth-watering kind that he couldn't hide. I imagined that was one reason gay men hit on him all the time.

"I can give up seeing other guys, James, but I don't feel the same about women."

"You want to have my baby but you think you're a lesbian?"

I shook my head. "Babe. Please. Stop."

James said, "If marrying you means I have to accept your having your female companion, I can do that."

My eyes widened in disbelief. Being with me wasn't that simple. I wanted to have sex with Domino. Not so much with LB. Most men didn't excite me enough to take off my clothes but what about the ones who did?

James knelt before me, pulled a small black box from his pocket, opened it. I swear, I was blinded by what must've been five carats.

"Alexis Crystal, will you become my wife."

I wasn't sure if my "yes" was for him, the ring, or the fact that I could have a female side. I wanted to invite James to the strip club tonight but that would piss Chanel off.

He eased the ring on my finger, then lay his head in my lap. "I love you, Alexis."

My eyes were wide. I didn't blink. "I love you, too, James."

I meant that. I truly did. Honestly. I did.

CHAPTER 32

Alexis

Getting rid of James after accepting his proposal wasn't happening. Dinner was remarkable. He had steak. I ordered seafood. Staff didn't ask us to leave after they'd closed. We left Ocean Prime at midnight.

I was cool with James taking me to his house. En route, I texted Chanel, My mom needs me. I won't be home until tomorrow. I need to see you. Can you come by at noon?

No part of my text was a lie. My mother always needed me and I didn't want to wait until tomorrow to taste my gurl's pussy. If I could warm Chanel up to the idea of a lifetime threesome, and our having a baby, maybe she'd give in.

Chanel replied, Sure she does.

Her text accompanied some level of disappointment and disbelief. I'd decided not to respond to her last night. Wasn't going to justify not making it to Pin Ups.

Dropping my cell in my purse, I said, "Babe."

"Yes."

"You sure you not going to change your mind about my having a female companion?"

James kept his eyes on the freeway ahead. We had about twenty minutes to go before we made it to Stone Mountain. "Have I ever gone back on my word?"

I had to ask, "Okay, so can she live with us?"

"You sure you want that? What if she wants to slide on my pole? You okay with that?"

Hell, yes. "Let me think about that," I said, not wanting him to believe he could have complete access to my woman anytime he wanted.

I hadn't told James what had happened to my mom. He'd be upset with me when he found out. I should tell him before we showed my mom my engagement ring.

"How's your mom?" he asked.

Damn, like he'd read my mind. "She's on vacation for another week. We celebrated her fiftieth last week."

"Damn! That's right. Shit. I forgot about my girl's big five-O." He reached for his cell.

I picked it up before he got to it. "Surprise my mother tomorrow. I want you to myself tonight."

A text registered on his screen: Hey Babe, Just landed safely in LA. Thanks for—I slid the bar. Continued reading: flying me in. Can't wait to see you again next week.

Oh, okay. That's why his phone had been on silent all night.

Another text from the same person named Cleopatra. This was a series of pics. The guy sitting in the driver's seat next to me was in the photos with a woman I'd never heard him mention. She was hot. Not ATL sexy. She had that Hollywood polished look. Neutral makeup on her vanilla skin. Pink lip gloss. Nude fingernail polish. I had no idea James was into anyone else.

My eyes bulged when the naked pic, no filter, popped up. I tossed my hair over my shoulder. Rocked forward. Leaned back.

"I'll definitely make it up to her," he said.

"To whom?"

He looked at me. I dropped his cell in the cup holder.

I thought James would never cheat on me. My ego was fucked. I had to up my game. A white woman named Cleopatra. That shit wasn't right.

Figuring I'd let him squirm a little, I kept quiet. I had the ring. I didn't see one on Cleopatra's finger. He entered his driveway, opened the garage door, then parked. Soon as the door closed, I waited for him to do the gentleman thing he'd consistently done.

I got out of the car. *Bam!*

I slammed his back against the car window, unbuckled his pants, unzipped them, yanked his underwear to his knees, squatted, then wrapped my lips around his dick.

"Damn, sweetheart!" he yelled, then moaned.

One squat after another, I sucked him in each time I went down. Adding the rhythm he liked with a slight twist of my hand, I hummed on his dick.

James shouted, "I getting ready to—"

I stopped stroking him, pressed two fingers to his frenulum, gave him a few seconds then I pumped his shaft and his balls, slid my hand to his head. I stood, grabbed two fists full of his button-up shirt, pulled him from the car, then I assumed the position. Placed my hands on the hood.

"Fuck me!" I commanded him.

Soon as he put the head in, I squeezed his dick with my pussy muscles. I didn't have shit to prove. He knew how good my pussy was. The shit that I saw on his cell was why I didn't trust men. They lived double and triple lives.

James would question himself on whether I'd seen the messages. He'd wonder what I'd do next. That's exactly how I wanted things between us. Arguing with James about Cleopatra was pointless. She was clearly his side. No amount of yelling, crying, or fighting would make him stop fucking her. I had too many other opportunities to trip. If I were going to get back at James, I'd have to find a way to fuck Cleopatra.

I wasn't into white women but I'd make Cleopatra an exception. Nor was I dumb. I assumed she knew I was the main. I was in no hurry to shake things up.

Had to secure my position first. I might have to hold in James's seeds and drop his baby sooner than I'd expected.

CHAPTER 33

Alexis

Noon.

Parking outside of Houston's on Peachtree, I selected James Wilcox from my phone favorites, tapped "Block This Caller." I had a valid reason to put James on mute. "Fuck you. Fuck you. Fuck you, James! And my father, too!" Men made me the way I was. If I didn't love dick, I'd stop fucking with dudes all together. James's ring was not going to be a noose around my neck. Let him fly Miss LA-ass back here and see what happens.

Bet that bitch don't have a Lexus convertible. Picking up the flowers I'd bought my gurl, I entered the bar, scanned the area. Chanel was seated in the first booth to my left. I reached for her hand. Gracefully, she stood.

"Damn, C. You're supa sexy today. You did all this for me?" If I had a real dick, it would be hard as shit right now.

My gurl stayed fresh. I wouldn't have any other type of piece in my collection. The time I invested in maintaining a head-turning appearance would never be wasted being seen with a guy that didn't keep his shit trimmed or a woman that looked like she'd showered, dressed, and forgot to comb her damn hair.

Swinging her long, straight, blazin' red hair over her shoulder, Chanel placed her hands on her hips, tilted her head sideways. The sexiest smile spread across her sweet, brown, full lips. "I'd do anything for you," she said, eyeing the bouquet in my hand.

"Yes, these are for you," I said, giving her a dozen peach roses. Gently, I swept her hair from behind her back, over her right shoulder. "Hold that pose." I took several pictures of her with my phone. Needed to update my collection of nude photos of Chanel and James.

The light blue dress she wore clung to her bodacious booty. I admired her naturally tiny waist, full cantaloupe-size breasts. The enhancements lots of females paid for in Atlanta, God had blessed my gurl with. If Chanel had more confidence than beauty and talent, she could have any woman or man she wanted.

Leaning over I placed the flowers on the end of the table. When I hugged my gurl I noticed she wasn't wearing a bra. Neither was I. Her nipples touched against mine, that shit ignited a sexual spark between my legs. I inhaled her perfume. Locked in her scent for three seconds, opened my mouth, then exhaled softly in her ear. We could sneak away to one of the private stalls in the women's restroom for a quickie. I could French kiss her while playing with her clit until she came on my finger.

Not today. I pressed my gold gloss to her light blue lip stain, then said, "Scoot in, baby. I want to sit next to you."

"You always have it together. I wish I were more like you," Chanel said.

No you don't. I nodded and smiled. "I love the shine. My gold gloss makes your blue stain pop."

She rubbed her lips together. "I love your rainbow."

My white mini halter dress had a colorful rainbow that started at the hem on the left side. It curved up and over my butt cheek, then stopped at the top between the split of my ass where there was a small glittering pot of gold C-notes. Pocket change would never give anyone access to this. Bands? Rolls of money. Yes.

The waitress filled two glasses with water, then sat the carafe in the middle of the table. I ordered two mai tais, the spinach dip, the off-the-menu chicken fingers with fries, and a vegetable plate for us. The way James ordered food, planned vacations, bought me a car and nice gifts, and the way he took charge outside the bedroom excited me. I wasn't giving up James for Chanel. I enjoyed being dominant with females but I didn't want to lead all the time.

"This is nice of you," Chanel said.

Damn, she was fine. I told her, "You're right. It is. And I'm going to start treating you better." Just because Chanel settled for my bull didn't mean I had to treat her like shit.

She'd think my spoiling but not sexing her today was quality time. Truth was I'd been fucking all morning and my pussy was sore. That was the real reason we were here. I didn't feel like licking her pussy or making her squirt. Didn't want her mouth on my clit for sure, not for the next twenty-four hours. And I definitely wasn't strapping on again today. My thighs were aching.

James enjoyed anal stimulation. I'd instructed my guy on the proper way to penetrate by taking his time. I let him do me first. Then, as our relationship grew, I gained his trust by promising that I'd never tell anyone. He agreed to let me try various plugs with him. The Assifier was ideal for his first experience. After he became comfortable with the feeling realizing it didn't hurt, I upgraded him to the skinny silicone three-inch. He enjoyed that, too.

Today I'd given him the five-inch. I was a little rough but he liked it doggie-style and missionary. His dick stayed hard the entire three hours we made love.

"What's on your mind, Alexis? You're here but you're not," Chanel said.

"I'm sorry, C. Just thinking about my mom."

A familiar voice distracted me. I gazed over my shoulder. I couldn't understand what he'd just said but I was almost positive that was him.

I told Chanel, "Excuse me for a second, C."

Facing the empty booth next to ours, I picked up my cell, stood tall in my five-inch gold open-toe stilettoes. I heard him say, "Babe, don't quit me. I know I can't be with you as much as we'd like but don't leave me. What do you need from me to stay?"

She answered him, "More of your time," then she stared up at me.

That definitely appeared to be the back of his head but I had to make sure. Bypassing the second booth, walking to the third booth, I stared into his eyes, stepped back, snapped a few pictures of them, then returned to my gurl. My back was now to his. Sipping my drink, I had nothing to worry about. He wasn't going to confront me. If she did, it would be the worst day of her life. I'd make sure of that. I did not wait for a female to strike first. The wrong look could set me off.

"Everything okay?" Chanel asked.

I told her, "It's good," as the waitress placed our food in front of us.

"Who's that? Why did you take a picture?" she asked.

If he were with his wife, Chanel would've recognized my sister, Mercedes. But the woman Benjamin was with had obviously been his side piece for quite some time. Just like seeing the texted photos of Cleopatra in James's phone, I had no intention of telling Mercedes anything. I'd give Benjamin that opportunity.

Chanel placed her hand underneath the table, then touched my clit.

"Damn." I'd hissed at her unexpectedly.

She jerked her hand away. "Sorry. Is that one of your guys? Is that why you lost focus on me?"

I kissed her lips. "Don't ruin it. Let's keep enjoying our lunch." Didn't want to spend James's money to waste time with menial convo with Chanel.

The guys at our end of the bar stared at us. Lust. I bet their imaginations had their dicks hard. Chanel tightened her mouth, narrowed her eyes, then scanned the lineup.

That was the level of insecurity I hated. It didn't matter what those men thought. They could go home, sex their woman (or man), jack off while recalling a picture of Chanel and me kissing in their mind. I did not care! She did. Seductively eating one fry at a time, I gave Chanel all the time she wanted to give those guys an evil stare. If her attitude hadn't adjusted by the time I was done munching, I was out.

Eventually, she asked, "So does this mean we're going to work on exclusivity?"

"I want you to take initiative in our relationship."

Chanel frowned, dipped a chicken finger, took a small bite. "So you're telling me you feel I'm not taking enough initiative by paying your rent?"

"No. I'm telling you. You're not taking any outside of paying my rent."

"Humph," she said, putting down her food.

"Yeah, marinate on that for a minute."

She became quiet. Started eating the cold spinach dip. Normally, I'd send it back. Request a fresh one. Too many didn't value their worthiness. They'd rather eat, drink, or pay for something they didn't enjoy than to speak up. If they didn't take it off my bill, I'd pay for it but that would be the last dime they'd get from me.

A text registered. LB had sent his sixth text of the day. I refused to acknowledge him until he called me. He only had forty-eight hours remaining for that opportunity. If he missed his window, I was blocking his number. Then it was on to the next.

Thoughts of Domino made me wet.

Stopping the waitress, I said, "Bring me the check and pack everything to go." Kissing Chanel, I asked her, "You ready?"

Her eyes shifted to the side, then back at me. "I want to finish enjoying lunch with you before we make love."

Make love? Really? That was not happening. Sleep was on my mind. I stared at her wanting to check her panties. *Don't trip, Alexis.* Chanel would never cheat. The thought of her being with another woman crept into my mind because of the photos in James's phone.

Benjamin and the woman he was with passed us. Seeing another person I never imagined having an affair step outside their relationship made me doubt Chanel's loyalty. The woman's hand was on the small of Benjamin's back. He had to feel my eyeballs on him but he didn't glance in my direction.

Mercedes should be less concerned with Sandara's selection of bed partners, Devereaux's engagement to Phoenix, our mom sleeping with Spencer, my personal lifestyle, and tend to her husband. Men strayed for two reasons. One, it was in their character. Two, their needs were not fulfilled by their spouse.

"Leave it," I said to the waitress, then told Chanel, "Today is your day. We can do whatever you want." I meant that.

Men were different from women. When they knew they were busted, they'd go from caring to not giving a fuck in minutes. Go from trying to explain the lie away to shutting down. It was easier not to communicate than to open up. Easier to lie than to tell the truth. Everybody was searching for their own happiness at the expense of others.

"I want to have sex with you on the gondola two hundred feet in the air. Pay the bill and let's go."

Chanel's decision wasn't the best, but this might not happen again. Riding a Ferris wheel immediately after consuming food, could get messy. Her assertiveness turned me on enough to do everything she wanted.

I nodded. "Let's do all that."

CHAPTER 34

Alexis

Chanel shocked me yesterday. She let loose like never before! Damn!I didn't have to do anything. She rode me. Went down on me. The body massage was fantastic but when my gurl caressed the arch of my foot, slid her tongue between my toes, then sucked my big toe like it was the head of a dick, I had a total body orgasm. I enjoyed every second. Chanel called in sick to the strip club. Stayed at my place. Danced for me. Washed my body with hers in the shower. Then she spooned me all night. Cooked me breakfast this morning and she fed me.

Chanel didn't need my permission to be sexually uninhibited. Why was she bottling up all that Good Good with her insecurities? If Chanel cared less, I know I'd care more. She was a keeper though. I may have to get on one knee, put James's rock on my gurl's ring finger, tell him to buy me another five-carat, then ask him to marry us.

Standing in the doorway of my bathroom, I asked Chanel, "You almost done?"

"I am done," she said. Turning sideways to avoid touching me, she exited the bathroom.

This was the foolishness I understood but hated dealing with. "I'll see you tonight."

Chanel dressed, then left. I heard her crying on her way out the door. We both knew the truth. Hot as last night was, I wasn't going to give up James.

I felt an empty space when she closed the door without telling me bye. Soon as she'd left, to balance out the love I was feeling for her, I shifted to the new person in my rotation.

I texted LB, We're still on?

He replied, I'm all yours.

Not hardly. Getting ready for my date with LB, all I could think about was how cool his friend Domino was. One week had passed since Fortune died. I wasn't an insensitive person all the time but truly I was glad Fortune would never inhale again. Mom didn't go to the funeral because there wasn't one. Word was once the autopsy confirmed Fortune had a heart attack, Fortune's wife cremated him immediately, then cashed in on the million-dollar life insurance policy she'd kept on him. If I married James, I was definitely getting seven figures of coverage.

I called my mom.

"Hey, honey! How are you?" she answered with a high pitch.

Okay, that was the I-just-got-some-real-good-dick sound. Not wanting to interrupt her flow, I lied, "I have to take this call. I'll call you back."

"All right, I love you. Bye, honey."

Domino had stayed by my mom's side the entire time after the incident. That proved he was special. What guy would do that for a woman he'd just met unless he really liked her or was he hiding out from that crazy bitch who cursed out my mom? If I ever met Charlotte, she had a backhand coming for calling my mother a bitch.

Regardless of our reasons, Mercedes, Devereaux, Sandara, and I appreciated Domino's caring for our mother. Mom needed someone to be there for her. Family was cool. But the touch of a loving man, not much compared to that.

If a man ever put his hands on me, I won't have to wait for Georgia to adopt the stand-your-ground law, I'd take his ass out. He'd be exactly like Fortune . . . one less breathing asshole.

I called LB, put him on speaker, then started brushing my teeth.

He answered, "Don't tell me something came up?"

I laughed. "No, I'm almost ready. Look, I have a question."

"Shoot."

I stopped brushing, then asked, "Who's Charlotte and what is she to Dom, I mean Spencer?"

LB became quiet, then said, "If I tell you, you can't tell your mom."

"Cool," I said. Turning off the faucet, I listened attentively.

"That's his girl but I think he's ending it."

"Why?"

All he'd said was, "A minor hiccup. Shit happens. That's Spence calling. I'll see you shortly."

LB should've kept his damn mouth shut if that was all he had to say. I hated people who volunteered information but declined to give details.

The guys I knew were better at keeping secrets than my female friends. Like my fiancé having a side chick across country. None of his boyz would've told me that but I'd bet all of James's friends knew about Cleopatra. Even if James were faithful, my being engaged to him didn't feel right. The best way for me not to have my indiscretions spread wider than my legs was for me to start keeping everyone out of my personal business.

I slipped into a lemon romper with a gold and silver beaded necklace. No five-inch stilettos today. My tan open-toed three-inch heels with the yellow ankle straps were the perfect match. Bending over, I hung my head upside down, fingered my natural strands, stood, then tossed my dark wavy hair behind my shoulders to create a sexy, untamed fullness.

This date was a good start for me to get back at my fiancé. I might take a total break from James and focus on Chanel. Maybe I should take a few days off from seeing Chanel to give her time to reflect on what she really wanted.

Oh, damn. I can't put Chanel on pause until after the fifth.

Turning up my music from my cell, I twerked in my bathroom mirror. Domino had that kind of attraction that made me want to rip his clothes off, throw him down, ride his dick, and make him cum.

Maybe LB would have the same effect on me. I doubted it. People either had chemistry or they didn't. Stepping onto my patio, I took a deep breath, glad it was Saturday afternoon. The sun was brightly shining; it was a blazing eighty-five. It was too hot for me. I went inside hoping whatever LB's surprise was did not require us to be outdoors. My cell rang.

"Hey, LB. You here?"

"Downstairs. Outside, sweetheart."

Perfect. Men needed to respect a woman's request.

"See you in a sec," I said, ending the call.

CHAPTER 35

Alexis

I could've invited him in but I didn't typically let guys inside my apartment until after they'd taken me out, I had their home and work addresses, I knew their mother's and father's first and last names.

Although LB and Spencer were friends, I still ran a background check on Lawrence Bennett. No failures to appear, misdemeanors, or felonies came up. I took one last look in the mirror, gave myself a confident smile, grabbed my piece, put it in my purse, then locked my front door.

Exiting the lobby by the leasing office, I saw LB facing the five-star mall across the street. Tom Ford, Gucci, Prada, Dior, and other high-end retailers were there. No Bebe's or Outfitters. I had to drive five minutes to Lenox or Phipps for my other favorite department stores. I lived in the heart of what had become known as the Rodeo Drive of Bollywood.

"Wow." His brows hiked toward his neatly trimmed hairline. He didn't blink.

Great! Especially for a first date, I always dress for the wow factor.

"Spence didn't tell me you were so beautiful."

What? "Stop acting like you didn't notice me at the restaurant with my mom and sisters last week. You were our waiter."

"I swear I didn't. I mean I saw you but I didn't. All I recall is all of you were attractive. Plus you were sitting and I was in customer-service mode. Anyway, you look amazing. You did all this for me?" he asked.

If he was serious, he truly hadn't checked me out. But I knew he was lying. I replied, "Of course I dressed for you." What difference did it make if that was what he wanted to think?

Opening his arms, he gestured for a hug, then whispered in my ear, "Thank you for asking for my number."

You're not the one I wanted but you're here now. Spencer could've given me a different contact and another man would be standing here. Hopefully LB wasn't one of those guys who stroked his own ego all the time by constantly reminding a female that he was not the one to initiate getting together.

"You look nice too. Love the shirt."

Men needed an incentive to do more and if LB planned on tasting my pussy, he was going to have to do a lot. A guy would have to be a real asshole for me not to compliment him at least once. Twice was optimal. Ego boosters prior to sex helped maximize a man's performance.

A real diva always allowed her women and men to like her more than she did them. Heartaches were for people who cared about breaking up. Once a dick walked out the door, I was done until it was time for me to cum on it again. Maybe my hard exterior was a shell protecting me from all the bullshit players in Atlanta. Never failed. The men I thought would never screw up always proved me wrong. Women cheated, too, but we were better liars.

Guys didn't have to do much to be presentable. LB had on blue denims, a tapered short-sleeved T-shirt that showed off his well-defined biceps. His shirt was tucked behind his big belt buckle that had a cross on it. The rest of his tee hung over the sides and back of his jeans. I gave him another hug so I could inhale his cologne again and press against his dick imprint. He didn't appear to be as hung as Spencer but I'd underestimated the size of a few guys. Depending on his expansion, his dick could be a keeper.

"You smell good enough to eat," I told him, sliding my hand down his spine to his butt. "Nice whip." It was true. His silver Mustang with black leather interior was hot.

I'd seen passive women in Atlanta get pushed out of the way in a nanosecond. A thirsty bitch would get drenched with semen and left ass up to dry. I'd never allowed either to happen to me.

LB opened my door, waited until I was settled into the passenger seat, then closed it. Easing on my sunglasses, I watched him proudly walk in front of his car. He was more attractive than I remembered. Depending on how well our date went, I might give slim sexy some pussy.

"Where to?" he asked, starting the engine. "I'll make three suggestions but before you decide, we're only dropping in for appetizers and drinks, then we're headed to . . . I can't tell you. What's it going to be? Ray's on the River, Cheesecake Bistro at Atlantic Station, 10th and Piedmont, or you can choose a different spot."

I laughed. "10th and Piedmont? Really?"

"No, I'm not gay. What difference does it make where we eat long as the food and drinks are good? If we go, you'll see for yourself that I'm not suspect. Down-low dudes don't take chicks to gay spots. Besides, I know how you females think every man in the ATL is bisexual, on the low, or straight-up gay. For the record, in case you're one of those females that try a bruh, all you need to know is nothing goes in my ass. Now where's it going to be?"

Something was going in his ass and he was going to like it. "Ray's on the River," I said, not wanting to deal with the weekend crowd at Atlantic Station. "We need to make time to visit my mom? I have to check on her." Actually, Domino was the one I wanted to see me.

"I can make that happen," LB said, stopping at the red light. "But we're going to have to cut drinks short. Cool?"

"Cool." But I wasn't asking.

He glanced at me, then shook his head. He valet-parked his silver mustang. The waterfall behind the host stand flowed down the wall. He had some class. I prayed he wasn't trying to impress me and this would end up being the best place he'd take me.

"Bar area, inside or out?" he asked, pointing to the right.

"Definitely inside."

He sat beside me at the highboy table. Scooted his stool so close to mine our thighs touched.

"Hope you don't mind but I like sitting next to my date."

Any closer he'd be on my lap. Exhaling, I moved my chair a few inches away from his. "This is better."

"That's cool," he said.

There was a moment of awkward silence until the waitress took our drink order. I hated when dudes got quiet and had that underlying pissed off attitude. A few pertinent things were discussed during our telephone conversations throughout the week. He'd grown up in a small town outside of Atlanta, called Warner Robins. His dad was a civilian employee for the Air Force. His mom managed the Carrabba's in Macon.

I'd told him the basics about my mom and sisters. Nothing to tell him about my dad except "I never met him." I knew his abandonment influenced my distrust of men. If my father could walk away from me without remorse, he represented a lot of men.

We ordered from the appetizer menu. Right now I was more enthused about my mai tai than LB. Hopefully that would change soon.

"So you graduated from Clark but you bartend at a restaurant. Why?"

He stared me down. "It pays the bills. That's why. Gives me flexibility to job-search." Sighing, he said, "Tell me more about yourself."

This dude had issues. I was here; I'd make the most of my time. He already knew I was in grad school. He knew where I lived. He'd informally met my mother and sisters. I told him, "I enjoy hiking, weekend getaways to places like the DR, Jamaica, Paris. New York and Miami are cool if I'm chilling stateside. Want to go to Dubai, Greece, Venice, Australia. And I'm passionate about everything I do." I looked into his eyes, then moaned, "Everything."

He smiled. I knew the second "everything" would get his dick hard. I wanted to let him know, "I love men with money who don't mind spending it on me," but I could sense my opening LB's wallet in that kind of way would've made him uptight so I asked, "Where are some of the places you've applied?"

"Applied?"

"Job. You mentioned you were looking."

"Oh, yeah. Chosen, um—"

I had to interrupt. "Really?"

Nodding, he said, "Really."

"The modeling agency, Chosen?"

He put his hand under his chin, turned sideways, looked up, then laughed. "Relax, girl. I invited you out."

I pressed my lips together and smiled.

"Damn, don't do that. That's the same exact way Spence smiles." He asked, "You ever think about living elsewhere?"

I shook my head. "I love ATL. Can't imagine being far away from my family."

I could have aunts, uncles, cousins on my father's side in Los Angeles, Chicago, New Orleans. Forget my daddy! Fuckin' deadbeat!

LB wrapped his arm around my waist, then drew me closer to him. What was up with his needing to have my body touching his?

Deciding to relax, I asked, "If you could vacation anywhere in the world, where would you go?"

"Miami."

"Stop. You're kidding, right?"

He shook his head. "I'm afraid to fly."

"So you've never been on a plane?"

Slowly, he shook his head.

"Do you like dating older women?"

"You wondering why Spencer is attracted to your mom?"

"I am."

"I've dated older but not more than three years. Spencer didn't start dating older until after his moms passed seven years ago. Venus Domino was his everything. She made a big deal out of everything. Christmas. Halloween. Thanksgiving. His and her birthdays. They went to the movies together once a month. Mother's Day he always designed her the coolest outfit to wear. Most of the times he picked out her clothes. All the things he did with his mom I've never seen him do on the regular with any female. Your mom is a good distraction from that crazy chick Char . . . I know I'm lucky to be close to and to have both of my parents living."

That was the most attentive I'd been since I'd spoken my first word over the phone with LB. I should thank him. Char was good enough for now. Charmaine? Charla? Charissa? I'd find out from Spencer who LB had referred to.

"How long ago did your last relationship end? Why? Do you still have sex with her?" I started massaging his hand, wrist, forearm, then caressed his fingers one at a time.

"Whoa, slow down," he said, laughing.

I let go.

"No, don't stop touching me. That feels great. I mean on all the questions."

Ordering another round of drinks, LB answered each of my questions. Three months. His ex had met some movie producer. And they hadn't had sex since she'd left him. He didn't seem bitter about her upgrade.

LB leaned in for a kiss. I gave him a sample of what he could get later if he didn't fuck things up. For the moment, he'd taken my mind off of Spencer.

"If we're going to make it to our final destination on time," he said, holding up two tickets, "we'd better get going."

This guy might be a decent catch. Someone new to have a lil fun with. Closing out the tab, we got back in his Mustang, then headed to my mom's.

CHAPTER 36

Spencer

"Would you mind going to church with me tomorrow?" Fabulous asked. Pinning up her hair she covered it with a cap.

Her naked body was close to mine. My dick pointed north. I gave Fabulous a long hug, then told her, "You are so beautiful."

Sunday morning service was about twenty-four hours away. Maybe stepping foot into a tabernacle would do my soul good. I was glad Fabulous had asked and that she wasn't telling me we were going to church. I had reasonable time to consider her request. Too many women in this Bible Belt had tried to force religion on me.

All that "I can't be with a man who doesn't praise the Lord. A man who doesn't believe in God doesn't belong with me." I hated that hypercritical BS.

I was a decent person who intended to treat others right but sometimes I failed. I didn't know a single person who came out of the womb a Christian. And the ones singing the loudest were lip-synching.

I held Fabulous's hand until she took two steps down into the bubbling water, then I did the same. The large pink shower cap on her head leaned against my chest. We were chilling in her Jacuzzi for the seventh or eighth time since I'd been here.

Cool jets of water pressurized a bruh's asshole. Warm water swirled around my nuts. I had to have the cleanest rectum in Roswell. I couldn't lie, my shit felt damn near sterile. Fabulous's ass eased between my inner thighs. I wanted to stick my dick in her back door.

I kissed the back of her neck, then asked, "You ready to try anal?"

She rubbed the outside of my thigh. "Almost. I won't make you wait much longer. Just not right now."

I'd never seen swivel barstools in a home Jacuzzi like the ones Fabulous had in her Jacuzzi outside by the pool. A wet bar in a Jacuzzi was the kind of shit I expected in Jamaica. Not at somebody's crib. This chick had her place laid out like a man cave.

Kicking back with my new side trumped sucking up liquor, watching sexy babes prance in front of me in shoestring bikinis while I was on vacation in Rio last year. I had to end it with Charlotte before I could ask Fabulous to be my woman.

"Let me know what you decide about church. Either way, I'm going," she said. Her hands were on my knees.

Nothing against getting the word in but I preferred to read the Bible. Do my own interpreting. A lot of these guys in the ATL were standing in pulpits, sitting on pews, humming along with the choir, shouting in response to the pastor's words, clapping their hands, stomping their feet, but soon as the doors of the church were closed, they were hitting the streets in search of something. Pussy. Dick. Alcohol. Drugs. God knew their hearts but they wouldn't think about the Lord until the following Sunday, or if they were cumming or they got into trouble.

Thinking of trouble I thought about Alexis. My dick got hard. "If going to church is what you want, let's do it," I told Fabulous. "I'm here for you."

She slid forward, put her hand underneath my balls. My head pressed against the opening of her rectum. *Damn!* I wanted in.

Leaning forward a little more, she asked, "Why are you so good to me?" then she started massaging my nuts.

Her nails grazed my asshole. Precum seeped into the water, I kissed the nape of her neck, then answered her question with one. "Why are you so good for me?"

Fabulous began crying. "I don't know what's wrong with me. I work hard. I raised my girls. I can do everything well except choose a man." She moved her hand. The back of her head fell against my chest.

Wanting her to put her hand back, I had to focus on her concerns. She'd shed a lot of tears over the last seven days. She hadn't gone upstairs since the day the coroners carried Fortune out in a body bag. I only went up there when she specifically needed something. We'd slept in the downstairs bedrooms. All four of them.

"It's time for you to close this chapter," I told her.

She stared over her shoulder at me. "What are you saying?"

"Not us. It's time to take Mercedes's advice and put your house on the market." Getting out of the house would be good for both of us but outside of church, I was not trying to run into Charlotte.

There were moments when the pain she'd shared with me had become my sorrow. If Fabulous could be that transparent with me, I was ready to level the emotions and open up.

I told her, "You're not alone. I feel lost at times. Can I share something with you?"

She gave a slow nod. I was glad she didn't face me. Looking into her eyes would make telling my story harder.

"I want you to share everything with me, Spencer. Even if this"—using the back side of her fingers she rubbed my chest in front of my heart—"is just for the moment. You have no idea how much you've helped me through this abusive situation."

"I was too young to protect my mom. But"—I exhaled—"you're a strong woman. My mom was too."

I didn't expect Fabulous to start crying again. I hadn't hit Charlotte but I knew I'd hurt my boo. Fabulous's tears were different from Charlotte's. My gurl cried to get her way. I hadn't responded to any of Charlotte's texts or calls since I'd deplaned. Fabulous was releasing pain.

Wiping Fabulous's tears with my wet fingers, I told her, "Let it out. Time heals all wounds." I just wasn't sure how long it took to mend a broken heart. Years? A lifetime? "God doesn't take any of us before He's ready. Fortune's time was up." I hugged her waist, pulled her back to my chest.

Exhaling, I tried hard to convince myself it was my mother's time. Silencing my sniffles, I let my tears flow because Fabulous couldn't see them falling onto her plastic cap.

"I don't know, Spencer. I don't know what to believe when it comes to men. What did you want to share?"

There was no easy way to tell Fabulous. "I was molested as a child."

Slowly she faced me. "Are you serious? A woman stole your innocence?"

I shook my head. Her eyelids stretched wide as I revealed, "My uncle. I've never told anyone. I just feel like you've shared so much with me that I could trust you. Please, do me one favor."

"Anything," she said.

"Don't you ever tell anyone. I never even told my mother. And please don't ever throw this in my face. Ever." In the heat of an argument, women had a way of using a man's weakness against him.

Fabulous sat on my lap, wrapped her legs around my waist, then kissed me tenderly. She leaned my head on her shoulder and the howl that came out of me was that of twenty years of pent-up shame, hurt, and anger. I cried like a newborn baby for at least fifteen minutes.

The doorbell sounded. Fabulous looked at me. I could tell she wasn't expecting anyone. "They can go away," she said.

I shook my head. "It's okay." I needed a reason to stop crying.

We put on our white bathrobes. Blake cleaned my face with a cool towel.

"You sure you want me to answer the door?" she asked.

"Let's go," I said then thought, oh shit! What if it's my boo? Heading toward the door behind Fabulous, I insisted, "Let me get that for you."

I couldn't put it past Charlotte to have figured out where I was. She had her ways. I had mine, too. Before peeping through the hole, I told Fabulous, "We're getting you a video surveillance system."

She frowned. "But I'm selling this place." Abruptly, she chuckled. I didn't understand the humor she got from my comment until she said, "Fortune is dead, Spencer."

I'm not but I might be if it's Charlotte, I thought.

The doorbell rang again. "I can hear you two. Open up."

Damn, once I saw who it was I wanted to close the door. "What's up, LB?" I looked at Alexis with that little-ass lemony outfit. Did that woman ever cover her ass? "Hi, Alexis," I said, swinging the door wide to let them in.

"You got it, Spence. We're just stopping by. Alexis wanted to check on her mom. Hell, I needed to check on you," LB said, then laughed. "You looking all like it's spa day up in here, bruh."

It wasn't Comedy Central up in here and I wasn't offended. Post my confession I could use a little humor. He was my boy and all. "Cool," was all I said.

Alexis hugged her mom. "You look good, Mama." She held on for a moment.

Fabulous embraced her daughter a few seconds after Alexis had let go. "I'm glad you stopped by, baby. Where are you guys headed?"

Alexis stepped to me, opened her arms, wrapped them around my back. "Thanks for taking such good care of my mother."

Her ear was pressed to my chest at the opening of the robe. I didn't want to seem rude, so I gave her a light one-arm hug. Those firm twenty-seven-year-old bra-free titties with erect nipples were damn near in my stomach, inches above my dick. She knew what the fuck she was doing.

I took a step back to give my dick some space. Picturing Alexis's pussy in front of my face that day we were on the porch, my shit started rising. These Atlanta chicks had their way of getting a man's dick hard on the under. The sensation started to make my pole hard enough to wave a flag. A snapshot of Fabulous's face a week ago made me go flaccid instantly. Calmly, I took another step back.

Had to be careful not to send LB any questionable signals. At least not from my standpoint. He could think whatever he wanted about Alexis. He had the gurl he wanted. I had her mother. This wasn't my first glimpse of the sneaky assertive side of Alexis but I was familiar with her kind.

"We're headed to . . ." Alexis paused, then looked at LB.

"Fine, it was supposed to be a surprise. We're going to—"

Fabulous interrupted, "Then don't tell us. We're going to church tomorrow. You're welcome to join us if you have time in the morning," she said, looking at Alexis then LB.

"Of course we will, Mama," Alexis said with no consideration for my boy. "Spencer, will you be there?"

I nodded.

The way she was wearing that sunshine on her face, the yellow dress was banging too. It was Atlanta. Women wore high heels, short dresses, with accessories to complement the unimaginable to Publix grocery store. Georgia peaches were beyond sweet. These females were straight ripe.

"Spence, you know you and Alexis live in the same building, man?"
Aw, hell no! I refused to say a word.

I looked at Fabulous. Not for a response for what I now knew she'd already known. Fabulous wasn't oblivious to Alexis's intentions. I understood why she didn't want me to know. Out the corners of my eyes, I saw Alexis staring at me with a closed-lip smile. I wanted to shake my head but I knew better than to do that shit.

"Guess not," LB said. "You ready?" he asked Alexis.

"Oh, yes. I'm definitely ready," she said.

Fabulous said, "Alexis, James called. He wished me a happy belated fiftieth. I understand congratulations are in order."

Flipping her hair over her shoulder, Alexis said, "Bye, Mama. Spencer, I'll see you guys tomorrow."

Watching Alexis jiggle her booty out the door, in advance of my arriving at church tomorrow, silently I asked God on the spot, "Please help me, Lord."

CHAPTER 37

Alexis

After closing my door, LB got behind the wheel. He was silent. Again.

Second shutdown. I supposed he was waiting for me to explain why no one answered his question. Obviously, my mother didn't want me to know. I had no idea Domino was my neighbor. Apparently it was news to Spencer as well. Knowing we were about two hundred feet from each other almost daily made sexing him more convenient.

I texted Domino, I'm in 408.

"Still not going to tell me where we're headed?" I asked, touching up my lipstick. I refreshed my perfume. A dab behind each ear. Never knew what new prospects may be at our destination.

"You might not want to put on too much of that fragrance," he said. "We're going to the Affordable Old School concert at Wolf Creek, baby! Whew!"

Okay, bipolar was one thing. I didn't know what was going on in that dude's head.

"You should've told me sooner. My mom probably has VIP tickets." I paused, looked at LB, then continued. "Please tell me you did not get lawn tickets."

Proudly, he said, "Yup. And I made us a tasty pasta, a salad, grilled chicken, and I premixed a special drink. Named it Lex because that rhymes with sex. And I had a dessert made especially for you."

I refused to ask what it was. Rolling my eyes in the direction away from LB, I saw Chanel texted Haven't heard from you. You mad at me?

I replied, Yes, baby

Cool Y

I meant, No baby. You wore me out. I'll call you in a few

You coming to the club?

I texted Chanel back, Definitely, as a message from James registered from his second cell number. He should've given Cleopatra that number. What's up Alexis?

I hit him with, Where you at? Atlanta? LA?

No immediate response from him but Spencer had texted back, I'm in 505.

Barely concealing my joy, I saved the unit number under his contact info. He was in building five. I was in four. Now it made sense. We parked on different levels, lived on separate floors.

"I'm your date. Not your phone. If you don't want to go, I can take you home," LB said, exiting the freeway.

Where'd that come from? No need to apologize for my divided attention. Everybody was glued to their cell phones nowadays and every person I was texting was more interesting than LB. Men did this shit all the time while on a date. They viewed naked pics, watched XXX videos, hit their main, their side, their main and their side when they were with another woman. LB shouldn't act as though he was the exception. I knew that nigga was emptying his balls somewhere.

We were a few miles away from the park. For the first time, I kept quiet. He could decide. I was cool either way. He continued driving ahead.

I texted my mother, Did you have two VIPs for the AOS today?

She texted back, Yes, table seven. You want me to text Jeremy?

PLZ Mama. TY

Hopefully, I could convince an officer to let us park in the lot next to the amphitheater. What I was not going to do was get on a shuttle or walk downhill in my stilettoes to sit my ass on grass.

I touched LB's thigh. He smiled. Men were so ridiculously easy. "I appreciate everything you've done. Pull up to security."

"Oh, you got it like that," he said.

"Officer, he's dropping me off," I lied.

Moving the orange cone, the officer let us in.

"Wow, that would never work for me," he said.

"After the night is over, you let me know if I got it like that," I told him as my mother texted, When you get there, go to will-call and tell Jeri Miles you're picking up my tickets.

TY Mama!

LB retrieved a small red cooler and a blanket from his trunk. "Leave the blanket," I told him, leading the way.

I gave LB's tickets away. Did as my mom told me, and we were seated at a table close to the stage.

LB said, "Dang, I need to hang out with you more often."

No . . . you won't. From this night forward, LB was strictly a pay-my-bills bottom bitch, in that order.

CHAPTER 38

Alexis

LB left his car in a "Visitors Only" space to escort me to my apartment.

"Thanks for a good first date," I said. Giving him a hug, I placed my palms flatly to his shoulder blades, meshed my breasts to his chest, then softly scraped my fingernails against his T-shirt. Barely touching my lips to his ear, I whispered, "You remember how to get out of here?"

His dick responded first. Of course he knew how to exit but I knew he didn't want to leave. He held me, tilted his hips toward mine enough to make sure I felt his hard, throbbing manhood. Why did guys think that was a turn-on for women? LB should try being more creative. I never removed my clothes without a purpose. Sex. Shower. Sleeping in the nude. Lounging around my place or James's. Sex only mattered when I wanted it.

Letting him go, I was excited that Domino lived in the same complex. My pussy puckered for Domino, not LB. There had to be one person out there who could totally satisfy me. It wasn't James or Chanel. And it sure in the hell wasn't LB.

I tried to recall if I'd ever seen Domino in passing. Couldn't say I had. Not many residents hung out. There were always empty lounge chairs poolside and on the rooftop patio. Most of my time was in transit to get a package from the office, mail from my box, or getting in and out of my car. I turned the key, opened my door.

LB said, "Up to the top floor, down to the first?"

"You got it," I said, gripping the inside lever.

"Hey, mind if I use your restroom before I go?"

Letting LB in, I said, "First right. Next right."

"Cool, thanks."

I connected the Bluetooth to my surround sound speakers, synched it with Pandora One from my cell, and selected Pray for Me Radio. I'd avoided that station for months thinking it was gospel. I enjoyed listening to the choir at church but spiritual hymns at home weren't my preferred. Pleasantly surprised to discover the countless classic slow jams I loved and lots of new panty-dropping songs on one station, this was my new favorite.

Imagining my tongue circling Domino's head, the walls of my vagina tightened, causing me to have a small orgasm. Performing cunnilingus made me cum. Doing fellatio made me climax real hard at times. Penetration was wonderful but not required for me to get off.

Damn, Alexis. I shook my head, wondering if I fantasized about sex more than most men. Would I ever be monogamous?

LB came out of the bathroom grooving. He had a nice flow to R. Kelly's "Marry the Pussy." He started singing all the words, real seductive. I watched him get down on both knees, crawl toward me, then he sang to my pussy.

She didn't twerk for LB the way she'd done when I put her in front of Domino. LB wasn't half bad and I was horny as hell. Thinking about Domino had made me hot. I decided to go ahead and give LB what he wanted.

I smiled, backed up. Dropping my romper to the floor, I pulled my thong aside. "Get your ass over here and taste this sweet pussy?"

He crawled toward me on all fours. I backed up. Played with my clit. Moaned. He came closer. Opened his mouth, stuck out his tongue. I squatted on the tip three times, released my thong, then pointed to my liquor. "Make us a drink. Surprise me."

Standing, he offered to make what we had earlier. I sat on my white leather sofa. Watched him maneuver his way around my bar. Chanel texted, You still coming to the club tonight?

I should but wasn't sure. My clothes were in the middle of the floor. Wasn't putting them or any others on right now. How long I remained naked depended on how good LB was in bed. Be there at 1 or 2.

Why so late?

LB handed me a much needed drink then sat beside me. Deciding not to respond to Chanel, I put my cell on the coffee table. Hell, my rent would be past due in a few days. Chanel was my bird in the hand. I texted her, See you shortly baby

I told LB, "Why don't you go upstairs, take a shower, select three toys from the chest at the foot of my bed, and get comfortable. I'll be up shortly." I could tell it wouldn't take him long to cum but I'd show him a few things I was certain he hadn't had done to him before.

Closing my eyes, I listened to Anthony Hamilton's "Broken Man." He made me think about James. Hadn't heard from him since my last text. I related to the lyrics of the song asking, *Will I ever love again?* I wondered how James felt about me. I'd toyed with his heart because he'd let me. I didn't have James on a full-time basis. So what? I sure as hell wasn't letting him go.

I wasn't jealous of Cleopatra. Whatever my mother told Domino regarding my engagement to James wouldn't change Domino's craving to stroke this pussy. Men were like that. Once their dick got hard there was only one way to satisfy the lust. Head-on!

I opened my eyes. Stared at all the paintings, statues, and furniture James had bought me. The white leather sectional. The white mink rug that Chanel and I had sex on last night. I picked up my cell, unblocked James's contact, then texted, Let's go to Miami next weekend

Three dots scrolled, disappeared. Scrolled again. Vanished. Then I saw his response, Can't. Taking LA to New York

Oh. Getting bold, are we? Whateva. I texted, Lunch tomorrow?

Busy. Can't.

Can't or won't?

You decide, Alexis. Does it matter? Do I matter?

Texted him back, CU2mrw. Brio. 3p. He'd be there.

A message from Chanel popped up. You on your way?

I tossed my cell on the couch, then headed upstairs.

LB was on his back naked. He'd blindfolded himself. His frame was nice. Pubic hairs neatly trimmed. I scanned his selection.

"Nice," I said. "Turn over so I can give you a massage."

Heating the paraffin wax on high, I removed my thong, slid it under his nose, then tossed it onto the bed. I stepped into the shower, washed every part of me twice. Lathered up my pointing finger then twirled it inside my asshole several times. Inserting my crystal wand into my vagina, I stimulated my G-spot while cleaning myself thoroughly.

When I entered my bedroom, LB was in the same position. Couldn't say he wasn't a patient man. Slowly, I trickled almond oil all over him. Rubbing his legs, back, arms, and ass, I spread his butt cheeks and sniffed his asshole.

"Damn, that shit feels good," he said.

"Just wait," I said, tying a silk scarf around his wrist. I did the same with his other wrist and his ankles, then tied each scarf real tight to a post on my bed.

As I knotted the last one, he said, "Whoa, wait a minute. What are you getting ready to do?"

"Nothing you don't want me to. You want me to stop?"

"Nah. Nah, I want to see where this is going."

"I didn't blindfold you."

"I know. You don't have to take it off. At least turn me over."

I whispered in his ear, "This'll all be over soon. Relax." He mumbled something. At this point it didn't matter. I massaged lots of almond oil until he was greased from head to toe, then I straddled him. My ass sat on the back of his head. As I faced his feet, I slid my pussy up and down his neck.

"Oh, shit," he said. "That's a first."

I stopped, picked up my thong, aggressively stuffed it in his mouth, then resumed gliding my titties against his back. I made certain he felt my nipples. Cupping my mouth to his asshole, I teased it, licked it, put my thumb in, then pulled it out.

Instantly, LB tightened his rectum. I gently dug my fingernails into the flesh of his ass. "It's okay. Just consider that your first unofficial prostate exam."

He moaned into the mattress as I poked him a few more times. A thumb in the behind was harmless. Grinding and wiggling my pussy down the center of his back, when I reached his ass, I rode his left cheek with my clit as though I was sexing his dick. The transition should help take his mind off of what I'd previously done.

"When I untie you, do you want me to fuck you like this, LB?" Pausing a few seconds to let him worry about what I was going to do next, I touched his asshole. I started thrusting my pussy hard, then said, "Or like this?" Massaging him real slow with my labia, I moaned real loud.

With my thong blocking his tongue, he could only grunt sounds. "Nod if you're okay," I said. Not looking for an answer, I didn't glance over my shoulder.

I got up, covered his ass with a thin layer of saran wrap, wedged the plastic between his cheeks. LB started jerking. Didn't matter. He wasn't getting up until I let him. I dropped a three-inch butt plug and a hand towel into a crockpot of nearly hot water.

Scooping the hot paraffin wax with a porcelain ladle, I spread his cheeks, then drizzled the hot wax along the crack of his ass and over his balls. He squirmed for a few seconds.

"You'll enjoy this more if you stop fighting the feeling." I lined his spine up to his neck with wax too. "You know you like it."

I put on my rubber gloves, turned off the crockpot, wrung the hot towel, flapped it open, then eased it onto his back. He flinched. After removing the saran wrap and wax from the crack of his ass, I tossed everything in the trash. Wet a hand towel and proceeded to cleanse his butt.

Spreading his cheeks, I licked his ass a few times while sliding my hand along his body to oil my fingers. Slowly, I twirled one notch then two of my fingers in and out of his rectum. He fought the feeling but what was he going to do. He'd never break free from silk scarves. Not in his position. I retrieved the warm butt plug, slowly eased it into his ass, then left it there.

Pulling his dick between his thighs, I sucked it until he came, which didn't take long. A few minutes later, LB was snoring. Rubbing his balls, I removed the plug, wiped his ass, then I removed the towel and wax from his back.

I showered, dressed, then headed to the club to see my gurl.

CHAPTER 39

Spencer

Alexis showed up at Blake's with LB. I could not believe she had on a short dress for church. At least it wasn't a halter. This one was lace, white, cropped sleeves. It wasn't see-through. Thankfully it covered her ass. Barely.

Her kind was normal for the ATL but I was . . . looking away I shook my head. My dick was too attracted to all of that.

"Morning, Spencer," Alexis said, then called out, "You ready, Mama?" She glanced at me, headed toward the kitchen. "I'm still thirsty, LB. You want anything to drink?"

I didn't understand why my boy looked at me then shook his head. Alexis couldn't see him. The grin on his face and the shine in his eyes made me ask, "What the hell did ole girl do to your ass?"

LB closed his eyes, exhaled, drooped his shoulders, then rattled his head. He looked at me. "I'm in love, man."

I whispered, "Get the fuck out of here. After one date?"

"I'd tell you all about it but she made me promise not to tell you."

"Me?" Knowing LB there was probably some shit he didn't want to tell a bruh like me having seen how I get down.

"Spencer," Blake called from the downstairs bedroom.

"Coming, Fabulous!"

Alexis peeped her head from the kitchen. "Spencer, come here for a second. Won't take long."

Maybe it was the cherry lipstick, her perfume that lingered, or the way she'd said my name. Foolishly, I went into the kitchen.

Alexis squatted, pulled out my dick, sucked it into her mouth three times. Three more times. The third of the third, I couldn't believe I came so fucking hard I almost screamed like a bitch. She swallowed, tucked my dick back in, wiped her mouth with a paper towel. She left the glass of orange juice on the counter.

"You drink it," she said, walking out.

I looked down toward my dick. "Nigga, what the fuck just happened?"

She was a real head master. There was no lipstick marks on my navy slacks or T-shirt. I circled the island twice, downed the juice. Let out a quiet, "Whooooo!"

I heard Fabulous ask, "Where's Spencer?"

LB answered, "In the kitchen."

Composing myself, I returned to the living room.

Alexis said, "Mama, you guys can ride with us," as though she wasn't asking.

The hell with that! I strolled into the living room. Blake looked incredible. She wore a coral fitted dress down to her knees. Pink heels. The colors were great on her.

Fabulous asked me, "You mind?"

"What?"

"Riding with Alexis?" she said.

Didn't want Fabulous and me to be on their schedule. Definitely didn't want to take a back seat to LB with his LED glowing ass.

"I'll drive. My car," I insisted. Picking up my car and house keys, I checked to make sure I wasn't missing one. The way Alexis sucked my dick a bruh could end up falling for her and not realize it until he was in too deep.

"I want to take you to brunch at the Ritz after church." I'd just made that up but it was a fantastic idea and the chances of Charlotte being there were slim.

Alexis could come back here after the service but my black ass would not be here. I did not trust my dick around her. Hopefully they wouldn't want to join us. I locked Fabulous's front door with the key she'd insisted I have.

LB opened his car door for Alexis, waited until she got in, then headed to the passenger side. Since when did he start opening doors for females?

"It's a beautiful day. Let's take my Benz." Fabulous reached into her purse.

"No." I opened the passenger door of my Range Rover, waited for her to get in. "You can give me directions to the church," I said, leaving the driveway.

"Or, you can follow me, Alexis," she said. "Is there something wrong, Spencer?"

"Nah" was all I'd said. My dick wanted to shout, "Hell, yeah!"

Fabulous must have sensed something wasn't right. She said, "I think LB and Alexis could make a good couple but he won't last. That girl doesn't like anybody. Man or woman."

"Or what?"

Fabulous instructed, "Turn right at the stop sign," then said, "My beautiful daughter is bisexual."

Lots of girls got down like that in the ATL but Alexis didn't seem the type. Oh, snap. That's why LB was all lit up. Lucky motherfucker. They probably had a threesome. On the first date? I was jealous. But if he knew what went down in the kitchen, he'd be pissed.

"She has a gorgeous stripper girlfriend, Chanel, who adores her. A man who worships her but she won't commit to him. She doesn't even wear the engagement ring he gave her a few days ago. What do you think she's in search of?"

Me, if I was lucky. If I'd said that aloud, it would be true and I'd get slapped upside my head. Alexis needed a real man to challenge her.

"She seems to have a male mentality," I said. "For some people it's all about the chase." That was understandable for dudes. I wanted to say, *For us,* but en route to church was not the time to spark our first argument.

"Maybe I don't have enough chase in me. What do you think?" Fabulous asked.

"Oh, you've got it. Where do you think Alexis gets it? You ever see dogs play when one provokes the other then runs away? That sparks the chase. And when the chaser loses interest, he's provoked again. Chases again. Men are supposed to pursue you but they need a reason."

Fabulous didn't have the right approach. She was nice but she wasn't exciting. I parked in the church's lot next to Alexis's door. LB scurried to let her out. I'd just noticed my boy had on the same jeans and T-shirt from yesterday.

Looking into Fabulous's eyes, I lied trying to boost her self-esteem, "You've got the right amount of everything."

This woman could be the best thing that's happened to me. If I could change one thing, it would be her overly generous spirit. I was offered the keys to her cars anytime I wanted. She freely handed me money to go get us food. I'd been by her side for one week and she trusted me with almost everything she owned. I'd planned on leaving her house and her house keys this evening.

Alexis stood in front of my car with her back to us. I swear that was a woman who knew how to bring out the dog in me.

CHAPTER 40

Spencer

I closed Fabulous's door, held her arm until we were inside. Sitting beside Alexis, we were at the end toward the center aisle five pews from the back exit. Intentionally, I'd let Blake sit on the very end in case she wanted to go up for altar prayer or some special offering. I wasn't in favor of having a minister lay hands on me for additional blessings. God gave me what He wanted me to have. What I did with it was pretty much the same as the people who'd thought they'd get more than their share.

I glanced around to see if I knew anyone. A few of these folks I'd seen at the restaurant, the mall, but I didn't know them enough to say, "I trust them." Just because it was church didn't mean half the congregation wasn't toting a piece on them.

Hearing the choir took me back to the days my mother and I worshipped together. In the middle of the bishop's sermon, I held Blake's hand. I whispered, "You good?"

"Yes. You?" she asked.

Not really. I should've been listening to the word but the truth was I was only here for Blake. Sitting next to Alexis was a major distraction. I felt Alexis's leg next to mine. I wanted to switch seats.

I lied to Blake. "I'm cool."

Alexis's shoe touched my shoe. I moved my foot away from hers. She placed hers closer. Touched me again. Okay. I wasn't going to play this game with her. Not here. Not now. She'd made it clear that she was interested in me but we'd made our choices. She was with LB. I was with Blake.

I'd missed whatever was said after Alexis distracted me. Truth was, I wasn't mentally present in the word. Had to concentrate on keeping my dick from rising. There'd be no hiding if this thang got loose. I was here with and for Blake.

When the bishop said, "Pull out your cell and tweet this . . ." that gave me the opportunity to check my phone. No text messages or missed calls from Charlotte. That bothered me more than if she'd blown up my car in the church's parking lot.

Finally, church ended. I didn't mind still being here but my praying for forgiveness for lusting for Alexis while I was sitting in the house of the Lord was the worst. It wasn't my fault. I couldn't call Alexis out. I was ready to go to Fabulous's place. Oh, yeah. Brunch. Whatever we did next, my time with Fabulous was almost up.

Soaking in Fabulous's essence while we chilled in her Jacuzzi one last time would be a great way to end a good week. I was going to miss her spot. Six thousand was a lot of square footage for one female.

Looking around the church I'd bet quite a few of these females who just finished praising the Lord had hit up a guy in their rotation during the sermon. What was Alexis's motivation for being with LB while pushing herself on me? I knew the answer well.

Ego.

"Let's say hi to the bishop, Mama," Alexis said, leading the way to the front of the church.

She was definitely a control freak and a real freak in one. Looking straight ahead, I focused on Alexis. LB was to her left. Blake was to my right.

Alexis's dress rested on the top of her ass. There was a subtle indentation that only a thong or no underwear could allow. I imagined circling my third eye around her asshole wondering if she were the type to strap on for her girl. Did she ride a fake dick or preferred penetrating pussy? Could she take it up her rear like a pro? She was so bad I'd almost forgotten where I was until I heard, "Alexis Crystal, it's good to see you and your mom."

LB was looking around as if he were trying to see if any other dudes were checking out Alexis. I was glad he wasn't tripping on me.

Alexis shook the pastor's hand. Complimented him on the sermon.

Alexis had my undivided attention until she turned to Blake and me. "We're outta here, you guys. See you later this evening, Mom." She winked at me, then said, "Come on, LB."

"Later, Spence," LB said, trailing Alexis.

Wow! My boy was gone. I prayed she hadn't turned him out.

As the pastor reached for Fabulous's hand, I checked out the people chatting with one another. A woman approached us, extended an envelope. The bishop smiled hard reaching for it. She pulled it back, gave it to Fabulous, then walked away.

I glanced at the bishop, and he stared at me. His smile vanished. Sounded like the whole church shifted to mute when he mouthed, *What's your name, son?*

My neck shrugged backward. He mouthed it again but he wasn't asking. Seems like he was trying to place me in his mind. As I faced the bishop, my eyes shifted toward Blake. She put the envelope in her purse, then smiled at me.

I was cool until the bishop stared deep into my eyes without blinking. Oh, wow. This nigga is a bishop. Really?

Blake pronounced, "This is my guy, Spencer."

While Fabulous was telling him my last name, he mouthed, *Leave her alone.*

He didn't want to go there with me. I stared him down, stood nose-to-nose, then I whispered, "You lucky we in church."

He never looked me in the eyes when he was fucking me in my ass. Faced me to my bedroom wall. My action hero, Superman, on my favorite poster couldn't save me. My dad could've but didn't! He knew what was happening.

So this is where he's been. I hadn't seen him since my mom left my dad seventeen years ago. This dude fucked me when I was a kid but he acted as though he didn't know me at all now? If he were so righteous. If he were a man of God back then as opposed to being a child molester. If he were truly his brother's keeper.

I wanted to beat his ass down!

"You okay, Spencer?" Fabulous asked, touching me on my bicep.

I gave her a serious look. "That's him."

She squinted. "Him?" Her eyes widened. "Him? Spencer, are you sure? There must be some mistake."

"Yes, son. You must be mistaken," the bishop said. Moving over, he greeted some woman. "Praise God, sister. It's good to see you back in the house of the Lord."

I wanted to strangle him with that cross and shove that Bible down his lying throat. Opening up to Fabulous took a heavy weight off my chest yesterday. If I hadn't released some of my anger I was sure Bishop would be laid out at the altar.

I nodded at him. I had a pine box in my heart for this nigga. The worst part was, he didn't care.

Shaking my head, I exited the church before I did something even the Lord might not forgive me for.

CHAPTER 41

Blake

Once a Christian always a Christian my behind.

I loved the Lord and the people who worshipped Him but some folks went too far with their phoniness. Being a saint wasn't in one's DNA like being black or white. All the years I'd attended my church, I'd never step foot in that one again. That man ministered to me, my children, my grandkids. The thought of what'd he done to a defenseless innocent child made me want to expose him.

The gospel message was separate from the deliverer but a rapist and a molester—pastor or not—Bishop was a person I no longer respected. Sure he could've repented and reformed but the fact that he showed no remorse toward Spencer pissed me off. I knew long as there was breath in our body everyone had the right to ask God for forgiveness.

Spencer was silent the entire ride back to my house. Refusing to go inside, he sat on the porch rocking back and forth. I made two martinis, went outside, handed him one hoping the vodka would relax him a little.

His fingers were interlocked face up. He shook his head, spoke toward his palms, "I'm good." I placed the drinks between our chairs, sat in the rocker beside him, then I touched his wrist. He pulled away, telling me, "Blake, you mind?"

Yes. I did. I wanted to be there for him the way he'd done for me.

"Blake! Do you mind! Damn! Leave me alone!"

I left the martinis on the porch in case he changed his mind. I needed to catch up to Mercedes, Devereaux, and Sandara. None of them were at church today. Seeing and hugging my grandbabies would do me good right now. Quietly, I left Spencer rocking with his thoughts.

Staring at my face in the mirror, I removed all of my makeup. The constant application of witch hazel had done an amazing job. The bruises seemed more like skin discoloration. I reapplied a light coat of foundation, a little eye shadow. I hadn't perfected all those strokes and blends the artist at Sephora showed me. The basics were fine. I didn't want to spend forty-five minutes to an hour applying makeup unless it was a special occasion.

I felt bad for Spencer. I knew he was hurting yet I could do nothing to alleviate his pain. Staring at myself in the mirror, I shook my head. If Spencer didn't love me, I wanted to know how he'd treat the woman that he'd fall in love with. I believed one day he might be mine but I didn't want to seem desperate. For what reason other than love would a man I barely knew tend to me?

Maybe I was doing it again. Falling for a man before I knew him and giving him all I had to offer. If Spencer was attracted to Alexis, even if she weren't my daughter, how could I compete with a twenty-six-year-old woman?

Exchanging my coral dress for a white jumper, I switched to my white and black Michael Kors bag, slid on my sunglasses, got in my Benz, then drove to the exit of my driveway. I glanced in my rearview mirror. He was still looking down, rocking.

"God, I love that man," I said, driving off.

There were many degrees of love. I didn't want to analyze how much, or how deep my feelings were for Spencer. Self-acknowledgement of my feelings was good enough for me.

Spencer knew how to contact me. I made sure the volume on my cell was turned up. He could leave my house or stay. He had a key to lock the door. If he called, I'd go back to hold him in my arms. The entire time Spencer was at my house, he hadn't started any arguments the way Fortune would've done. I wasn't sure which was harder to deal with. A man that shut down or one that bitched more than me?

Tears flowed. What if he was testing me? Giving me the option to be by his side the way he'd been there for me and I'd abandoned him. Wow. I wasn't five minutes away from my house and my heart ached for Spencer. I made a U-turn, headed back home, parked in the driveway, walked up five steps onto the porch.

This time I refused to walk away. I stood in front of Spencer, opened my arms. "The world can wait."

For the first time since he'd sat there, he looked up at me. He stood. Hugged me, then started crying on my shoulder.

"You have no idea how fucked up it is to have a man stick his dick in your ass against your will. I was a kid, Blake. I should've laid his ass out across the altar. But all I did was walk away. I'm feeling like a bitch right now for punking out," he said.

"You could never be that. It wasn't your fault."

He yelled, "Then who's to blame! Huh? Tell me! Who's to fucking blame!"

I refused to let him go. His concerns were valid. The one thing no one should ever question was who was wrong for abusing a child. "Shh." I held him tight. When I touched the back of his head, he cried louder.

After about ten minutes, he started sobbing. I whispered, "You don't have to say a word. Let's go inside. I'ma fill the tub so we can zone out."

"Everything okay over there, Blake?" Tom was standing in my driveway.

"Yes, Tom. We're good."

Tom made an about-face, then headed across the street. Spencer entered my house.

My Jacuzzi had become our sanctuary. A place where we could lay our heads, clear our minds, and open our hearts to each other. Turning on the surround sound I played his favorite smooth jazz CD.

Spencer settled into the water. I sat naked on the side of the tub with my feet in the water. I rested the back of his head on my stomach, dipped the sponge in the warm water. Gently, I washed his neck, shoulders, back. I scrubbed his chest. With each stroke, I stayed well above his waist. This moment was not about stroking his dick or his ego.

He dunked his face into the water. "Get in. I need for you to hold me."

I eased into the water, sat behind him. I wrapped my arms around him. He gripped my biceps. This was the type of man I'd longed for. Sensitive. Caring. Open.

We chilled. Our energies comforted each other. The connection felt spiritual.

Spencer whispered, "Thank you, Blake."

I could trust this man, and love him hard.

I cried. He cried.

I whispered, "Thank you, too."

CHAPTER 42

Spencer

Just as I dozed off, my cell rang. Looking at the caller ID, I smiled. Fabulous was lying next to me asleep. "What's up?" I eased from underneath the covers, tiptoed to the living room.

"Can you be here in two hours? I need you."

Now who needed whom? I didn't want to argue or debate, I was happy somebody genuinely wanted me.

I replied, "You got it. See you in two."

"Thanks."

"No. Thank you," I said, ending the call.

One of the many things my mother, Venus, taught me was being courteous to the right people at the right time is called respect. Pride ain't worth a dime if you have to step on others to get it or to keep it.

I shook my arms, wiggled my body, tilted my head side to side, then proudly entered the bedroom. Fabulous's eyes were wide open. "Who was that?"

"I've got to go. I'd planned on leaving today anyway." That was the truth.

"So you're not going to tell me who it was?"

Telling her my boss, Derrick, needed me wasn't a problem. I didn't want Fabulous to show up at my job. Not that it'd be a problem for Fabulous to chill but I'd been with her long enough. A brotha needed some space. And I mean what if Charlotte decided to drop in at the bar?

I opened a new pack of boxer briefs, held up two pair, then asked her, "Black or red?"

I'd been here so long, I'd run out of the new clothes I'd bought at Cumberland Mall and I had to order more underwear online and have them overnight-expressed. All my dirty laundry was in a trash bag. I could've used Fabulous's washer machine but I didn't want to.

"I have business to tend to," I said, giving her a kiss.

Fabulous hugged me. "You're leaving me," she said with a sad face.

I imagined she didn't want to be home alone. "Maybe one of your daughters can come over."

She let go. Turned her back to me. Wrapped her arms around her pillow.

Not committing to a day or time, I said, "I promise I'll call you."

Softly, she said, "Sure."

I was not going to let her make me feel bad about doing what was best for me. Damn, I'd been with her eight, nine, ten days. Shit, I'd lost count. I didn't want to be insensitive. Refusing to let her make me feel guilty, I kissed her lips, picked up my cell, then headed to the bathroom.

Derrick giving me time off was the proper response to Charlotte's behavior. The way I'd dismissed Charlotte was a mistake. What if she was parked in the lot waiting for me to return to work? I'd better call her ass.

Noticing the date, I realized the fifth was yesterday. Signing in to my online business account, I saw one of my tenants hadn't paid their rent. I should employ a management company to take care of my properties for me. I hated being a bill collector. I texted my renter, Your rent is past due. I'll wave the late fee if you pay by COB today. I didn't want to put a notice on his door but I would, first thing in the morning, if necessary.

Showering, I wondered, could I love two women at the same time? Yes, I believed so. I'd been there once before while I was in college. Could I be in love with two women at the same time? Absolutely. The lying, cheating, and breaking their hearts wasn't worth it.

I dried myself, dressed in the bathroom, then opened the door. Fabulous wasn't in the bed or the bedroom. Praying this wasn't going to be some a-thin-line-between-love-and-hate shit, I called out her name.

There was no answer. I entered the living room. She wasn't there. Checked the kitchen. No Fabulous. I wasn't going to play games. Walking out the front door to my car, I heard, "Want me to come over to your house?"

Shit! She scared me. I watched her rock back and forth.

"Not tonight. I'll call you."

Real sexy, she said, "You'd better." Then she said, "I love you."

"Cool. I gotta go." Driving away, I glanced in my rearview. Fabulous was waving at me. I tooted my horn as I exited her driveway. Stopping at the stop sign, I called Charlotte.

No answer.

I left her a voice message. "Hey, boo, Listen. I know I was wrong. Call me when you get this message."

Ending the call, I wondered, why were women so emotional? They could go from hot to cold or the opposite in a split second. Cry on a dime. Curse me out in a second.

Parking in the garage at my building, I surveyed my surroundings, got out of my car. Constantly, I glanced over my shoulder until I made it to my front door.

I changed my clothes, called Fabulous. She didn't answer. *Damn!* What did I do to her? I grabbed my cell and keys, then opened my front door.

Wham! My head snapped to the left. *Wham!* My head went to the right.

"You bastard!" Charlotte yelled. "You motherfucking bastard! I hate your ass!"

She raised her hand to hit me again. I snatched her wrist. She swung at me with her other hand. "Fuck! Bitch!" I dropped my phone and keys in front of my door, caught her arm in midair. Shoved her back against the wall in the hallway.

"It's over between us! You're crazy. I can't deal." I was serious this time.

Tears poured down her face. "You don't know what happened to me in Vegas. I had no money. You have no idea, Spencer. You didn't even care enough to check on me. You could've paid for the room so . . . so . . ." She screamed, "I wouldn't have had to do those . . ." Her words trailed off.

Staring at her with wide eyes, I didn't know what to think. Had some guy taken advantage of my boo? I got angry for a moment. What if Charlotte had made this shit up?

"Let me go!" Charlotte yelled, struggling to free herself.

I let her go. She faced my door. I stepped in front of her, blocked her entrance. No way was she getting into my place to break up my shit again. Pissed off as Charlotte was she might take a knife to my furniture, rip out the cushions, then attack me.

True. I could've made sure she had a place to stay. After I saw Fabulous's face, I wasn't tripping off of Charlotte. I took a deep breath. I was about to be the biggest sucker or the worst ex Charlotte has had.

Charlotte might've had an incredible time in Vegas or the unimaginable could've really happened to my gurl.

Kissing her lips, I told her, "Boo, it's over between us. For real this time."

"Hey, Domino."

Aw shit. I was already knowing who that was. Turning, I saw Alexis. I shook my head. She was sexy as hell. Another short-ass dress. Candy-apple red. Blue high heels. Her legs were shiny sexy. Hair flowed down her back.

I looked at Charlotte, then told Alexis, "This is my ex, Charlotte."

"Oh, really?" Alexis said, moving in closer.

"Ex my ass! Who's that bitch?" Charlotte asked.

Wham! Slam! Slap! Slam! Wham! Standing inches from Charlotte's face, Alexis said, "Call me a bitch again."

Wham! She hit Charlotte again. "That's for calling my mother a bitch, bitch."

Oh, shit. I sensed some shit was about to go down but I had no idea Alexis got down like that. I put my back to Charlotte, stood in front of Alexis.

Charlotte screamed, "Kick her ass, Spencer."

Was she serious? Did Charlotte believe for a second I wanted some of what she'd just got? It wasn't cool that a female had smacked up on my gurl, I meant, ex-gurl, but Charlotte needed to know everybody wasn't backing down from her.

Alexis reached into her purse, pulled out a brown band, gathered her hair, secured it into a ponytail. She dug in her bag again, pulled out a 9mm, tried to move me out of the way.

"Nah, now this is what's not going to happen," I told Alexis. Calmly, I said, "Put your gun away. Don't make me take it from you."

Alexis said, "I dare you, bitch."

Did she just call me a bitch? She could talk shit but there was no way I was going to let Alexis shoot Charlotte.

Charlotte's eyes narrowed. Her face turned bright red. She stared at me. I wasn't sure what she expected me to do. She'd showed up at my front door unannounced, hit me in my head twice, now she wanted my protection.

Alexis stepped back. Held the gun with both hands over her right shoulder. Damn, she looked like one of those women who could lure a man into bed then kill him. She lowered her piece to her side.

I had a flashback of her sucking me off in her mom's kitchen.

Charlotte said, "We're done. I won't bother you ever again. You're not worth it."

Hell, I'd almost forgotten Charlotte was here.

Hunching my shoulders, I said, "Cool." She'd made my decision to be chill with Fabulous easier. Alexis made it harder.

"You can have him," she said to Alexis, then stumped away. Her legs wobbled. Each step Charlotte took I thought she was going to fall.

"I don't need your permission, bitch! Don't bring your ass back here or let me catch you anywhere near my man!"

All I could do was shake my head. I didn't want to laugh but soon as Charlotte was out of our sight we busted up.

Alexis put her gun in her purse, then strutted away, jiggling her booty.

I'd be telling the truth if I'd said, "That shit turned me on!"

CHAPTER 43

Spencer

Glad to be back at work, that was the craziest episode ever. Charlotte's wylding out almost made me late.

I wanted to tell LB what had happened but he wouldn't believe me. Hell, if I weren't in the mix of that situation, I wouldn't believe it either. It felt good shaking my first drink.

Pouring a vodka martini, I thought about Fabulous. I'd texted her in transit. She hadn't hit me back. I understood. After putting in QT between her legs, I'd probably fucked up her head.

"How was it?" I asked LB. We hadn't spoken since church yesterday. "Alexis, what's she like, dude?"

"Man, thank you," he said, gnawing on his knuckles. Any harder and my boy would've drawn his own blood.

"Damn. Like that?"

"All the way freak, man. Alllll the way, you hear me." His eyes rolled to the top of his head. He moved to the opposite end of the bar.

Tending to my customers, I didn't want to mess up again or give Derrick a reason to come for me. Checking out the female who just squatted on the wicker stool in front of me, I tapped the bar once, then said, "What's your pleasure?"

As she ordered, my dick got hard. I swear that nigga couldn't stay focused.

LB stood next to me, then whispered, "I'm tapped out, bruh. She's all yours."

Tapped out? I pictured Alexis sucking me off in seconds. I was going to have to have a talk with my dick about that shit. He was not a one-minute man. But that Alexis had given me the best nut I'd busted from a quickie.

I took a few orders, mixed, poured, and served drinks. Chatted with a few of my regulars.

"I missed you the last few days. Did you go on vacation?" she asked as I placed her usual, a glass of cabernet, in front of her.

"Nah. Had to take care of some things." That wasn't exactly a lie. "You're looking good."

"Not so bad yourself," she commented with a wide smile.

This one was harmless. She had so many dickatunities it was redickulous. I watched her come in here, sit alone, busy herself on her iPhone and laptop writing them nasty books. Never failed. A guy would sit next to her, offer her a drink, and end up paying her entire tab.

I wasn't supposed to be jealous of LB, but a part of me was. I was surprised Alexis let my boy hit it on the first date. I mean her mom giving it up was understandable. Fabulous was fifty but Alexis was so fine every dude had his eyes on her.

In between servicing customers, I pressed LB for details about what Alexis had done. Blow by blow that shit blew my mind.

I whispered to LB, "You let her do what to your ass, man?"

"Wasn't like I let her do all the other stuff. After I let her tie me up I didn't have a choice."

Hot wax. Massage. Hot towel on his back. I wanted all of that but she could squash that butt plug shit. I was no stranger to a finger in my ass. That was cool. Objects were not.

Wondered if my boy knew she was into females and she was engaged. Wasn't my place to tell him. I was more concerned about Alexis checking me than I was with LB questioning my source.

"When y'all going out again?" I asked.

"I invited her out this weekend. She said she had to get back at me. Don't try to push up on this one, Spence. I like her too much."

I didn't want to do Alexis's nasty ass. After all the shit LB told me, I had to!

CHAPTER 44

Alexis

The sixth had come. My rent wasn't paid.

Walking up to my door, I removed the plastic bag that hung on the knob. I knew what was in it. A collection notice for $2,000, plus a $150 late fee. I went inside, texted Chanel, Come over before you go to work.

Sitting on my couch, I kicked off my heels, went to the kitchen, mixed a drink. Thank God I was almost done with school. Graduation was next year. The lovers in my life today would be gone by the time I walked the stage. Not because they wanted out. I needed to draft more players. There wasn't room on the home court for everyone. Maybe I'd do like James. Date a white person who lived out of state.

All I have to do is get through this semester and the next one and I'm done. Applying for a job wasn't a bad idea but being on a schedule other than school wasn't for me. I'd rather use my title of Dr. Crystal to lure in a class of men wealthier than James. Like team owners. Let my new crew fulfill my desires.

Chanel replied, I can't keep letting you break my heart.

Women. One minute they were in love, then they were confused. Chanel wanted to end it but not really. She sent that response to get my attention. I sighed.

So she didn't forget. Chanel intentionally didn't give me her tips Saturday night. She did not appreciate that I'd gotten out of my bed, sat in the club, watched her perform, followed her to her house.

What was I to do? I couldn't bring her back to my place. LB was still tied to my bed. I told her I'd spent Sunday with my mom. That was mostly true. Just not the part when I'd texted, *I'm spending the night.* I'd spent the night at James's house.

I opened one of the drawers to my coffee table, placed a big black dildo on the sofa beside me, removed my clothes. Lounging back on a gold pillow, I turned my video camera toward me. Looking at myself, I softened my eyes, pressed record, waited a second, then said, "We miss you, baby. Wanna see how much?"

I circled the eight-inch dildo around my tongue. I licked the corona, then slowly lowered my mouth over the head. Opening wide, I let saliva roll off the tip of my tongue onto the top of the head and down the shaft. I teased my clit, slid the wet dildo in and out of my pussy. Letting go, I forced the dildo out using my muscles. Captured it lying between my thighs. The head touched my vagina. Picking it up I braced my knees to my ears, pushed it all the way in my asshole. Took it out. Held it up. It was clean and shiny. Making a pouting face, seductively I said, "We're ready for you and only you."

Ending the recording, I replayed it twice.

Perfect first take.

I texted the video to Chanel, this new girl I'd met, LB, and James.

James texted back. Rent check? Rain check.

Cute, Wilcox. Your days of having the pleasure of my fucking you in the ass are limited. I could pawn his ring but I was sure that wasn't going to be necessary. I always got whatever I wanted. My last resort would be to charge my rent to the credit card James gave me for incidentals. Quickly, I decided against that. I didn't want him to cancel my card.

I hit a few other options in my rotation. The two over fifty would give me the money in cash today but I didn't enjoy sexing either one of them. They were my backups.

Sending the video to Spencer wasn't necessary. Men talked more than women and I was certain LB had told Spencer what I'd done to him and I was positive he'd show the video to Spencer for me.

Mercedes texted, We're meeting at Mom's house. She needs us. See you then in an hour.

Good, hopefully Spencer would be there since we got rid of Charlotte's ass. I texted, LB, Is Spencer at work?

Nah. Why you asking about him?

I was going to drop by the bar with my mom, I lied.

Come see me.

I'm headed to my mom's. She won't come if Spencer isn't there.

If I told Mercedes I needed two grand for school, she'd pay it directly. She might need her funds to pay for her divorce when she found out Benjamin has a mistress. Devereaux had it but didn't have it to spare. Sandara, the thought of her finances made me shake my head.

LB texted back, Damn, that video got my dick hard as concrete. Can I cum over after I get off so you can finish what you started doing to me? I close tonight and I'm off tomorrow.

I'd already grown bored with him. He had no imagination. I'm a little short on my rent. Will you help me out this one time?

He replied, How much?

Two Gs.

He texted, Damn!!!!! That's a little?

I'll give it back when I get my student loan next week.

Next week?

Yes LB. Next week, I lied. I didn't have any student loans.

Cool if I can do half? I don't have 2Gs.

That's cool. He was probably telling the truth. I didn't know or care what he'd have to do to get me the cash.

He texted back, See you tonight.

I didn't respond. It was best to let him send the last text. I might have to strap-on for him tonight. But that was only if he had my money in his hand. Men lied to get laid more than women.

Chanel texted, I stopped by the office and paid your rent plus the late fee. Come see me at the club tonight.

I called the office and confirmed, then I texted LB, My family made plans for tonight.

What about the check?

Check? Since you're off in the morning, we can go to your bank. I can pay my rent then we can hang out during the day and have all the fun you'd like tomorrow after I get out of class.

Class would allow me to ditch LB for the rest of the day if I wanted to. I didn't get a response from LB. Didn't matter. It was his money until he'd give it me.

Heading out, I decided to check if Spencer was home. I knocked on his door. No answer. I knocked again.

He opened the door. His body was wet. A black towel was wrapped around his waist. OMG! He looked delicious.

"Hey, Alexis. What's up?"

"Just dropped by to make sure you're okay. Mind if I come in?"

He smiled. "Yes. I do. I'm headed to your mom's," he said.

"Me too," I said with a sexy smile.

"Then I will see you there." He closed the door in my face.

Thinking he was playing, I waited . . . and waited. Why was this bitch acting brand new? I was not knocking again.

I left.

CHAPTER 45

Blake

I refused to chase another man. I'd rather be alone.

Seemed as though Spencer wanted out and a call from whoever that was gave him a reason. It took a lot of willpower not to call or text him but I made it through the night, this morning, and this afternoon. I hadn't gone upstairs. That was one thing I appreciated Spencer doing for me when I needed something.

His leaving had an upside. Last night I'd spoken with each of my daughters and I'd told my girlfriend Echo everything that had happened starting with Fortune's death.

Standing in my doorway, I watched Echo park her car in my driveway. She would've come when I called but she was in New York. She hurried up the stairs.

"Blake, you should've called me sooner," Echo said, hugging me. "I came straight from the airport."

I wrapped my arms around her. We rocked side to side. "Things worked out the way they were supposed to. I'm glad Fortune is dead."

"You don't mean that," she said, letting go.

Yes, I did. I was relieved. His dying wasn't my fault. His being gone was like a burden lifted from my life. All the tears I'd shed for him while he was here had drained me. Not one teardrop fell from my eyes for that man since the day he'd died and it would stay that way until the day I died.

I told Echo, "Honestly, I do."

She looked at the pictures on the mantel. "Oh, my gosh it's been so long since I've been here." Echo picked up the photo of us together at a Falcons versus Saints game. We had lots of fun that day. We always had a good time wherever we went.

"This was five years ago but I remember it well. We got our ass *whupped*," Echo said, then laughed. "Have you been to any games since this one?"

Admiring my girl, she was still inside-out beautiful. Her round face blended her cheeks with her chin. Her nose was flat, wide, with no bridge. Her marbled-shaped chocolate eyes beamed with energy. She hadn't gained a pound. Still had that perfect size fourteen. Small waist. Gigantic booty. Itty-bitty titties.

"I went to a few with Fortune. The ones I'd bought tickets to." Disgust rose in my voice. That man was dust and the thought of his selfish ways still angered me.

Echo placed the frame back in the lineup. "Let it go, Blake. Don't let hatred eat away your soul."

She was right. "I like your purse. What designer is that?" I asked.

She handed the tan bag to me. "Long as it looks good you know I have no idea. You tell me."

I placed it on the table behind the sofa. "It doesn't matter."

Her maxi sundress dragged on the beige carpet. Her B-cup boobs sagged a little. Were those her areolas I could see? Shaking my head I couldn't miss the red panties. Maybe her breasts appeared small because her ass was so big.

She was the one friend that I had who was optimistic ninety percent of the time. She wished people well when they spoke ill of her. Uplifted her man in positive praise through their toughest times even after he'd cheated on her.

If Echo couldn't help a person become better, she didn't stand by to watch them fail. Guess that was why she'd stopped hanging out with me. I missed being in her presence.

"Not that I need to say it but make yourself at home. Let me get some champagne. I chilled it just for us," I said, heading into the kitchen.

"When do you go back to work again?" she shouted from the living room.

"Not soon enough! In six days! I'd go back today if I didn't have to list this property and purchase another one."

"Shut up! You're selling your house! Are you staying in this area? You should buy the house next door to us."

We'd been friends for thirty-five years. Part of the reason I hadn't reached out to her until now was it was hard for me to be happy seeing her in a healthy relationship knowing mine was screwed up. Her friendship always remained in my heart even when she wasn't in my life.

"I'm tired of the commute. I'm going to buy in Buckhead." That was one reason. The other was I'd be in the center of the social environment where I'd met Spencer. Hell, if he was that attracted to me and he was the bartender, I could sit at the bar and meet all types of men.

"Don't sleep on Smyrna, it's safe. Buckhead has too much crime for me."

"Buckhead isn't that bad. You're talking about all of Fulton County," I said.

Echo replied, "Okay. You're going to have to keep all of your guns loaded and one in your purse."

Echo was friendly but she would shoot back if necessary. The gun collection she and her husband owned was impressive. All this talk about firearms reminded me I was overdue for a few rounds at the range.

I placed the open bottle in the ice bucket, carried the two flutes, handed her one. "Mercedes is coming by with the Realtor later so I can sign the listing agreement. Knowing my daughter she's probably already found me something."

Echo's being here made me regret that I'd sacrificed my relationship with my best friend for a man. A man who was never a friend to me.

"Not calling you for years won't happen again," I told her, squeezing her hand.

That was the truth. She gripped my fingers. "You my girl, Blake. Sometimes we have to figure things out, our way, you know. In our own time. Your relationship with your man wasn't about me. Neither my number nor my address changed. You knew where and how to contact me."

It took us two hours, plus one and a half bottles of champagne, to catch up.

"You're so assured of yourself. How do you stay happy in your marriage and grounded in your personal life?" I asked, sipping on a mimosa.

Echo grabbed my hand, sat my drink on the coffee table. She escorted me to the full-length mirror on my wall. "Take off your clothes," she said.

Glancing around as though someone could see us, I frowned and smiled at the same time. "You can't be serious."

She lifted my dress, pulled my panties down to my ankles. Slipped my dress over my head, flung it to the couch, then unfastened my bra. I didn't resist. Echo wasn't bisexual.

Standing before her naked nervously I laughed. She didn't.

Echo removed her clothes. "Look at us, Blake. We are fifty and sexy as hell."

"Oh my goodness. I missed your fiftieth!" I wanted to give her a hug but opted to wait until my clothes were back on.

Echo shook her head. "This isn't about me. You've got to give praise to the Lord. I thank Him every day for my healthy beautiful body. It's not what it was five years ago and it won't be what it is now in five years but I still look good." She twirled, then continued, "These titties hang a snatch but so what. This juicy phat ass has dimples but I don't care and neither does my husband." She slapped herself on the butt, then smacked mine. "Don't wait until you're on your way out to appreciate what you have."

Echo's comment reminded me I needed to call Brandon. Lunch with him before returning to work was a must. It dawned on me we didn't meet up for drinks after my makeover. He had no idea all I'd endured and he was probably distracted by some new guy.

"You're right," I said, admiring my smile. My teeth were even; my mouth was attractive enough to please a much younger man. My neck, nipples, breasts, stomach, curvy hips, and thighs were caressed by Spencer.

Echo and I put on our clothes, then we sat on the sofa. I picked up my mimosa.

"Honey, I had a twenty-seven-year-old in my house for a whole week after my fiftieth birthday. He just left yesterday."

Echo smiled. "So the truth comes out, bitch. That's why your ass didn't call me when Fortune died. Before I forget, I need to borrow one of your handbags. You're probably still not using most of them anyway."

I pointed to the bedroom in the back. "Help yourself. There's more upstairs. I'm going to refresh our drinks." I was so happy she'd come to visit.

I chuckled. None of us gave a damn that Fortune was dead. Returning to the living room, I reclaimed my seat.

"This one okay?" Echo asked, knowing I didn't care. I also knew I'd never see that purse again. She never returned the items she so-called borrowed. I'd used that purse for church this past Sunday. After what I'd discovered about the bishop, I hadn't planned on using that bag or wearing the clothes I had on again. I didn't want anything to remind me of what the bishop had done to Spencer when Spencer was a boy.

Echo opened the purse. "Oh, here," she said, handing me an envelope.

"I'd forgotten she'd given me this." There was nothing written on the outside. I opened the envelope and unfolded a letter. My mouth hung open.

"She, who?" Echo took the letter and check from me. Her jaw dropped. She read, "Dear Blake, This is a thank-you offering for your taking care of my trifling husband. I knew you wouldn't take it if I'd handed it to you so I asked a member to give you the envelope. You did me the biggest favor one woman could do for another. I know how much of an asshole my husband was but he'd never hit me. Sorry for that. No woman deserves to be abused. If it weren't for you I wouldn't have enjoyed the last five years with my cub (lol). We married the day after Fortune died. Enough about me. Here's a little something for your troubles, sweetheart. You've earned it."

I was speechless.

Echo said, "Now this is what I call high class but let me rewind. He did what to you?"

I nodded. "He beat me because I'd put his ass out. He came back and—"

Echo held up her hand. "Wait, how did his wife find out?"

"I imagine she ordered the police report."

"You should've told me, Blake. I'm your friend."

I wanted to cry. I stared away from Echo.

Echo gave me a hug. "It's okay. We can talk about it when you're ready."

I told her, "Not that I need it but I never expected a cashier's check for a hundred thousand dollars. Girlfriend, I'm taking you on a vacation. Anywhere you want to go. I'm serious. Now back to Spencer. He made love to me yesterday. The kind that made me cry, then he left."

Echo smiled. "Girlfriend, he gave you that I'ma-put-it-down, you-gon'-fall-in-love dick. You probably just hadn't had any good dick in five years. Those tears were pent-up pussy juice flowing from your eyes."

Echo could always make me laugh and smile. "I love you so much."

"I love you too, Blake."

"You think I'm being foolish."

My friend shook her head slowly. "Your problem is you don't believe you deserve him. If you have feelings for Spencer, let him know. If he's feeling the same, great. If not, thank him for the dick and ask if you can have some mo'."

I had to laugh, then sip my drink. I knew Spencer had sworn me to secrecy but Echo was my best friend.

Echo's cell chimed as though she'd tapped her glass twice with the handle of a spoon. I waited as her gaze scrolled across her screen. Standing, she said, "Blake, I hate to cut our girlfriend time short, but I have to leave. I'll call you later."

Maybe the interruption was a sign that I wasn't supposed to tell her about Spencer. I escorted her to the door, put my hand on the knob, cracked the door. But I valued her opinion and there wasn't anyone else I'd tell.

"This will only take a moment. Let me ask you something."

Echo stared into my eyes. She remained silent.

"What would you do if you found out our bishop molested your man when your man was a child? Would you still go to our church?"

Her lips parted. She paused, then said, "God is my every—" Her jaw dropped, she frowned. Blurting, "Shut the hell up! Your guy told you that *our* bishop molested him!"

I nodded.

"Girl, to be continued. I wish I didn't have to leave but I've got to go. I'll call you soon as I get in my car."

When I opened the door, I thought I'd die.

Echo glanced at me through the corners of her eyes, then quietly excused herself.

Spencer stared at me with tears that didn't fall from his eyes. His lips, those lips that generally curved into a closed smile, pressed tightly together. He dropped a dozen red roses and a Saks Fifth Avenue gift bag at my feet.

Tears filled my eyes. His cologne greeted my nostrils. His face was freshly shaved. His locks were gone. Oh, my, God. Had he cut them for me? His red button-up was nice, crisp. I was dying inside. The lump in my throat didn't make me speechless. The one thing he'd asked me not to do, I'd . . . I'd . . .

Shaking his head, he walked down the steps as Alexis got out of her car.

"What's up, Domino," Alexis said. "By the way, love the new look."

She had on a short, sexy, black lace halter dress that draped her hips. She opened her arms to him for a hug. What if . . . What if he had sex with Alexis?

He opened his arms, wrapped them around my daughter's waist, looked over his shoulder at me. His hands cupped Alexis's butt, underneath her dress. Sliding his hands up her ass, I saw her gold thong. She didn't protest.

Loud enough for me to hear, he told my child, "Hit me up later if you want to come by."

I know I wasn't right. But what he'd told her was wrong.

CHAPTER 46

Spencer

Women, I swear I'd never trust another one of them! I punched my steering wheel. The horn blasted.

"Fucking bitch!" After all I'd done!

She probably thought I was wrong for feeling up her trifling daughter in front of her. At least I didn't do it behind her back. Like mother, like daughter. Yeah. "The hell with both of them."

I'd finally made up my mind that Fabulous was the one I wanted to date and she go and do some foul shit like that. That woman leaving her house didn't know me but she knew some dude had fucked me in the ass when I was a kid. She couldn't even look me in my face.

That shit right there was unforgiveable.

New clothes. Burberry Touch cologne. Fresh flowers. I'd done all that for Fabulous. For what! Women loved bragging on what a guy did for them. I knew she was feeling some type of way when I chose work over laying up with her for the what, ninth night in a row? See, women quickly forget all the considerate shit.

Speeding to merge onto the freeway, I swerved. I almost collided with a white Benz zooming by me. I did a double-take thinking it was Blake trying to catch up to me. It wasn't that bitch. If it were, I would've caught up to her just to flip her off.

Spencer. My mother's voice echoed in my ear. I knew it was Venus. She was trying to calm her baby boy down before he injured himself, or someone else.

"Mama, why?" Why were women so heartless? "They don't make 'em like you anymore," I cried aloud.

How many others had Blake told? Who would I serve at the bar not knowing if they knew my deepest secret?

I pulled off at my exit, dried my tears, stopped at Tower Liquor on Piedmont. After picking up a 375ml of peach vodka, I drove up the street to Piedmont Park. Got out of my car, sat on the lawn, stared up at the sky. I held the bottle in my hand between my knees.

"Why am I so fucked up in the head?"

I uncapped the vodka, swallowed a mouthful, twisted the top back on. Instead of alleviating my problems, Blake made it worse. I hadn't bounced back from feeling emasculated at her church.

"If I'd never tapped the fucking bar twice, I wouldn't be here."

What was the purpose of my trying to do right? Females. I shook my head. I unscrewed the cap, pressed the bottle to my lips. Maybe this shit was karma. Get-back for how I'd mistreated Charlotte. She was the one that screwed dude and ruined our good thing. I knew I could've done a better job of helping Charlotte while she was grieving over her dad but she sought comfort by opening her legs for dude? Finding that shit out gave me unnecessary grief.

Women didn't understand that pussy wasn't sacred unless they had a man that gave a fuck. Fuck Charlotte. Fuck Blake, too!

Charlotte hadn't contacted me since Alexis smacked her. I hadn't reached out to Charlotte either. Some shit was easier not to deal with. Probably how my bitch-ass dad, Conner Rogers, felt about me and my mom. Perhaps it was best for me to let Charlotte be. Let that sleeping female dog lie to some other dude.

I was nicer than the average guy in the ATL. Some of these hoods had zero mental when it came to their girl fucking around. If their girl slipped up, their girl would get one of two things. Cut off. Or beat down. Sometimes both. Some of these females were on a leash so short they couldn't turn around to take a piss.

A text came in from Alexis. Still wanna hookup later?

Sure was my response. Why not? If she was tossing up pussy, I'd take it.

Sweet. I'll hit you when I'm leaving

I texted her back, Leave now, to irritate Blake.

On my way

That's what was up. My kind of girl.

Blake didn't suck dick better than Alexis but the chemistry I had with Blake made each moment special. A call came in from her. I declined it. She called again. I hit decline again.

Now you want to talk to me. What the fuck she got to say now? She hadn't called my name when I walked away. Didn't text or dial my number until Alexis had probably left or said, *I can't stay long.*

A brotha like me got pussy on pause. Did Blake have a clue how many numbers I received from females and dudes on a daily? At the end of my shifts, tips were green but I tossed every contact a guy gave me. I was molested but I wasn't gay.

What was Blake going to say if I'd answered? *Spencer, I'm sorry.*

Fucking straight she was sorry. Or was she going to beg me, *Please don't have sex with my daughter.* I didn't owe Blake any consideration. Just like Charlotte, Blake handed a brotha a get-you-some-new-pussy pass.

If Charlotte hadn't messed up, I wouldn't have done Blake. If Blake hadn't screwed up, I wouldn't be on my way to give her daughter the Spencer special.

The one and only thing I begged of her not to do, she'd done. Her betrayal gave me the right to do whatever the fuck I wanted. I turned the bottle up again. Again. Until it was half empty. Got back in my car, then called my boy, LB. I didn't know what made me hit him.

"Hey, what's up Spence?"

"Nothing much, man. Where you at?"

"Work. For another hour. Dude, you sound over the legal limit. Where you at? You good?"

"Nah, man, but I'll be straight in an hour or so." I couldn't share my truth with him. Boy or not, dudes never knew what to say to one another about male-on-male molestation. Now, if a female had taken my virginity, he would've known that a long time ago. "I'll hit you tomorrow, bruh."

Ending the call before I said some shit about Alexis, I drove to my place wondering if I'd ever settle down. Marry. Have kids. Blake could never make me a father. Alexis could. Alexis was high maintenance though. That was okay. I had enough money to take care of her the way she'd like. Couldn't take my money with me. Learn that from my mom when she willed me everything. Might as well make somebody happy. Have a kid or two to pass my funds on to.

I got out of my car, went inside my apartment, showered, and started preparing for a freakfest showdown with Alexis.

CHAPTER 47

Blake

I had all of my daughters, grandbabies, Phoenix, and Benjamin at my home.

Despite Alexis's blatant disrespect, I was not going to let her ruin the surprise birthday party Mercedes had planned. She really got me by having it on a Monday. Mercedes had mentioned there were surprise guests coming. Since the children were here, I'd ruled out strippers, though that would've been entertaining. Maybe I'd go to a strip club with Echo to have fun this weekend.

Suppressing the hurt in my heart for betraying Spencer, I hugged Alexis. I whispered in her ear, "This is the one and only thing I ask of you regarding Spencer. Please don't have sex with him."

Letting go, she stared into my eyes, then said, "He's more my type, and a little closer to my age, Mama."

Where did this defiant child come from? I wanted to slap her. "I'm not asking."

"Asking what?" Sandara said, hugging me from behind.

Alexis raised her brows to Sandara, eyed me, then walked away. "Benjamin, glad to see you don't have any competing commitments tonight." Alexis patted Benjamin on the back.

I scolded her, "Watch your mouth and your tone, Alexis."

Benjamin replied, "It's okay, Blake. We're all adults."

Alexis smiled at me then strutted into the kitchen. What had I done to her?

Sandara picked up Brandy. Twirled her around. Brandy laughed.

"Do me," Brandon said, jumping high in the air.

"Stop it!" Mercedes told them. "Go sit down."

"Let 'em enjoy themselves," Benjamin said.

Mercedes's lips became tight.

"Fine. Kids, do what your mother told you. Go outside and play," he said.

Mercedes's mouth drew closer together. She never spoke a word.

Benjamin exhaled. Remained silent. What the hell? Those two were having a standoff? If anyone had a right to be pissed, it was me at Alexis. I held Mercedes's hand. Benjamin went outside.

"Come with me," I told my daughter, leading her to my bedroom.

"Mama, everything is fine. I don't have time to chat," she said, standing in the doorway.

I pulled her into the room. "Now, Mercedes, you volunteered what I hadn't asked, that means I'm right. Out with it," I demanded.

Her dreamy eyes and full lips were expressionless. "Mama, really. I have too much to do. We can talk tomorrow."

I closed the door. "What's going on between you and Benjamin?"

She flopped on my bed. "Fine. Since you insist. Lately, things seem different."

"What do you mean, 'seem'?" I asked, holding her hand.

I could see my child was hurting. I was too. My job was to be here for her. Not fill my head with worries about Spencer that wouldn't allow me to hear what she said.

Mercedes shook her head. "Can't put my finger on it."

"You think he's cheating?"

"No. He'd never do that. It just seems like we're growing apart and I don't know how to get us back to where we were."

Tears clouded her eyes. I just hoped her sorrow didn't blind her judgment. Mercedes believed no other woman could ever come between Benjamin and her. I knew better. Her I'm-the-only-one-in-this-family-with-the-legal-right-to-change-my-last-name attitude might make her cover up her problems. She probably knew more than what she'd admitted.

Mercedes was not for being embarrassed or having others in her business. She stood. "Mom, I've to check on things."

"The best advice I can give you, sweetheart, is never underestimate what your man will do."

Firmly, she replied, "Husband. He's my husband. I'm not Alexis. Benjamin is not Spencer. And you've never had a husband. No disrespect. But you're not qualified to give me advice."

The last part was unnecessary but she had a right to feel however she wanted. Alexis was a woman and Benjamin was a man and everyone was capable of cheating. I told Mercedes, "I'll be out in a minute."

Men didn't need a reason to cheat. For some, sexing more than one woman was in their nature. I called Spencer a few times. Each time my call rang once then went to voice mail. No need to leave a message. Obviously, he wasn't ready to speak with me. I put on the best smile I could, then went into the living room.

Sandara took my cell then said, "Mama, we have a surprise for you. I'm your social media and personal assistant tonight. I need you to go change your clothes."

"Where are my grandbabies?" I asked, looking around in search of Alexis.

Devereaux answered, "They're outside playing. Alexis is watching them."

Hearing that Alexis was still here made me exhale. Strangers dressed in tuxedos entered my home carrying trays of food. Some guy rolled in cases of champagne. "Child, what are you doing?" I asked Mercedes, moving out of the way of a three-tier cake with red and white frosting.

"What you deserve and what I can afford," Mercedes commented.

Was I the only one who noticed Benjamin rolled his eyes at Mercedes after she'd made that comment? I prayed they weren't having financial problems. I did not want to go back to signing checks to help out my children.

"Why are you still standing here, Mama?" Sandara asked. "Go. Guests will be here in an hour."

I smiled. "Guests, huh?" I'd never had a birthday party that I hadn't given myself. Cake and ice cream depending on how much money my mama had at the time. There were too many of us for my mom to afford eight parties a year.

"Yes, guests," Devereaux replied. "Now, go get dressed. Call me when you're ready for me to do your hair and makeup."

"Seems like someone should've bought me an outfit for whatever this occasion is," I said, smiling.

"Oh, I did. I forgot it's in my car. I'll bring it in in a moment," Mercedes commented.

Oh, my, goodness. If Mercedes had picked it out, I prayed it wasn't anything up to my neck and down to my knees. Heading toward my bedroom, I thought, *This is not the time to beat myself up over a mistake,* then I heard Mercedes say, "Alexis, where are you going?"

"I'll be back," Alexis said.

Sandara replied, "You're lying. I can tell the way that you said it."

I stopped, turned to look at Alexis. She eyed me for three seconds, then walked out the door. I closed my bedroom door. I wanted to call Spencer then realized Sandara had my phone. That gave me a reason to go back into the living room. "Where's my cell?" I asked her.

"Mother, will you please go get ready?" Mercedes protested.

Holding open my hand, I wiggled my fingers. "Anyone know where Alexis is going?"

"Who cares," Mercedes said. She took my phone from Sandara, slapped it in my palm, escorted me to my bedroom, and closed the door. "Don't come out again. I'll bring you your clothes."

I didn't want to celebrate my birthday without Spencer. I texted him, Please come back. We can talk about it.

While I showered, my stomach felt like it was trying to eat itself. I turned off the water, rubbed the towel between my legs. There was no stimulation. The Jacuzzi hadn't been used since the last time I'd shared it with Spencer.

"Knock. Knock." That was Devereaux's voice.

"Yes," I answered, wrapping the towel around my body.

"Are you decent, Mama?"

I unlocked the bedroom door.

"Good, you're done with your shower. Your guests are arriving. Sit here," Devereaux said.

She pinned up my hair, then layered on foundation. "Is Spencer coming back?" she asked.

I snapped. "Is Alexis back?"

"Not yet. But of course she's coming back. Call her," Devereaux said.

Reluctantly, I dialed her number. It went directly to voice mail. I called Spencer. Again. One ring, then my call went to his voice mail.

"She's not coming back." I powered off my cell. "Spencer isn't coming back either."

"Mama, no. After all Spencer has done for you, Alexis wouldn't. He wouldn't. We all know that man loves you." She did a few more strokes with a brush. "All done with your face." Using a wide-tooth comb she swept my hair to the front, then to the left, last to the right. Devereaux fingered the roots, then teased the ends.

Sandara entered the room holding two hangers and the Saks bag. "Ready to see your outfits?"

Raising my brows, I told her, "I hope so. Let me see what's in the Saks bag first."

Sandara removed the tissues, unrolled a pink corset with an hourglass shape. After opening the other tissue, she held up a pink skirt that had wide peach stripes.

"I love it. I don't need to see the others. Give that to me."

While I dressed in the clothes Spencer had bought, Devereaux paired my birthday attire with my peach stilettoes. This wasn't the right time to tell any of my girls about the hundred grand Vanessa had given me. Just in case my event didn't fit comfortably into Mercedes's budget, I didn't want her arguing with Benjamin over money. I was giving Mercedes a check for five grand.

Devereaux opened the door. Everyone yelled, "Surprise!"

Scanning the faces, I began to cry when I saw Ruby, Carol, Peter, Walter, Teresa, Kevin, and Kim. Their children were here. Friends I hadn't seen in years. Echo was here holding the purse she'd borrowed earlier. When I saw Brandon, I almost screamed. I covered my mouth.

Mercedes said, "Happy fiftieth birthday, Mama. I love you."

"I love you, too," Sandara said.

Lots of "I love you" and "I love you, too" flooded the room.

Mercedes's friend, Dianna Crawford, the Realtor, approached me with a handsome man in tow. "Blake, this is your buyer. He's offered what Mercedes said you're asking. I can get the escrow started in the morning and I have a few properties to show you tomorrow."

Knowing Mercedes she asked for more than market. I was ready to move forward with getting out of this house. Especially if I was going to be here by myself. Pointing at the DJ in the corner, I said, "Hit it!"

The photographer took lots of pictures of me with my siblings, my children, minus Alexis. This was almost the perfect birthday.

The only two important people missing my celebration were probably together. My front door opened, and my jaw dropped.

Billy Blackstone looked sexier than I ever remembered.

CHAPTER 48

Spencer

The sexy sound of a single fingernail pecked three times on my door.

A rat-a-tat-tat followed. I placed my right eye to the peephole. Did she ever have an off day? Licking my lips, I admired the halter clinging to her firm tits. Her cleavage sparkled with glitter. Some of the sparkles had gotten on my shirt earlier. I liked that, so much that I'd put the same clothes on after I just got out of the shower.

The last time I'd left her standing outside my door, I was tempted to let her in. Let her suck me off the way she'd done in her mother's kitchen. I'd made the correct decision that time. Although I was pissed at Blake, it wasn't right to fuck her daughter. I could do the morally correct thing and leave Alexis standing on the other side of my door.

"You done watching me, Domino? I can feel you staring," she said, sliding her tongue out of her mouth.

Her tongue was a pretty shade of pink. Clean. Bet both sets of lips were soft and sweet. Her closed-lip smile mirrored mine. I loved Atlanta women. Most of them were tasty chocolate, darker than me. I wasn't that red brotha. I was a shade or two tanner. My skin was that cocoa color.

I let her in. Soon as I shut the door, she put her purse on the bench, pushed me against the wall. Shoved her tongue into my mouth, suctioned my tongue into hers. Abruptly she stopped. Stared at me while unzipping my pants. She yanked my boxer briefs to my knees.

"Whoa, slow down. We've got all night to do this. Let's chill," I said. Cupping my hands under her armpits, I lifted her up, pulled up my underwear.

"Your place is fresh," she said, looking around.

Damn, she smelled great. Fuck it. I removed my pants. "You can leave your . . . nah, scratch that. Give me your purse."

Surprisingly, she picked it up, then handed it to me. Yep, it was weighted. I opened the closet, placed it inside. My dick was on swole. I gripped my shit. I sat on the built-in granite countertop where Charlotte and I occasionally ate. I didn't have to ask Alexis to give me what I wanted. Alexis whipped my shit out, started bobbing and slobbering.

Abruptly, she stopped, went to the fridge, filled her hands with crushed ice. Eating a mouthful, she rubbed her hands together, then emptied what was left of the chips into the sink. Making her way back to my dick, she pulled up a barstool, sat in front of me, spread my legs, then she wrapped both hands around my shaft.

"Oh, shit!" That felt incredible. I almost blasted in her face.

I watched her gaze up at me. She opened her mouth so wide that I saw her tonsils. My shaft disappeared inside. This was some *Animal Kingdom* action. I could feel my head in her throat. Slowly, she eased my dick out, stopped at the frenulum, circled the tip of her cool tongue under my corona. She slid her hand down past my nuts, then made a fist. I swore my dick grew another three inches. She pumped three times really fast, then stopped. The visual of my cumming in her face, on those titties, in her ass, was climactic. My shit grew hard, thick, and long but that nigga was prepared not to cum quickly. I pressed two fingers at the base of my shaft.

Alexis snatched my hand off of my dick. When she started bobbing and slobbering again, this time only taking in my head, I . . . Fuck it. I yelled like a bitch. "I'm cumming! Awwww!"

Cum shot into her mouth. She kept going. My next, "Awwwww!" was louder than the last. When she swallowed my dick and my cum at the same time, my third shout was damn near soprano. "Awwwwwww! Fuck!" I pushed her ass away.

How the hell she'd done that without making a mess? Beast bitch. Best bitch. I'd definitely met my match.

"What you got to wash this down with?" she asked, licking her lips. "Make us something."

I slid my ass off the countertop as though I didn't have a spine. It wouldn't be cool to let my boy, LB, eat in that spot again. There weren't any seeds for me to clean up. I tucked my dick inside my underwear, put on my pants, and fastened my belt. Still had on my shirt. Damn.

"What you want, gurl?" She could get the whole bar and keys to my Range Rover right now.

Flipping through my cable channels, she selected Pandora's love songs. "Surprise me."

Was I supposed to go over and eat her pussy? Was I to make this drink first? Filling a glass with ice, I shook my head. I added orange Patron, pineapple Cîroc, and pineapple juice, covered the glass with a shaker. Mixed the contents well, then drained it into one glass. No more ice for that beast. I needed her to catch up to my consumption of alcohol or at least try.

"Here you go, boo."

She laughed. "No ice. That's cool. Where's your drink?"

I had something for her. Later. Real sexy, I answered, "I want to taste yours," smiling at her kitty. I slid open my patio door. "Let's sit out here." A brotha needed some fresh air.

I wasn't intimidated but females like Alexis made a bruh man up on his sex game. I wondered if LB had learned anything new. I sure did. Ice wasn't new to me. It was her chilling her hands that got me off. I'ma have to try that on . . . damn, I didn't have anybody to try it on. Damn sure nuff wasn't spittin' Alexis's game back at her. That was for lames. I had to come at her with some dumb shit.

The view of the swimming pool below was calming. Shooting fountains accented with red, green, and gold lights arched high above the platform recycling water back into the pool. The three-story waterfall sounded like waves washing ashore.

Taking her drink, I took a few swallows, then placed it on the table.

Alexis and I sat quietly until she asked, "So why did you leave my mom's? Did you know all of her brothers and sisters were coming to celebrate her birthday?"

Wow. "No. I knew Mercedes was giving her a party. I didn't know who all was going to be there." A part of me wanted to let go of the mistake Blake had made. But she'd proved that I couldn't trust her. My not being there would've never happened if she'd kept my situation between us.

"Why did you leave the party?" I asked. "I know it wasn't for me."

Alexis twisted her lips sideways, then sighed. "If I share something with you, you promise not to tell my mom."

I nodded. "Straight" was easy to say. She hadn't asked me not to tell anyone at all. I positioned my chair in front of hers so I could look into those hazel-green eyes of hers.

Alexis took a deep breath. Her eyes shifted to the right, then back at me.

"Take your time. We've got all night," I said, wondering if her culinary skills exceeded her fellatio talent. Hopefully she could make a brotha some pancakes in the morning. The way she worked her mouth, some of that couldn't be taught.

The white of her eyes slowly changed to red. Tears coated those beautiful irises. Patiently, I waited to hear what was troubling her. I knew she had a soft interior underneath that tough shell. My weakness made me vulnerable, too, at times.

"Don't let the circumstances dictate your emotions." I gave her the advice I struggled to implement in my life.

Her lips quivered. "I feel like a dude sometimes."

No shit? I wanted to cosign but I could tell she was serious. "What makes you feel that way?"

"My dad."

I shook my head. My lips tightened. I had to chill. This wasn't about my fucked-up past. "What about him?"

"That's just it. I have no idea who he is. None of us communicate with our dads. I feel it's my mom's fault I don't know my dad."

"If he didn't step up, that's not your mom's fault." I had to defend Blake on this one.

I saw the pain in her face as she struggled to hold back tears. I knew that feeling.

"I don't know why I'm even telling you this. I'm probably not making any sense," she said. She became quiet. Stared toward the blue water.

I opened my arms to her. She stood, walked around the table. I scooted my butt across the cushion until it was against the arm of the wicker chair making enough space for her to sit with me.

Pretty sure it wasn't intentional, but Alexis tilted her hips, positioned the crack of her ass over my dick. I felt her thong. We faced the pool. I cuddled her in my arms. She leaned the back of her head onto my chest.

I wanted to fuck her. The intimate urges made me want to forget I'd sexed her mom. At the moment, honestly I didn't give a damn. All that I'd done for Blake. I had no regrets. I was where Blake had forced me to be.

"Girls need their father. Boys need their mother," Alexis said. She became quiet again. Picking up her drink, she started gulping.

"Hey, slow down," I said, not wanting her to become sick. Not at my spot.

She handed the glass to me.

I wanted to know why she was hurting. Her pain had a similar intensity as mine. Deeply rooted from childhood. I tried storing my excruciating mental reels into the area of my brain responsible for losing memory, then erase it for good. Problem was, physical abuse could never be permanently erased. The little boy inside me cried for the little girl inside of her.

"You ever asked your mom where he's at? I'm sure she knows."

"If she knew, I shouldn't have to ask. She likes to pretend he doesn't exist," Alexis said, sniffling.

Yeah, I could relate. That was how my dad had done when his brother penetrated me. He acted as if I didn't exist.

Alexis started crying. "My birth certificate reads 'father unknown.' "

Damn! That was fucked up. I became chilled for a moment.

"Is that why you're here with me? To get back at your mom." Getting caught up in a game of get-back was not my intent. If Alexis and I had a cutthroat agenda, Blake would have two knives to her back and not know it.

Alexis shook her head. "I don't know. I don't know why I mistreat James and Chanel. They're good people. They're good to me."

"Who's Chanel?" I asked as if I didn't already have insight about their relay status.

"My girlfriend. She's gorgeous. Nice. One of the sweetest persons I've dated."

I wanted to ask, You have a pic? But I had to ask, "You love her?"

Alexis shook her head. Took the drink from me. Swallowed more alcohol, handed me back the glass.

"So why are you with her?" I took one swig, put it down.

"The same reason I'm with James. They take good care of me. I give them someone to love. Fair exchange. Everyone wants to be taken care of, right? Even Charlotte. Even you."

I could argue who takes care of James and Chanel to take the spotlight off of myself. I could think what Alexis had said was horrible. But her truth was what I was in search of. Someone to take good care of me. Loving them wasn't necessary.

"Have you ever tried to find your dad on your own?"

She shook her head. "I checked into it but it's too expensive. I wouldn't know where to start. That, plus, I know it'll piss my mom off."

Money didn't appear her real concern. I wasn't buying that a woman with her degree of treachery, with a master's under her belt and nearly a doctorate, didn't know how to locate a person. Alexis seemed afraid of rejection. From James, Chanel, her dad.

"And if your mom found out about our being here together. You don't think that would make her angry?" I asked, fingering Alexis's long, dark, wavy hair.

It smelled sweet like Charlotte's. I had to apologize to my ex. I wasn't going to bring Charlotte up with Alexis but the way I allowed Alexis to handle Charlotte wasn't right. I should've protected Charlotte.

Charlotte was wrong for showing up unannounced. I was wrong for not shutting Alexis down. Blake was wrong for divulging my secret. Alexis was wrong for being in my arms. Two wrongs never ended right but I wasn't ready to let Alexis go.

Aw, man. If I could get my dick sucked that way every day. I shook my head.

"What?" she asked.

Not sure if she was responding to my last question or inquiring about what I was thinking, I said, "Oh, nothing."

"Hmm. If you say so. Right now, I honestly don't care about my mother's feelings."

"Tell you what. I'll pay for you to find your dad and I'll help you. Whatever it costs, whatever it takes, I got you."

Alexis sat up, faced me. She spoke fast. "You're not just saying that. How can you be sure it's not too much if you don't know the cost?"

The only reason I told Alexis my story was because she'd opened up to me. I let her know how my dad beat my mother. How he'd beaten me. How my mother left him, started over, built a miniature empire, then killed herself. Maybe my mom felt like once she knew I was financially squared, she could get some rest.

I left out the part about my being molested. Not because I wasn't going to share. This time I became angry. "I pray I never run into that son of a bitch. I'm a man now. I'll beat his ass for all the times he hit my mother. She was nothing but good to him."

Softly Alexis said, "Spencer, I'm so sorry. Listen at me yapping it up about my problems. Do you think everybody's childhood is fucked up?"

I shook my head. There were people like my boy, LB, who had a great upbringing. His parents were still happily married. He was a cool dude. Seldom saw him get upset with customers that I would've refused to service.

"I do believe that if a person lives long enough their life is going to eventually be fucked up on some level. Relationships. Jobs. Finances. We either had 'em. Got 'em. Or we're gonna get 'em."

I didn't want to go all the way in. I doubted Alexis had more integrity than Blake. But Alexis was transparent. I'd expect her to draw a weapon. Not Blake.

Alexis stood. I stood.

She strutted through my living room, went into the bedroom. I followed her.

Slowly, she bent over, stepped out of her gold thong. Stuffed it into my mouth. I pulled it out, stuffed it into hers. Staring into my eyes, she took small steps as she walked in circles around me. Three times. She flung her thong somewhere. I didn't care where it landed. I wanted to keep it.

She stopped in front of me, unbuckled my pants, pulled my boxer briefs to my knees. Scanned me head to toe, grabbed my dick. Held it. I coughed for her. She gave me a closed-lip smile.

I was not a big-dick black man on her auction block. One thing Venus Domino taught me was, *Son, always know your self-worth.*

I held Alexis's wrist, broke her grip, licked the inside of her palm. Curling my tongue to her index finger, I drew it deep into my mouth. She was definitely a different kind of lover. If Blake ever questioned me, I'd never blame my intentions on alcohol. This was some shit I wanted to experience.

She shoved me onto my bed, then straddled me.

Damn, she was stronger than I'd imagined.

I kept still while she undressed me from the waist down. She rose on all fours like a cheetah, leaned forward, swept my body with her hair, licked my face, then stared into my eyes. I still had on the red button-up I'd bought for Blake's party. The vodka had me buzzin'. In a good way.

Alexis gripped the insides of my shirt, yanked in opposite directions. Buttons flew. I grabbed her halter dress. Ripped the lace down the middle. Her nails dug into my chest. Not enough to draw blood but it hurt so good I grunted from my gut.

"Shut the fuck up, bitch," she demanded.

That was the second time she'd called me a bitch. I liked it. Biting my bottom lip, I flipped her onto her back, squeezed her breasts. Her eyes narrowed, lips parted. She exhaled. The pain and pleasure showed in her face as she took a deep breath, held it. Her eyes widened. Yeah, I'd met my match but I'd never admit it.

"Damn Domino," she said, exhaling.

"Shut up, bitch," I said, choking her with one hand. With feathery strokes, I played with her nipple.

Letting go of her throat, I smashed her titties together, twirled her nipples between my thumb and pointing finger. She let out a whimpering moan.

Narrowing my eyes, I stared into hers. Damn. She was so beautiful. Slowly I closed then opened my eyes.

My dick was flaccid. *What the fuck, dude? Get up, nigga! Get up!*

I stroked my shit. This was the pussy I'd fantasized about. Dreamt about. Spreading her thighs, I stiffened my tongue, flicked it in an upward position against her clit. Then I suctioned her clit. Taking more of her into my mouth, I swallowed the sweetest nectar I'd tasted. I sucked her engorged shaft like it was one of her fingers.

Gripping her hips, I pulled her to the edge, I got comfortable on my knees. My shit never stayed soft. This was a first. Getting up, I told her, "Sit on my face." That way I could stroke my dick while she rode my face. This nigga was going to get hard.

I propped my head on a pillow. She straddled my face, put her pussy in my mouth. I sucked her clit for almost an hour. My mouth never tired. My dick never got hard. I decided to put my finger in her ass.

She started leaking into my mouth. I pushed my finger deeper into her rectum. More fluids flowed. This time into my ears. Shit felt eerie. Like I was underwater. If I stopped, I'd mess up her flow. I penetrated her asshole like I was fucking her until she . . . *gushed* in my mouth.

Damn, that shit turned me on. I had to block my airway to keep her juices from going down the wrong way. Alexis reached behind her, touched my dick. She got up, took off her torn dress, tossed it on the bed, put on my shirt.

That shit turned me on. Her breasts were partially exposed. Her heels were still on her feet.

I put on a pair of sweatpants, and followed her to the living room. She hadn't turned around. When I saw her ass barely covered with my red shirt, my dick started rising. Opening the closet, she removed her purse. Held it by the straps. I pulled down my sweats, tugged on her purse. Dropping it to the floor, she turned around then bent over.

For the first time, I penetrated her real slow. Her pussy was wet and tight. I teased her clit. She leaned on the stove. I pressed my chest to her back, teased her clit as I continued grinding deep into her pussy.

A condom was necessary but not readily available. There was no way I was pulling out. Couldn't take the chance that my manhood wouldn't hang in there long enough for me to continue what I started. Didn't want to lose this opportunity.

I howled like a wolf in heat in the middle of the night releasing what seemed to be all of the seeds left in my nuts. She waited a moment then pushed my dick out with her muscles. Semen dripped from her vagina onto my hardwood floor.

Alexis wiped herself with a paper towel, tossed it in the trash. My dick hung south but that motherfucka felt fantastic! I pulled up my sweats. She picked up her purse, closed my shirt, placed her hand on the knob, opened the door.

Damn! I did not expect to see my boy, LB.

His eyes went up and down Alexis's body. Her thong was still somewhere in my apartment.

"I stopped by to check on you, man. You ain't have that much to drink that you got my girl up in here. Why the hell she wearing your shirt, bruh?"

"Hey, LB. It's not what you think. This is my shirt," Alexis said. "Come with me."

My boy gave my crotch the evil eye, then followed ole gurl. Whateva. I went to my bedroom, got in my bed, stroked my dick while replaying that last scene in my mind.

Should we pretend what just happened didn't? Technically, we had sex. We didn't make love. Okay, fuck it. We did it. I was not going to mess up a sexual high feeling guilty about what Blake could have prevented.

I turned off the light, buried the side of my face into the pillow, then slept like a baby.

CHAPTER 49

Blake

Last night with my family was epic.
That many relatives hadn't been under the same roof at the same time since our mother's funeral. And seeing Billy Blackstone. OMG!

I wasn't sure if Mercedes found and invited him because she didn't want me to date Spencer or what. All I knew was I was happy he was here! It was my party and Billy turned out to be the perfect present.

"Well, top of the morning indeed," he said in his deep sultry voice. Gently, he fingered my hair away from my face. He rubbed his hand over my hair, then kissed me. "You are amazing. I want you to know I had no intentions of making love to you. I came to wish you a happy birthday, and to tell you something."

Darkness made way for the sun beaming through my blinds. For the second day I woke up in my bed but last night I was not alone. I didn't ask Billy if he wanted to make love again. I pulled back the sheets, climbed on top of my first love.

"Tell me later. We don't have much time. We still have to be quiet though," I told him. "I have no idea who stayed or who left."

I felt like we were back in high school. His dick seemed bigger than I remembered. Felt better than I could recall. But he wasn't better than Spencer. Grinding my hips I wondered if Spencer and Alexis had sex.

"Blake, you are just as beautiful as the day I first laid eyes on you. No, I take that back. You look better now."

"Thanks," I said, winding counterclockwise, then clockwise. I was excited!

His dick filled me up in many ways. Not the way Spencer's did. There were no tears on the horizon for Billy. All smiles. I gathered my hair on top of my head, posed, then let it fall. His fingertip touched my neck, slid between my breasts, touched my navel, then teased my clit. "Are we going to see each other again?"

Billy had aged gracefully. His gray and black hair was cut low. I rubbed his head. Billy answered, "I don't know. Maybe."

I thought he'd ask me a follow-up question. When he didn't, I told him, "Don't let this be our last time. I hope this is the beginning of something special." I looked into his eyes and smiled.

Billy smiled right back at me, then said, "Okay. I'll let you take the lead."

"Oh, no," I said.

"Oh, yeah." He thrust his erection deeper inside of me. "You're good at taking charge."

I knew he had options of seeing other people. This was Atlanta. We both did. What I didn't know was what type of relationship he wanted with me, if any. Not wanting to come across desperate, I focused on climaxing.

"Damn, I'm cumming . . . again," he said. His mouth opened. I placed my hand over his lips, muffled his grunting.

I closed my eyes and enjoyed the moment. I came on his dick. My orgasm wasn't explosive but it was pleasurable. If things didn't work out with Spencer, Billy could be my backup.

Climbing off of him, I said, "We need to take a shower and get dressed."

I went first. I was not getting sexy. I slipped on a black T-shirt, fitted black jeans, and flat black sandals with a one-inch heel. I waited for Billy. Watched him put on his tailored tan designer suit from last night.

"I don't know who's here but you're welcome to stay for breakfast."

He kissed me. Shook his head. "I already had breakfast and dinner and not in that order. Thanks. I wish I could stay but I have an early appointment with my attorney."

I did not want him to leave thinking I would be the one pursuing him. I told him, "Call me later." Later could be today, next week, or never. I told him the truth. "It was good reconnecting with you. Take care of yourself."

Billy frowned. "You act like we're never going to see each other again."

"You decide," I told him. "Oh, what did you want to tell me?"

"Not the right time. You'll find out soon enough."

"What's that supposed to mean?" I asked.

He opened my bedroom door. The smell of bacon floating under my nose brought back memories of when I was a kid. I was shocked to see Mercedes passing by.

She stared at Billy. "I didn't invite you as an overnight guest. Did you tell her?"

Billy shook his head. "I'll let myself out."

"Do that," Mercedes said.

"No, Billy. Wait." I went back into my room, picked up my cell, then escorted Billy to the front door. "Don't worry about Mercedes. She's being protective. What is that you wanted to tell me?"

He shook his head. "I'll tell you when the time is right."

I could not be bothered with the shenanigans. I watched Billy get into his car. Turning to get another whiff of the bacon, I bumped into Mercedes.

"Thank God all of my cousins have left. You embarrassed me, Mother. This is why you have a hard time finding a good man. You haven't seen Billy in years and you opened your legs for him. No gratitude or loyalty to Spencer for being here with and for you."

Mercedes didn't have the details on my situation with Spencer. Billy was my first love and I didn't see any harm in sleeping with him after my birthday party. "Spencer made his decision not to come back. I made mine. Let it go, Alexis."

"I'm Mercedes," she said, exiting my front door.

I'm the mother. She's the child. I yelled out, "Wait until you turn fifty!"

I was as done with Mercedes as she was with me. To make sure she didn't feel I was indebted to her, I'd write her a check for ten thousand. I went into the kitchen. My oldest sister greeted me. She was sixty.

"Morning, party girl. I saw Billy leaving," she said teasingly. "Was he one of your presents?" She whispered, "Was it still as good as high school?"

"Morning, Ruby." I wasn't a little girl anymore. I nodded real slow. "You up early. I heard all of the kids left."

"They claimed they had things to do." Using a spatula, in one sweep she flipped the row of strips in the cast-iron skillet. I'd forgotten I had that skillet.

"Cooking for all of us brings back so many memories, Sis," she said. I smiled. "What. You mean all of *us* are still here?"

Carol, Teresa, and Kim dragged in. "I'm getting too old for these late-night-shindigs-get-up-early days," Carol said. She was fifty-eight and the second oldest.

"I'm so glad all of you came," I said. "I wish I could turn fifty all over again tonight."

Ruby laughed. "Me too! You think that Mercedes was taking no for an answer? Out of all your girls, Sis. That's your right hand. We sat up talking a long time last night. Keep her close. She needs you."

Mercedes didn't need anybody. Ruby wasn't one to interfere but she was always there when I needed her. Frowning, I wondered what Mercedes told Ruby.

Ruby asked, "Why you acting like that man didn't die in this house?"

Okay, I wondered what else Mercedes told Ruby.

Kim chimed in. "I wanna know did you get some dick from Billy last night?"

"Last night? You mean this morning, too," Ruby said. "He just left."

Shaking my head, I smiled. "Where are the fellas?"

"Where else," Teresa said. She was a year younger than I. Her fiftieth was a year away.

"Uh-huh. Don't try to count the bruhs out," Kevin said. He was the baby boy. Forty-seven. Kim was the baby of us all. Forty-six.

Peter and Walter marched in. We stood around the island. Ruby stirred a large pot of grits. "Breakfast is ready. Everybody hold hands, let's give thanks and y'all go sit at the table and wait for me to serve you."

I hadn't used my dining table for a gathering since Alexis got her master's. I hadn't seen nor heard from her since last night. I had a feeling that was the last I'd see of Billy. I wanted to let go of Ruby's and Kevin's hands, get in my car, and go to Spencer's.

"Heavenly Father," my oldest brother, Peter, said. "We thank You for family, our health, friends, and this food. Bless the preparer, the parents of the pig, and the pig."

We laughed.

He continued, "Dear God, we ask that You watch over our sister, Blake. Be with her in those moments of silence when no one except You will hear her cries. If there should be any one of us in need of a special blessing, I ask that they receive it. When each of us depart to our destinations, I pray that we arrive safely, Heavenly Father. Thank you for allowing each of us to be alive and well. I pray for Your continued mercy and forgiveness for our sins, Dear Lord. In Jesus's name we ask these things of You."

Everybody said, "Amen."

Walter, my brother who was a year younger than Peter, said in his Georgia accent, "Boi, you should've been a politician, instead of a doctor. You still long-winded. Now Ruby gotta reheat them grits."

"You have a wonderful wife," Kim said. "That's why you don't know that those grits are still hot as hell. Ask my ex-husband. He tried that mess like Fortune. The Crystals don't play that."

Okay, so everyone knew that Fortune had beaten me but no one said anything directly to me. Fine. I knew we still had that kind of one-for-all, all-for-one family. They knew Fortune was married. None of them condoned nor condemned my choice to be with him. And none of us cared that he was gone.

I said, "Don't start none." In unison everybody said, "Won't be none." That was one of our mother's favorite sayings and the confirmation I needed to know they still had my back.

The youngest and oldest men sat at opposite heads of the table. One at a time, Ruby prepared our plates.

I thought, *Thank You, Lord.* If it were meant for Spencer and me to be together, we would. But in this very moment, I was thankful that blessings were all around me.

CHAPTER 50

Blake

Ruby stacked the dishwasher with plates, silverware, and glasses. Carol pitched in by hand-washing pots and pans. Truthfully, I was ready for them to get out.

Soon as my siblings left my house, I was in transit to Spencer's house. I dialed him twice. Same old crap. One ring. Voice mail. Spencer could choose not to answer the door like he'd done with his phone but I'd followed a car into the complex. Waited on the fifth floor until a person finally exited the building.

I knocked twice on Spencer's door, then waited. No answer.

Knock. Knock. My knuckles hit harder this time. No response.

"Spencer," I called out, not caring whether or not his neighbors would hear me.

I heard the lock click. My heart pounded. When I saw him, I froze.

He stood before me. Dripping wet. A red towel tied at his waist, the imprint of his hanging manhood commanded my attention.

"I'm up here," he said with a closed-lip smile. "You coming in?" Walking away, he left the door opened.

Slowly, I crossed the threshold where it had all begun. Ten days ago felt like an eternity.

"Lock my door please," he said, sitting on his sofa.

I placed my purse on the blue bench.

Spencer propped his feet on the coffee table. He folded his arms across his bare chest.

I wanted him to hold me. There were words that needed to be spoken. Obviously, he wasn't going to go first.

"I'll start," I said, sitting on the edge of the sofa.

"Rightfully so," he said.

"Spencer, I love you."

He smiled. Laughed once. His neck swayed back. "Oh, really?"

"Yes, really," I said, sadly hoping he'd feel that I was sincere. "You mind if I stay here for a while?"

He frowned. "Stay as in live here until you sell your home or you mean visit for a while?"

"Visit."

Spencer hunched his shoulders with folded arms. I tugged to pry them apart. He shrugged. "Don't touch me, Blake. You have a strange way of showing love," he told me, staring ahead. "Today's not good. I really don't want to see you. I have nothing to say to you. You need to leave. I have to go to work."

Wow. I know I made a mistake but did I deserve this? I touched him. He pulled away.

"Look at me. Please, babe."

His eyes shifted in my direction. I thought his closed-lip smile when he'd opened the door meant we were somewhat cool. He let me come in. Now he was stone cold. I shouldn't have come yet I couldn't go.

"What?" he said with an attitude. He shook his head, exhaled a puff of air. "I swear. I can't stand the sight of you right now."

If his intent was to make me feel like shit, he'd done that. "I apologize."

"For what?"

Shaking my head, I kept quiet.

"What if I told you, 'I fucked Alexis.' How would you feel?"

Tears clung to my eyes. I wanted to slap him. "You wouldn't do that to me."

Spencer didn't know Billy but what if I answered Spencer, "We'd be even," and left it at that. The probability of Billy meeting Spencer was slim but if he was serious. Alexis. She was the flesh of my flesh.

His arms unfolded. His hands gestured toward me. He yelled, "How the fuck you think I feel? I never thought you'd do what the fuck you did! I asked your ass not to." He shook his head.

I jumped. Moved away from him. Stood. Backed up. Calmly, I said, "Please don't yell at me."

"No, fuck you, Blake!"

"Spencer, please stop," I begged.

"You show up at my place unannounced," he said. I stared at the veins popping out in his neck. "Acting all cool and shit like nothing fucking happened. And you want me to . . . what the fuck you want from me? Dick?" He unwrapped his towel, then wrapped it back. Shook his head. "You will never get this dick again."

I was more concerned about how nervous he made me when he yelled at me. I didn't think he'd hit me after what he'd told me about his mom. I knew I should leave as he'd demanded but I had to be sure what he'd said was what he wanted. Leaving wasn't what I wanted.

Shaking his head, he said, "What?! You think I'ma lay hands on you? Never that. Believe that. I asked you what you came here for?!" He stood. Opened then tucked the red towel tighter to his waist. Sat. Crossed his arms again.

Damn! He had to let me see the dick. That was on purpose.

"You're telling the truth. I was trying to deny it but she was here." I sniffed the air. "Yep, I smell Alexis's perfume," I said. "I see her glitter on your sofa." I looked at my hands. There were a few specks on my fingers.

Silence divided us. Spencer didn't confirm nor deny. I wanted him to tell me he didn't fuck my daughter. Even if it were a lie I needed to believe he'd never do that to me. To us.

I walked into his bedroom. The fitted sheet near the headboard was wet. The flat sheet on the floor sparkled. I picked it up; tossed it onto the bed. A gold thong fell out. The dress she'd worn to my house yesterday was ripped and on the floor. I picked up the thong, stormed into the living room. I hurled it in his face. It fell to his lap. He placed it beside his thigh.

Calmly, he said, "Get out of my house," without moving.

"You did fuck her! You bastard! You fucked my daughter! How could you do that to me!" Standing directly in front of him on the other side of the coffee table, I started crying. He scanned me from head to toe. For the first time, I wished I'd changed into something sexier before I'd rushed over here. I must've looked a hot mess. That was how I felt.

Earlier I was surrounded by people who loved me. This, I didn't know what this was. But I knew what it wasn't.

He pressed his lips together, and his eyes glazed over with tears that didn't fall down his cheeks. He curled his fingers into a fist, pressed his thumb to his mouth. Pointing at me, he said, "You have a lot of nerve."

I was not going to be outsmarted by a guy who was young enough to be my son. "What do you want to do?" I asked him. "You want to call it quits. You want me to leave?"

He nodded. "Yes, I want you to leave."

"I want to hear you tell me we're done and you'll never have to say it again." I stood still. He didn't move. I sat beside him. He stood. He opened his door.

Drying my tears, I had to take this one like the grown woman I was. I picked up the thong, put it in my purse. I walked toward him.

"I love you, Spencer."

He leaned over, passionately kissed me. We held each other. Our tongues traded places. I cried. He gently pushed me to the other side of the threshold.

"I'm gonna miss you, Blake. Take care of yourself."

Slowly, I shook my head in disbelief as Spencer closed his door. No one could hear me screaming, *I hate you!* inside my head but in my heart, I loved him.

It was time for me to have a woman-to-woman talk with my daughter. Instead of exiting in the direction of my car, I went directly to Alexis's apartment.

CHAPTER 51

Alexis

Bam! Bam! Bam!

"What the hell?!" I opened my eyes, checked the time on my phone. "Damn. One o'clock in the day?" I couldn't believe it. I stared at my cell. Shit! I'd overslept.

LB was buried under my sheets like a Chihuahua.

Three missed calls from Domino. I hoped he hadn't shown up at my door unannounced to talk about last night. What was done was done.

I had zero respect for LB though. Any guy who would knowingly feast behind his boy was stupid. He couldn't possibly believe he'd gotten my pussy that wet that fast. The person at my door definitely wasn't Chanel or James. They'd never have shown up without permission.

Returning Spencer's call, I put my cell on speaker.

Spencer answered, "Hey, Alexis."

I asked him, "What's up, Domino?"

"Your—"

Bam! Bam! Bam!

I interrupted him. "Hold on a sec."

Uncovering his head, LB leaned close to my phone, then asked, "You want me to get that, sweetheart?" Then he puckered his lips toward mine.

What?! That was a bitch move by LB. I shoved his face away with my hand. He didn't realize neither Domino nor I gave a damn about his being at my house.

Firmly I told LB, "Do not touch my doorknob. What you need to do is get dressed. We have to get to the bank before they close at four."

LB was not supposed to be here and I'd missed class. We were supposed to hook back up later. But it was my call, I'd let him stay, so I had to be cool with it. By the end of this day, I was going to make him wish he'd never met me. LB was taking me to his bank, keeping his word to drop a grand on me, then he didn't know it but he was taking me shopping. He was going to carry my bags. Staring at him, I wanted to strap on and fuck the shit out of him and not in a sensual way. I was pretty sure I'd told him to leave my house at some point.

He frowned. Stared at my cell. "You don't need me with you to deposit *your* check."

"No, bitch. I need you with me to cash it." What if his check wasn't negotiable? The thought of what I'd done to the last guy who tried to play me surfaced.

Ma, I swear I left the money on your nightstand. Maybe I left it in the bathroom. I'm not sure. Maybe you move it.

A man who offered three or more explanations for one situation was lying. My misplacing fifteen hundred dollars in my house never had and never will happen. The cash was on my nightstand when we got in my bed. I noticed it was gone after he'd left. That meant, he'd pocketed it. Once he'd gotten what he came for, he tried to play me for a fool. No one uses Alexis Crystal.

The next day I'd dressed super provocative. Put on the highest spiked heels I had, my red power suit, strapped my piece to my thigh underneath my skirt, went inside his corporate building, bypassed his secretary, entered his office, then locked his door. There was no gratuitous pussy or dick-sucking in store for him. I came out with three grand, cash.

Bam! Bam! Bam!

LB got out of bed, put on his clothes, then headed downstairs.

Damn. Whoever it was they were determined. Better not be that bitch Charlotte. I went downstairs naked.

"You can't open the door like that," LB said, staring at me.

It could be a number of pissed-off lovers. Next time I moved, I'd make sure the building had real security. I peeped through the hole. What did she want? I opened the door.

She stormed in. Looked at LB. "So you're fucking both of them?" she asked.

Pretty much. What was it to her? My pussy wasn't hers.

"No, ma'am," LB answered.

I shook my head. This guy here was the worst.

"I'm not talking to you," my mom said to him, then rolled her eyes at me.

I laughed at her. "Seriously, Mother. You left your house in jeans and a tee. You look a hot mess. You're never going to keep a younger man if you don't get yourself together."

"Copy," LB said.

Exhaling, nonchalantly I asked, "What's up, Mom." She had no idea how done I was with the Spencer situation. I was the one who told her not to have sex with Spencer.

Her comment didn't get a reaction from me but it made LB swell. "Is that true? You did Spence?"

"Don't mind her," I said, making my way to my refrigerator. "Mom, you want something to drink? LB?"

"I'm good. I'll get out of y'all way," he said, trotting upstairs.

He didn't have anything to get upstairs. I followed him. He handed me a robe. "Don't you think you should put something on?"

"Thanks. I'll catch up to you later. Don't disappear," I told him. I grabbed the nape of his neck, kissed him hard, then pushed him away. Heading back down the steps, this time he followed me.

Standing in my kitchen, I looked at my mom sitting on my sofa and said, "What's up, Blake?"

I hadn't called my mom by her name in a long time. Her hair was slicked back the way it was on her birthday, except not as neat. No lipstick or lashes. It was obvious she was in a hurry to get to Spencer's. The way my mom looked right now, stressed and no makeup, I'd give her fifty-four easily.

"Call me Blake again."

This wasn't about what I'd called her. I was tired of being respectful to her when she'd disregarded my wishes to know my father.

"Blake. You're not bold enough to do to me what Fortune did to you."

"I'ma let myself out," LB said.

"Yes, do that," my mother said.

"Don't hold on to that check too long," LB said, closing my door.

My mother didn't wait for me to sit beside her. She met me in front of the stove. I had a flashback of Spencer hitting this Good Good in his kitchen.

I folded my arms, sighed heavily. She came to my house. If she didn't say something soon, I was going upstairs to take a shower.

"Did you fuck Spencer? Yes or no?"

Matching her obnoxious tone, I asked, "Who's my daddy? You know where he's at? Yes or no? I'm serious. You tell me the truth. I'll do the same."

Her game was straight old-school. If my mom had tried this approach on an ATL female, she'd be in the emergency room at Grady's. I swallowed a mouthful of juice, walked around her, sat on my sofa, turned on the television for a welcome distraction. Even if she told me, I'd never tell her what happened between Spencer and me.

She sat on the edge of my couch, turned toward me. "So you want to play games. So this is why you're upset with me? You want to know where to find your dad?" Digging in her purse, she threw my gold thong in my face. "You left something at Spencer's last night."

It fell in my lap. "Yeah, I'm sure they only made one of these. Good lookin' out." Glad I'd gotten one of my favorites back, I set it aside. Started flipping through channels. "You act like because you don't want to tell me, I don't have the right to know. It's your fault I'm this way. If you're not going to tell me who my father is, just leave, Mom."

My mom sighed, moved closer to me. She placed my head on her shoulder. I stayed there. I loved my mom. I'd never tell her the details of what had transpired with Domino.

"Baby, I know I didn't make the best decisions. Your dad was married when I conceived you. His wife was pregnant. Everything was good until I told him I was pregnant too. He swore I did it on purpose. Then he told me you weren't his and to never contact him again. Later he agreed to a paternity test to prove he was right. He was wrong. So I'm sure who he is. I don't know where he's at."

"So that's where Sandara gets poor judgment from. You."

"That's not fair, Alexis."

"You're the one who's not fair."

"Fine. You wanna know his name? It's Conner Rogers. I honestly have no idea where he's at. After he said don't contact him, I didn't. That's the truth."

Knowing it would piss her off, I told her, "If you don't mind. Spencer said he'd help me find my dad."

"You know what. Things are over between Spencer and me. But don't involve him in the search for your father. That's my responsibility. I'll help you."

Lifting my head from my mom's shoulder, I hugged her. "I'm sorry, Mama, for talking to you that way. I won't involve Spencer. You still want to know if we did anything?" I asked, breaking our bond.

My mom exhaled. Nodded.

"Promise me you won't get mad at us."

"I guess that's a yes."

"Not exactly," I said.

"If you're going to lie, Alexis. I'd rather not know. It's not that serious anymore." She stood. "I'll see what I can find out about your dad between house hunting and the end of my vacation."

I escorted my mom to the door. "Mama?"

"Save it, Alexis. I don't need to know. It doesn't matter."

It did matter. I told her, "Spencer is in love with you. I wanted to have sex with him but his dick didn't get hard. And anytime a man's dick does not get hard for a woman he's trying to get it up for, that means he's in love with someone else. Give him time to get over whatever you did."

"He told you?" she asked.

"Told me what?" Now I was curious to know why he was upset with my mom.

"Nothing." My mom kissed me on the cheek, then left.

Texting Spencer, I lied to my mom. Told her we wanted to but didn't do anything.

He hit me back, Cool

I was hoping he would've said, "I'll tell her the truth." Being cool with it meant he still wanted my mother. I wasn't done with his dick.

I showered, dressed, went to LB's bank. Cashed his check without being questioned, then drove to James's house.

After all the madness, I had to fuck somebody to release my frustrations.

CHAPTER 52

Blake

Sitting at the bar, I knew I shouldn't have come here.
I promised I wouldn't chase another man. Again I'd lied to myself. He shouldn't have mentioned he had to work today. I had things to do but I'd put everything on hold to see him, including furniture shopping. Instead, I ended up at his apartment, my daughter's apartment, and now I was at his job. Waiting on him.

Dianna Crawford had three properties scheduled for me to see in Buckhead. I asked her to reschedule until tomorrow. I wasn't in the right frame of mind to make a decision that didn't move my relationship with Spencer forward. Not being chill with him, I didn't feel like doing anything, including being in this seat.

A text came in from Echo. Meet me for drinks. My treat. I'm at Twist. Not wanting to say yes or no, I'd respond later. Right now I couldn't move from this stool.

I didn't want my girlfriend to know I was emotionally caught up this soon. Being in a funk was my choice. I should have accepted Echo's invitation, gotten my ass up, gone across the street, and enjoyed happy hour. Maybe I'd have met someone new.

I wasn't sure why the restaurants called it "happy," when neither the food nor the drinks were discounted. Georgia had a law. If happy hour was offered one day, it had to be extended seven days a week. They'd changed the no sale of alcohol on Sundays. They could permit bars to select days that were best to lower the cost of food and drinks. Saving a few dollars didn't matter to me. I was rattling on in my head to pass time.

I was going to profit four hundred thousand on the sale of my property. Plus, I'd deposited the money Vanessa had given me. A half a million for my birthday wasn't bad so why was I soaking when I could be anywhere in the world having a great time?

There were other options outside of meeting Echo and waiting on Spencer. I could walk to a different restaurant or I could drive home if my blood level wasn't already over the limit. I chuckled at the thought that, if they were the only two who knew I was behind bars, who'd bail me out first? Spencer? Or Alexis? I replayed my earlier conversations with them.

"Another?" LB asked.

His interruption was timely. Momentarily he'd stopped me from trying to justify why pursuing Spencer was necessary. Didn't want to let my Nikko go. Didn't want an old-ass man or one my age. Why did mixologists offer alcohol to patrons who clearly didn't need another drink?

Staring at LB, I shook my head then nodded.

Mimicking me, he asked, "Is that a yes or a no?"

"Yes."

LB was an attractive young man. He didn't have sex appeal like Spencer. That was my opinion. I watched him pour the vodka over ice, shake the contents, then fill martini glass number three. He garnished my drink with three olives then set it in front of me.

"You want to order something to eat?" he asked in a suggestive tone like I needed to consume food.

I shook my head. I didn't have an appetite.

Before LB had met Alexis, his life was probably normal. Uneventful. Underneath his professionalism I could tell there was something he wanted to say but hadn't. My daughter didn't want LB. Spencer didn't want Alexis. Hell, Spencer might not want me. I prayed that wasn't true.

I exhaled, wondering if any two people were truly satisfied, in love, and faithful with each other. Why was being happy with one person so damn difficult?

"He won't be here for another three hours. You sure you don't want to order something to eat?"

Slowly, my eyes closed then opened. I nodded. "I'll wait." Spencer was worth it. I was more sad than inebriated. That could change once this glass became empty. "You okay?" I asked him.

Slowly looking away, he bit his bottom lip. "Let me check on my other customers. I'll be back to answer that."

He seemed sad too. Almost two weeks ago, LB was our jovial server. Bright. Bubbly. Eager to serve. Now he was tending to tables in the bar area and pouring drinks like it was a chore. As though he'd rather be someplace else. I saw the disappointment in his eyes. His other customers may have not noticed. They were greeted with a wide smile. But the eyes didn't lie. I was certain LB saw the hurt in mine, too.

Tapping on my Facebook app, I busied myself with following Sandara and a few of my friends. I saw a post on Brandon's page. I had the urge to reply and congratulate him on his new boo but I knew by the time I returned to work next week he'd have another man and a new side dude.

LB placed an order of fried zucchini fingers sprinkled with Parmesan cheese, in front of me. "Eat something, please."

I nodded knowing I wouldn't but his gesture was considerate. "Do you want to tell me something?"

He looked up. "Not sure if it's appropriate."

Reassuring him, I said, "Sure it is."

"Alexis borrowed a thousand dollars from me today, now she's telling me it was a gift."

I pressed my lips together to keep from laughing.

He became quiet. "Excuse me. I have to close out a customer."

I think he left out of embarrassment. Pulling out my book, I wrote a check for one thousand dollars payable to Lawrence Bennett. That child worked hard for his money. Maybe I should tear it up. Teach him a lesson. That wasn't the smartest idea considering at some point I might need him more than he needs me. I resumed scanning my news feed on Facebook.

Sandara had posted pics from my party that made me smile. That pink corset was sexy. The skirt kissed all of my curves. The top pushed up my boobs. I exhaled. Another generous gesture from Spencer.

Zooming in on my face, I noticed a few crow's feet around my eyes. My breasts could sit higher. My ass could be rounder. Waist smaller. I was definitely investing in cosmetic surgery. Echo didn't know yet but post-op she was going to have to care for me.

Mercedes would talk me out of it if I told her. Alexis would make me feel stupid for trying to have the body of a thirty-year-old. Sandara and Devereaux would support me. Was I considering this hoping Spencer would be more attracted to me?

Scanning the sixty-nine comments, I scrolled down, paused, then read, "The most beautiful woman in the world deserves all the happiness her heart can hold." When did he become friends with my baby?

Billy Blackstone and Sandara? Friends? Why? I looked closer at some of the other pics with both of them in it. *Okay, Blake. Stop it. You're reading into things because of Alexis.*

My breathing became heavy. Was Billy trying to tell me he knew Sandara?

I scanned and saw another familiar person's comment. "Sorry I missed the party." When did he befriend Sandara? I realized why Mercedes didn't care for social media. I'd never thought to look up Spencer online. I was tempted to view his page and send him a friend request.

I definitely didn't want to be like Brandon. When he was blocked by a guy he'd watch their pages from his other account. I was so obsessed trying to figure out what to do next that I hadn't noticed he was behind the bar until I heard, "Hello, Fabulous."

I didn't move my hands or my head. Butterflies swarmed my vodka-infused stomach. As I slowly looked up, my heart pounded. "I have to go shopping tomorrow for furniture for my new home in Buckhead. Wanna go with me?" What I really meant to ask was, "Wanna move in with me?"

He smiled. "You don't want that."

On the inside, I cheesed a wide smile. How was it that seeing his face, hearing his voice, changed my sadness to joy in a split second?

Speaking low, I answered, "Please, Spencer. You don't know how disgusted I am with myself. I miss you so much." I blinked to wash away the tears before they'd plop into my drink. "Whatever happened between you and Alexis, I don't care. I don't want to ever lose your friendship." *Okay, now I'm sounding desperate.*

"You drove?"

I nodded.

"You valet?"

I nodded again.

He took my drink, then said, "You're in no condition to drive. Give me your ticket. I'ma get you an Uber ride."

"I can call my daughter, Mercedes."

"I got you," he said, tapping on a few keys.

A few minutes later he escorted me to the black town car parked outside the Nike store. "Did I embarrass you? Is that why you're sending me away?"

That closed-lip smile surfaced again. He placed a folded piece of paper in my hand.

"Make sure my girl gets to her destination safely," he told the driver.

Spencer closed my door. I stared at him until he was out of sight. Unfolding the paper, I removed a key card, then read, "Presidential Suite."

The driver pulled up to valet at the Oriental. The attendant opened my door.

"There must be some mistake," I told the driver. I refused to get out of the car at a five-star hotel.

"This is your destination, ma'am. It's all taken care of," he said, holding the door open.

Standing in the lobby, I fingered the key. I made my way to the top floor. First, I knocked on the door. There was no answer. I knocked again, waited, then I used my key to access the room.

I gasped when I saw red roses everywhere. The Jacuzzi wasn't in the bathroom, it was inside the bedroom filled with water and lots of white petals. Oh, my, God. Douche. I probably needed one. I hadn't used a condom with Billy. Spencer hadn't done all this not to have sex with me. *Damn, Blake.* I wished I'd kept my legs closed last night.

Lingerie and a pair of red boxer briefs were on top of the king-size bed. Red stilettoes were propped up in a box at the foot of the bed. Champagne was on ice. I picked up the teddy. Underneath there was a handwritten note.

Fabulous, I miss you. Truly Yours, Spencer Domino

I went into the living room. The skyline downtown was beautiful. The Georgia Power building stood out. If there was any way I could've known Spencer would do all of this for me, I wouldn't have given myself to Billy.

I hurried to the bathroom, turned on the faucet, let the water get hot, lathered up a face towel, then swiped front to back between my legs. Sniffing the towel, I inhaled afraid that Spencer would notice if he went down on me. Wishing I'd worn a dress, I removed my jeans, cleaned my pussy properly, then put my clothes back on. I heard the front door. Oh, no. I searched for a place to put the wet towel, the only place he wouldn't go. I put it in my purse. I spritzed perfume in the air, then waved my hand to spread the fragrance.

"In here, babe!" I called out. Taking one last glance in the mirror, I wished I would've taken more time to put on my favorite lashes.

The bathroom door opened. Spencer entered the room. "I knew you wouldn't start without me."

I smiled at him. "I haven't told you but I love the way you look without your locks."

He nodded. "Too much crazy energy. It was time. I want us to start over."

I agreed. "How? When did you have time?" I asked. "I mean, to do all of this."

"We make time for the one we love. LB gave me a heads-up that you were getting wasted at the bar waiting on me."

I laughed. "Can't argue the truth. Oh, no. I forgot to give him his check." It was probably soggy inside my purse.

Spencer kissed me, then said, "My truth is, I think I'm falling for you, Fabulous."

CHAPTER 53

Spencer

Earlier LB had texted me a pic of Fabulous with Heads up. She's at the bar getting blasted. She's waiting for you.

Guys didn't hold grudges like women. LB was starting to see Alexis wasn't serious about him. I could've put him on that but he wasn't feeling me. It was best he came to his own understanding that Alexis was using him. Giving her that G made bruh wake up.

Zooming in on the photo, I saw that Fabulous's slicked-back ponytail was a straight mess. Her eyes were glazed like an old-fashioned doughnut. She still had on the same black T-shirt so I assumed she had on them jeans from earlier. Knew if we were going to get cozy, she needed something sexy. If she was going to hang with me, she had to up her wardrobe.

I could've gotten an attitude when I saw her at the bar. Could've called in sick and left her sitting there all night. I could've worked and ignored her all night. Let LB keep servicing her until she couldn't walk a straight line from the bar to the hostess desk.

For sure, I didn't have to worry about Fabulous pulling a Charlotte on me by causing a scene. Instead of doing any of that, I'd opted to surprise Fabulous. This was my last and final attempt to splurge on her. If this fell apart, I was done. Solid. No coming back.

There was one more special thing I'd planned for her today. Thankful the concierge coordinated having the flowers and champagne delivered to the suite. That gave me time to pick up the sexy gear that I'd laid out for both of us, then I made my way to Costco and picked out a diamond ring. Just in case things didn't work out, I could get my money back based on Costco's hassle-free return policy.

It was time to remove the small white box from my pocket. This was not a get-down-on-one-knee occasion. I sat on the couch beside her, held the box in front of Fabulous.

She began crying hysterically. She smashed her lips to mine. "Yes. Yes, I will."

She honestly thought I'd ask to marry her when the only thing I was certain of was she was a liar. "Whoa, Fabulous. Chill. Let me finish."

This wasn't my first time getting a woman a ring. Her reaction was the same as the other two. They were probably still wearing theirs. I should've given Charlotte one. In retro, I was glad I hadn't. Would never put a ring on a female's finger if some other dude ran up in her after me while we were supposed to be chill.

Truth be told, I'd still fuck her. I just wouldn't ice her. I'd never ask Fabulous for my ring back but if she ever gave it to me, I'd accept that and move on.

Waiting for Blake to calm down, I told her, "This is not what you think. It is not a proposal. I'm not asking you to marry me." I had to make my intent clear. Didn't want her telling anyone we were engaged.

"Okay. Okay," she said, eyeing the box, not me. She started breathing heavily, fanning herself.

Damn, she was fifty, not fifteen. I know some other nigga had to have iced her. "Before I put this on your finger, I have to ask."

"Anything. What is it?" Her eyes were still fixated on the box.

Holding her right hand, I said, "Look into my eyes. I'm up here." I gave her a moment to focus, then continued. "Whatever you do, don't lie to me." It didn't matter what she said. The look in her eyes and feel of her hand the moment I asked the question would give me my answer.

I didn't understand how guys could put any type of ring on a potential and not ask, "Since the first time we had sex, have you had any type of sexual contact with any person other than me, male or female?"

She took a deep breath. "I wouldn't do that to you."

I dismissed the inhale as nervousness. I followed up with, "So no other dude has put his dick in your pussy, mouth, asshole, ear, none of that?" I was real serious.

Her hand froze but didn't tremble. Her voice lowered but didn't crack. "No, Spencer."

Venus Domino taught me, "If a woman lies to you once, she'll lie to you again."

I believed my mom. Fabulous wouldn't tell me something that wasn't true over a ring. She didn't seem like the type of woman to lie and try to take it to her grave. Not about something she knew would end our relay.

Placing my hand on the box, I thought that if I ever found out she was lying, I would make her suffer. In the worst kind of way. I said, "This is a relationship ring." Opening the box, I asked, "Fabulous, will you be my lady?"

Nodding, she started crying again. "Yes, Spencer. I'm honored to be all yours."

I hoped she hadn't left out the part, "Starting here and now." I used to believe a woman's tears meant she cared for me until I learned women cried when they were happy, sad, pissed off, confused. Heard older women take men through changes just because they're going through what they call "the change."

We'd only known each other a short while but females were the best when it came to lying. I was smart. But a woman like Alexis would keep her brain cranking to stay one up on brotha and a female. I'd finally let go of my reservations and decided to give Fabulous one more chance.

I swooped her up, carried her to the bathroom, then I undressed her. She undressed me. I knew for sure, this woman truly loved me. I believed that Fabulous would do anything I'd ask and things I wouldn't have to ask of her she'd handle like a woman.

I hadn't heard from Alexis since her text about not telling Blake the truth about our having sex. Fabulous should've inquired if I'd sexed anyone other than her. The platinum one-carat eternity band probably made my indiscretions with Alexis insignificant.

A ring was an incentive for a woman to do right by her man. "You ready to get it in?" I asked her.

Fabulous smiled. Wrapped her arms around me. "This is the best time of my life."

A brotha couldn't lie. Hearing that shit made me feel good inside and out. My dick got hard instantly!

Holding her hand, I waited until her body emerged into the water. I got in, sat behind her. She held up her right hand. Smiled. My ring looked good on her finger. We chilled, sipped champagne. It was quiet. I liked that. We didn't have to say much.

Fabulous already knew the most secret part of my life. I frowned. Breaking our silence, I asked, "Baby?"

A notch above a whisper, she said, "Yes."

"Tell me your deepest, darkest secret."

"Hmm." She scratched the back of her head. "I don't have any."

Not believing her, I said, "Everybody has at least one."

"Not me. At least I don't feel that I do. I've had ups and downs. Reared my children on my own. Maybe not telling Alexis who her father was but I don't consider that a secret. I didn't tell any of my daughters."

"Ever been arrested?" I asked.

She shook her head.

"Ever been almost arrested?"

She laughed. "No."

"Ever done anything that could've gotten you arrested?"

"Sex in a car when I was sixteen."

"Now we're getting somewhere. With whom?"

"Billy," she said.

"Billy who?" I asked.

"Blackstone."

"Dude that you told me was your first? That dude in the pictures on Sandara's Facebook page?"

"Yes."

"He was at your party, right?"

Exhaling, she answered, "Yes, Spencer."

"Have you fucked him, since the first time we had sex?"

"I already answered that," she said, then asked, "You ever been arrested?"

"Nah. Too smart for that." Just in case she fucked his ass last night, I said, "I have one more question."

"I'm listening," she said.

"Can I fuck you in the ass tonight?"

CHAPTER 54

Blake

Losing my anal virginity at fifty? *Ou wee!*
I couldn't believe I'd agreed to do this. I took a deep breath.
Tried convincing myself "Yes, you can" was the right response.

A part of me should be thankful that Billy's leftover semen hadn't
ended up on Spencer's dick or his lips. I felt bad lying to Spencer.
The possibility of losing him made me do it. Men lied to me all the
time. I'd never confess. There'd be no way for him to find out. Mercedes wouldn't tell him and even if she did, I'd deny having opened
my legs for Billy after my party.

It was more complicated than an open-and-shut conversation.
Wait. I was not with Spencer at that time so it shouldn't matter that I
was riding, grinding, and having fun with another man. He'd done
some things with my daughter. I was sure of that. The way I saw it now
was we were even.

Spencer led me to the bed. Our bodies were dripping wet.

"Stand right there," he said, pulling a bottle of baby oil out of a
black bag.

Drizzling oil all over our bodies, he massaged me from head to toe.
I started rubbing oil on him. Our four hands gliding all over one another excited me. I grazed his full sexy lips with my slick fingers. Rubbed
my hands all over his head. There was something about touching his
scalp that made my pussy pucker.

He touched my lips, then kissed me. Oil coated our tongues. A flashback of Fortune's greasy body crept into my mind. I squashed it as though I were stomping on a Georgia bug.

"Lie face down for me Fabulous," he said, positioning me in the center of the bed. His hands glided up and down my back. Parting my cheeks, I felt his tongue tease my asshole with a single lick. His finger probed a little at a time.

Was I supposed to take an enema? I hadn't eaten since breakfast. My sister Ruby had done it up with those grits and homemade buttermilk biscuits.

"Relax," he said. "I know what I'm doing."

That was not my concern. Taking a deep breath, I exhaled as he pushed in more of his finger.

"I'ma get a towel. Don't move."

"Okay." That was a good idea.

He returned. I felt a hot towel sliding between my ass.

"I'm getting ready to put on a condom, then I'm going to stick my head in," he said. "If it gets uncomfortable, let me know. I'll give you a moment but you're taking all of this dick tonight."

OMG! Was I ready for *all* of him? "Okay, just the head."

He didn't answer. I wanted to please Spencer. When he penetrated me, my rectal muscles automatically contracted. He paused, then pushed a tiny bit. Waited then did the same again and as he began massaging my back and shoulders I began to relax. His hands on me helped release some of my discomfort.

Halfway in, I started to worry if I was going to crap on myself. "Is it safe to go deeper? I mean what if, I—"

"Have to shit," he said very matter of fact.

I nodded.

"It's not my bed and it's not yours. You're doing fine," he said, sliding in more.

"Oh my God," I thought, praying I didn't embarrass myself.

It felt strange. Like pressure, not pain.

He kept massaging. Eventually, I realized I'd gotten through most of it. Hopefully the worst of it was behind me. The strange feeling gradually changed from discomfort to erotic pleasure. My body relaxed. I started moving my ass toward him.

"That's it, Fabulous. Give me that ass," Spencer said, slapping me on the butt.

That felt good too. Was he turning me into a freak at my age? I chuckled.

"What's funny?" he asked, slapping me harder.

The sting redirected my attention to him. I submitted to his every stroke, slap, and to his fingers squeezing my ass.

"You like this big dick in your ass?"

Uh, "Yes." When he thrust deeper, this time I moved forward.

"Bitch, back your ass up on this dick like it's yours."

Anal was new to me. His calling me a bitch in bed, I didn't mind that.

Slap! "You heard me, bitch. Back my ass up!" He gave one quick thrust then slapped me again. "Play with your pussy."

Soon as I touched my clit, he pressed his thumbs into my lower back right above my ass. "Spen-cer! Baby, I can't take . . . Oh, my God!"

Spencer didn't ease up.

"I!" he yelled, holding on to my side. He thrust again and again each time pulling me onto his dick. "Fabulous, I'm cumming!" His body shivered as he continued to yell my name.

I said, "Baby, I'm cumming with you."

CHAPTER 55

Spencer

"This was very thoughtful of you. Saying thanks isn't enough." Acknowledgment was always appreciated. The red jumper I'd bought for Fabulous fit her well. I didn't want my lady to have a repeat of the night we'd met and have on the same clothes today that she'd worn yesterday. Besides, she needed to leave that T-shirt and those jeans in the trash where I'd put them.

Venus Domino taught me, "If you're going to start something, pay attention to the details, and finish strong."

I kissed Fabulous. "Get used to my being good to you."

She slipped on her sandals. I shook my head, stared at the heels.

"You can't be serious," she said with a smile.

I nodded. "Heels, babe."

Closing the suite's door, she said, "Please let this be the beginning of a beautiful friendship."

I didn't know what prompted her to say that shit. That wasn't cool. Fabulous should choose her words more carefully. In our situation, friendship was understood. When a woman used the word *friend*, guys didn't view ourselves as a longtime partner. The ring I'd placed on her finger should've made it clear I wanted to be more than her friend.

I handed the valet a ticket for Fabulous's car. "You mind dropping me off at Lenox?"

"Drop you off? I thought you were going furniture shopping with me."

What gave her that impression? See, women made up shit in their heads then act as though a real conversation had taken place. I didn't want the feelings we'd exchanged last night to grow old by hanging out all day.

Let a brotha miss you for a minute.

"I have a few things to do. I'll catch up to you later."

"Like what?" she asked, driving down Peachtree Street in the opposite direction of where I'd left my car.

I wished she'd let it go. "Where are you taking me?"

"So you can surprise me but I can't do the same for you?" She smiled. Continued driving.

Exhaling, I decided to chill rather than be pissed off. She was right about my plans for last night. "This is not the beginning of my conceding."

"I know. But I can't promise I'll never kidnap you again. And I told a little tale."

Here comes the bullshit. I stared out the window.

"We're not going furniture shopping, yet. I wanted to get your opinion on something."

She turned onto a side street. Made a few more turns. Drove up to this ridiculously sick mansion. I couldn't lie. Fabulous's red Ferrari belonged in this circular driveway.

"No way," I said.

"Maybe. Let's see if you like it. Dianna is waiting inside to give us a private tour."

When a woman opened the double French doors, the foyer was bigger than my bedroom. Damn near larger than my apartment.

During the tour, Fabulous said, "This is too much space for one person. If I make an offer on it today, I want you to think about moving in with me after the closing."

I'd never lived with anyone but if we were going to make our relationship last, I told her, "Okay, I'll do it." I think the house convinced me more than she did.

The crib was two stories. I think I counted six bedrooms, two full kitchens. There was an in-law unit, a finished basement, a tennis court, swimming pool, and Jacuzzi out back. "I can see you now. Teaching your grandkids how to swim and play tennis."

Fabulous held my hand like she was the proudest woman in Georgia. If I took her up on her offer, I had enough funds to leave at any time. I owned shit Fabulous knew nothing about. Planned on keeping it that way.

In front of Dianna, Fabulous said, "I love and want to be with you, Spencer."

That wasn't chill but I wasn't going to check my gurl on it in front of Dianna. Just as Fabulous was getting ready to kiss me, a call incoming registered on her phone. She looked at the number, then said, "I have to take this."

Her brows drew closer together as she nodded. "So soon. Really? Already? You're sure? You're positive?"

With each question, I became more concerned. "Everything okay?"

Dianna's eyes were fixed on Fabulous's face. Both of us waited for a response.

Blake nodded, then continued her conversation. "I'll take care of everything. Thanks. Bye."

"What is it?" I asked.

"That was my attorney. He's located Alexis's dad."

"Damn, that was fast." Instantly, I began to worry about how Alexis was going to handle this. I knew she said it was what she wanted but was she mentally prepared? I wanted to be the one to tell Alexis but being that Fabulous and I were official, I had to respect the parental line.

Dianna said, "I have to show another property and seems like you guys have to handle some serious business." Walking us to the car, she said, "Blake, take your time. We can look at more properties when you're ready."

Hell, I was ready to sell my place and make an offer. My apartment building, I'd never sell but my house in Stone Mountain was negotiable. I was renting that, too.

Fabulous told Dianna, "Don't tell Mercedes about this house."

Dianna zipped her fingers across her lips, then pretended she'd thrown away the key that was still in her hand. I opened the car door for Fabulous, then sat in the driver's seat. No more pit stops.

"This happened too fast. I don't know if I'm ready," she said. "Please don't say anything to Alexis. I'll arrange for them to meet once my, I mean our, house is furnished. It's best if he meets Alexis at our place. That way if anything goes wrong, I'll have you there for support."

"Cool." And crazy.

Fabulous was going to put off letting Alexis meet her biological father until after she'd purchased a home? That meant she really didn't want Alexis to know she'd found him.

"Oh, if you want, after we close on the property you can have your furniture delivered to our home."

Not really hearing much of what Fabulous had told me, "Cool" was all I said. The night Alexis opened up to me, shared her feelings about her father, that brought us closer together. Sex with Alexis would never happen again. And while I would always cover up the truth to Fabulous, in my heart there was a special place for Alexis.

Fabulous asked, "You all right?"

If I was going to be her man, I was going to be the man. "Yeah. I'm good. How soon can you arrange for that face-to-face for Alexis?"

CHAPTER 56

Alexis

"Will you marry me?"

Chanel sat next to me at Legal Sea Foods restaurant. A cute diamond, almost half the size of the one James had given me, was pinched between her thumb and pointing finger. Her makeup was professionally done. No blue lipstick. Today she'd worn a shade of deep red.

"C, it's not that easy."

"You don't love me?"

I lied. "Of course I do but this won't work long-term and we both know it."

Politely, she said, "Excuse me." She nudged my thigh, scooted closer to me. "I need you to move. I'ma go," she said.

I'd never seen her this heartbroken. I pleaded, "C, please. Don't leave. Let's talk about it."

"I'm done talking." She started crying and talking loud. "You don't want me. You don't want me to leave."

I kissed her. "Man, I never said I don't want you. I love you, C." If I had to lie to keep her, that was exactly what I was going to do.

"Move, Alexis!"

Damn. I wasn't the type to beg. My ego wouldn't allow that. I moved. Chanel placed the ring in my palm, stood in front of me.

"Keep it as a token of whatever you thought we had."

I'd created a monster by telling Chanel to take the initiative. She'd stopped crying but I felt her pain. I felt bad, for her. She was a sweet gurl but marrying Chanel would make me the babysitter to her emotions. I was saving that energy for the real deal. I watched Chanel walk away. I was in the moment of missing Chanel until a text came in from Domino.

I hadn't heard from him in a month. He hadn't ventured to my side of the building. I had no reason to go to his apartment. My mom had shown all of us the ring Domino had given her. He'd moved in with her so I'd stopped visiting my mom as much.

Wasn't sure how to break the news to either one of them that I was four weeks pregnant and keeping it. I should've told Chanel about the baby. This kid, I thought, touching my stomach, could have two daddies and two mommies. Maybe a kid was what I needed to focus on what was important in my life. The only person I'd told was Tréme.

Domino's text read, You chill

If I was not going to interfere with Spencer's relationship with my mother, I was going to have to block his contact. Soon as I'd finished editing Domino's number, a call came in from James.

I answered, "What's up?"

"Hey, Alexis. I made reservations for us to go to the DR in two days. I love you. I want to marry you. I'm not taking no. I've already packed your bags. And, yes, we are going there for our wedding ceremony. The arrangements are solid."

"What about LA?"

"Alexis, I, love, you. No more excuses, sweetheart," he said. "I'm sending a car for you tomorrow evening. Bye."

What had gotten into him? I was down for the getaway. I was not interested in the "I do" part.

I left the restaurant, drove to Mac's liquor store, bought a chilled bottle of champagne. After driving downtown, I parked, paid for a ticket to ride the Ferris wheel. I got into a gondola with the Ferrari leather seats and glass floor.

Spending time alone to reflect on what I was doing with my life was what I needed. Why was I so heartless? I really needed to meet my dad. Not communicating much with my mom, she'd probably forgotten about her promise to find him or she was glad I'd stopped asking. I wasn't going to take Domino up on his offer to help me find my father.

I popped the cork, took a sip straight from the bottle. I was hurting. I didn't think Chanel was ever coming back to me. I'd played one time too many with her heart.

A call came in from my mom. Guess I'd thought her up. I let it go to voice mail. She called again.

I answered, "Hi, Mom."

"I found him. Be at my house tomorrow at noon."

Wasn't expecting her to say that but it was what I'd asked my mom to do. I sipped from the bottle.

"Tomorrow at noon, Alexis."

I wanted to say something but I couldn't.

"Bye." My mom ended the call. Sounded as though she was angry with me. I called Chanel. I wanted her to go with me. She didn't answer. Fine.

I sent her a text, So we're done?

Chanel didn't text back.

Unblocking Spencer's contact, I texted him, I need to talk.

Can't. Ole gurl got me on lock. She's right here in my face. I was trying to see you tonight.

You still can.

Can't. She made dinner reservations. I'll see you tomorrow when you get here.

So, he knew too. I blocked his ass again.

I continued to drink. Didn't want to call LB. Wasn't sure why but I did.

He answered immediately. "Hey, Alexis. You got my money?"

I'd forgotten all about his thousand dollars. He wasn't getting it back. I told him, "No." He ended the call. I was glad I'd used a condom every time with him.

I was certain my mom had either told my sisters or she was going to tell them about my dad. I dialed Mercedes.

"Hey, I was getting ready to call you," she said. "Are you doing okay?"

"No." I started crying.

"Where are you?" she asked.

"Downtown. Close to Legal Sea Foods."

"Meet me there. I'm on my way."

CHAPTER 57

Alexis

I got off the Ferris wheel. Left the bottle of champagne on the floor.
Walked a few blocks to Legal Sea Foods. Sat at a table in the bar
area. Ordered a shot of chilled tequila. Probably shouldn't have mixed
that with champagne and pregnancy but in the moment I wanted to
drown my sorrows.

Mercedes, Devereaux, and Sandara rushed through the turnabout.
Lately I'd distanced myself from them but I was glad each of them was
here for me. They all hugged me. I started crying uncontrollably.

"You're brave," Sandara said. "I will never ask to see my father. Obviously, he doesn't care about me and he doesn't know his grandkids.
I bet when his ass gets old and his dick stops working and he's on his
deathbed he'll try to find me but it'll be too late." She started crying.

"Let's sit in that booth at the end," Devereaux suggested. "We don't
want to be the center of attention."

Honestly, I didn't care. I sat on the maroon vinyl bench. Mercedes
sat next to me. Sandara and Devereaux sat on barstools on the opposite side of the table.

Mercedes said, "You are not going to meet him alone. We'll all be
there with and for you tomorrow. Of course by default Spencer will be
there too."

I'd just sucked him off and swallowed his seeds a month ago and he
was living with my mother. That was fucked up. I hated both of them!

Mercedes said, "Since we're all together, I want to let you guys know that I think Benjamin is having an affair."

I wasn't expecting that. Nor was I going to be the one to admit I knew anything. I questioned, "How can you be sure?"

"'I think' means I'm not sure," she retorted. Mercedes snapped her fingers. "Bartender, we need a round of drinks over here."

Wow! "You know I am not one for being embarrassed in public either." I had to tell Mercedes, "Popping your finger at the server was rude. That's not like you. Don't give Benjamin the upper hand." I wondered how she'd feel toward me if she knew I saw brother-in-law on a date and didn't tell her.

Mercedes stared at me. She didn't respond.

"I wonder what my dad looks like. What if he doesn't accept me, you guys?"

Mercedes sarcastically said, "Don't give him the upper hand."

"Okay, I feel you." I decided this was definitely not the right time to tell them about the baby. I might have to rethink having it.

Devereaux asked Mercedes, "What will you do if you find out he's seeing someone?"

"I'm not certain. But I'm making sure everything we own is on financial lockdown. Any advice?" she asked, then added, "Not from you, Sandara."

"If you can give me some, I can do the same," Devereaux added. "I think Phoenix is cheating too. With a man."

My jaw dropped on that one. "Not with a man," I said. "I'd know if he were gay."

Each of them looked at me. I said, "Don't act surprised. Y'all know a whole lot of these ATL men have side chicks. But Phoenix is not doing a dude."

"Then why won't he walk me down the aisle?" Devereaux asked.

"For the same reason none of Sandara's baby daddies take care of their kids," Mercedes said. "Because you don't make him."

Sandara rolled her eyes at Mercedes. "Well, we see how marriage is working out for you and your husband." Sandara dragged out the word *husband.*

Suddenly, my issues about meeting my dad faded into the background. I took Chanel's ring out of my purse and put it on my finger.

No one noticed. There were several conversations happening at the same time. I'd become more concerned about how badly I'd treated Chanel.

I texted her, You okay. I'm going to come see you tonight.

Sandara stared at Mercedes. "Next time you invite someone to Mama's party, check with me first to make sure he's not one of my children's father."

No fucking way! "Say, what?" I damn near dropped my cell on that one.

The madness made me stop to think when was the last time we'd all gathered for girl talk. Mercedes and Devereaux, their confessions didn't surprise me. Sandara. I couldn't believe any of what I'd heard. I was ready to leave for James to take me to the Dominican tonight.

Devereaux told Sandara, "Just so there's no confusion, are you saying that Billy Blackstone is one of your children's father."

Sandara hunched her shoulders.

Mercedes shook her head. "I'm sure more now than ever, the wrong woman took me home from the hospital. I can't be the daughter of a woman that gave birth to y'all. You know Mama had sex with Billy that night and that morning. I heard them trying to be quiet. Sandara, that's the lowest of lows to sex a man that's been with your mother."

I wasn't sure I wanted more details on that one. Mercedes cut her eyes toward me.

I told her, "Don't go in on me 'cause I'll do more than hurt your feelings."

Sandara cried, "Don't judge me. How was I supposed to know?"

I asked, "Which one is lil Billy?"

"Tyson."

Damn! That was my favorite nephew. I had to know. "How did the two of you hook up?"

Sandara said, "Mercedes, how did you find him?"

Mercedes snapped back. "On Facebook."

"Uh-huh. And since you're so thorough, did you check out his friends?"

Damn, Baby Sis was on a roll.

Sandara added, "I had no idea that was Mama's Billy."

I felt it coming when Mercedes asked, "So you slept with him, and you didn't use protection. God gave you beauty but He didn't give you an ounce of sense."

"He doesn't know," Sandara said.

I asked, "If Billy doesn't know, how do you know for sure he's the father?"

Shaking her head, Sandara said, "I don't know for sure."

"Child, don't you ever go on *Maury*. I think you're over the limit on how many guys they can test," Mercedes said. "I'm glad we didn't ruin Billy's surprise for Mama with all this foolishness."

"What surprise?" I had to know.

Mercedes looked at Sandara. "Don't tell Mother you slept with him."

"I just wanted to piss you off. I never had sex with that man. He's just my Facebook friend," Sandara said.

I was so ready to leave the restaurant. I rolled my eyes at Sandara, Mercedes, and Devereaux. "What's the surprise if there is one."

Mercedes said, "Billy bought Mama a dog for her birthday."

"A what?" Devereaux said.

"That's not a bad idea," I said. "Maybe I'll get a dog."

"Child, you don't need anything dependent on you," Mercedes said.

Devereaux chimed in. "Changing the subject. Don't tell Mother any of our problems. Let's agree to support one another and get through our crises together."

We all agreed to that.

Marrying James seemed like my best option.

CHAPTER 58

Blake

The meeting with Alexis and her father should've been at a different location. Not at my, I meant our, new home. The energy in our space was peaceful.

Watching the Falcons game, Spencer asked, "You sure you want me here when he comes?" He picked up the pillow beside him. Stuffed it behind his back. His naked body was sexy against our white satin sheets. He loved the way they felt next to his skin. I loved the way he felt next to mine each night.

"For the tenth time, yes I do." I stood in the mirror styling and restyling my hair trying to decide which one made me look younger and hotter.

Secretly, I wanted Conner to see how well I was doing. Despite his disowning our child, I'd made it. I was the branch president of an international financial institution. Plus, I wanted him to see I wasn't alone. I had a ring on my finger and a young, handsome man in my bed every night.

"I'll think about it. This game is getting good."

I believed the real reason Spencer didn't want to join us was Alexis. They hadn't seen each other since he'd moved in. That was fine with me. But it wasn't okay that I'd seen Spencer every day and hadn't made time for my child.

"I didn't want us to meet at a public place in case things got out of control."

"Blake, it's not a problem. I'm right here."

Spencer was kind of like my security. I had no reason to fear Conner. Alexis? If this didn't go well, she might try to attack me. She already blamed me for everything. Surely Conner wouldn't raise a hand to our daughter, although lately there were a few times that I wanted to slap her in the mouth. Calling me by my first name.

"It's not your prom or our wedding. Stop messing with your hair and get dressed before I put you on your stomach."

My eyes softened. Oh, my! Anal sex with him was the best. I tossed my hair over my shoulder.

In a way, this meeting was more about me than my daughter but I'd never admit that. I walked into my closet to put on my control-top panties and push-up bra. I chose a sexy red dress that hugged my curves. My open-toe sling-back heels were cotton candy pink.

Sitting at my vanity, I took extra care doing my hair and makeup. I had on my Front Row Lash Love dramatic eyelashes. I even dabbed the sweetest perfume behind my ears. I didn't want Conner back. I wanted him to regret not leaving his wife for me.

"Dang, Fabulous. You on one," Spencer said, staring at me.

"What do you mean?" I put my hand on my hip. "You think it's too much?"

He scanned my body up and down. "Whateva. I'm definitely staying up here out of your way," he said, lying across the bed.

His naked body was delicious. I wanted him to bend me over, push up my dress, pull down my control top, then put his dick in my ass. He could do all of that after this meeting was over.

Spencer came to me, placed his hands on my hips, then gestured for a kiss. I turned my head offering him my cheek. He shook his head. Got back in bed.

"You want him that bad?"

"I don't want him at all," I said.

"You want something. Hope you get it."

Was Spencer jealous? If so, that was good. Maybe Conner would make an attempt to offer taking me out on a date. If Conner didn't raise a brow, that would defeat my primping-with-the-intent-to-rub get-back in his face.

"Alexis and I need you to be in the room with us when he walks in," I said. "Can you please get dressed?"

"Sorry, I don't have a tux," he said, rewinding the last play.

Exhaling, I told him, "Fine."

"Cool. Holla *if* you need me. What's my name?" He switched to Pandora. Played our favorite song through the surround sound from his app.

Spencer stood behind me. Wrapped his arms around me. He didn't have to say, "I love you." I felt it.

The doorbell rang. "That should be Alexis. Can you turn down the music so you can hear me when I call you?"

"When you call me. You're not slick. You want to showcase a brotha. Text me when you're done impressing him," he replied. "I might surprise you." Spencer clamped his fingers behind his head, crossed his feet at the ankles, switched back to the game.

Spencer hadn't officially moved in with me. Some of his clothes, all of his furniture was still in his apartment. That was okay. He was here.

I went downstairs. Checked the setup I'd put on the coffee table in case anyone needed to join me in having a drink. Posing in the standing mirror by the door, I fingered my hair, took a deep breath. "After twenty-six years."

I opened the door, and it was all four of my daughters. "I wasn't quite expecting all of you," I said, stepping aside.

Alexis scanned me from head to toe. "You're overdressed. He's not coming to see you. He's here for me."

"And I'm here for you too," I said, opening my arms for a hug.

I'd let the rolling of her eyes slide this time. Giving my daughters a hug, something about each of them seemed different.

I frowned. Scanned their faces. Tight eyes, lips. "What's wrong with y'all? Oh, so now each of you want me to find your fathers too?"

Shaking my head, I should've anticipated this. "Fine." I picked up my cell, dialed my attorney. "You were right. We need to find the rest. Let's get this over with," I said, ending the call. "Everybody satisfied now. If it doesn't turn out the way anyone expects, all I ask is that you don't blame me."

They sat on the same sofa. Alexis shared the middle with Sandara. The adjacent couch was empty.

I looked at them. "Okay, what is it? Somebody say something, dammit. Is my outfit that outrageous?"

"Fabulous! You okay down there?" Spencer asked.

Alexis's stare sent chills through me.

I called out, "I'm good. Thanks for asking, babe."

The sound of the doorbell brought relief. I wanted to get through this meeting, get Conner out of my house, and have a heart-to-heart with my girls. "Alexis, would you like to get the door?"

"You got it. I'ma sit here with my sisters."

I'd done enough. They came to my house with an attitude. I could show them attitude. I sat on the sofa, crossed my legs.

The doorbell rang again. We all sat there.

Spencer came down the stairs. "What's going on? Is someone going to get that?" He waited. I got up and stood by him. I stared at Alexis. She stared at me.

The doorbell sounded again.

"Guess it's going to be me." Spencer placed his hand on the door-knob. He looked at Alexis.

She hunched her shoulders.

Spencer opened the door. Conner was dressed in black slacks. A black button-down shirt. His broad shoulders were wide. His waist, slim. His eyes locked with Spencer's.

Spencer stared at me. His eyes narrowed. "Blake, is this some type of joke?" He looked at my girls then back at Conner.

"No, Spencer. It's not a joke. This is Alexis's father."

"No, Blake. That's my father."

BABY, YOU'RE THE BEST

Mary B. Morrison

ABOUT THIS GUIDE

The suggested questions that follow are included to enhance your group's reading of this book.

Discussion Questions

1. Children who have never met their mother or father, how do you think this impacts their values and character?

2. How do you believe your childhood shaped your present state of mind as it relates to your relationship(s)?

3. What's your comfort level with sex? What is your favorite sex scene in this book and why?

4. Which characters have got game, who's playing games, and why?

5. The original title of this book was *Single Moms.* Do you know that seventy percent of African-American women are single moms? Are you aware that more than fifty percent of African-American marriages end in divorce? And fifty percent of African-American women never marry? Based on statistics, what do you think is the main factor contributing to the breakdown in communication in the African-American community?

6. Which characters are in search of love? Someone to love and love them back? Give examples based on the characters' actions.

7. Should Alexis have bothered finding out who her father was? Was she prepared?

8. We may all agree that Alexis is not the caretaker of anyone's heart. In fact, she derives satisfaction in dominating others but accepts no responsibility for her actions. Can you give examples of people who do the same or similar?

9. Is sex a weapon? Can sexual ties bond individuals to the point they feel like they want to die if it ends? Have you ever suffered

depression as a result of a breakup or divorce? How did you find the strength to overcome?

10. Is love an in-the-moment connection? How can a person sex one person today, then a different person the same or next day and waver between the two?

11. Do you believe monogamy is natural? Why do people cheat? Have you cheated on someone you love?

12. Women dating younger men. Do you have a preference? How old was the youngest person you've dated? Based on your dating experiences, what's the difference in maturity between a younger man and an older guy?

13. Is a younger person better at sex? Why? Or why not?

14. Should the daughters share their relationship problems with their mother? What advice do you think Blake would give each one?

15. Accidental incest. A daughter getting impregnated by her mother's ex-boyfriend. Do you think it happens in real life? Who's to blame when this does happen?